TO DIE FOR

Recent Titles by Tessa Barclay from Severn House

The Crowne Prince Gregory Mysteries

FAREWELL PERFORMANCE
A BETTER CLASS OF PERSON
A HANDFUL OF DUST
A FINAL DISCORD
TO DIE FOR

Romance and Saga Titles

THE DALLANCY BEQUEST
A LOVELY ILLUSION
RICHER THAN RUBIES
THE SILVER LINING
STARTING OVER
A TRUE LIKENESS

TO DIE FOR

Tessa Barclay

This first world edition published in Great Britain 2007 by
SEVERN HOUSE PUBLISHERS LTD of
9–15 High Street, Sutton, Surrey SM1 1DF.
This first world edition published in the USA 2007 by
SEVERN HOUSE PUBLISHERS INC of
595 Madison Avenue, New York, N.Y. 10022.

British Library Cataloguing in Publication Data

Barclay, Tessa
   To die for
   1.   Crowne, Gregory (Fictitious character) - Fiction
   2.   Forgery of manuscripts - Fiction
   3.   Murder - Investigation - Fiction
   I.   Title
   823.9'14 [F]

   ISBN-13: 978-0-7278-6471-0   (cased)
   ISBN-13: 978-1-84751-012-9   (trade paper)

All Severn House titles are printed on acid-free paper.

Typeset by Palimpsest Book Production Ltd.,
Grangemouth, Stirlingshire, Scotland.
Printed and bound in Great Britain by
MPG Books Ltd., Bodmin, Cornwall.

One

Ex-Crown Prince Gregory von Hirtenstein and Countess Zalfeda were looking very handsome together as they drove towards the charity ball. He was in dinner jacket and black tie, light-brown hair recently barbered; the countess was wearing a little black dress of considerable style, pretty shoulders showing off above the black silk, a pink carnation at her bosom.

They were both thoughtful. She was congratulating herself on having looked up this friend-of-a-friend on her visit to London. He was telling himself that Liz Blair was likely to be at this affair and wondering whether he wanted to see her.

The countess was almost a stranger to him, though they had a few things in common. They were both descended from old nobility, both expatriates and rather hard up. The prince made his living by arranging concerts and recitals of classical music. The countess was personal assistant to an eccentric old lady at whose behest she'd come to London.

'And so the ball is on behalf of needlewomen?' she enquired.

'Garment-workers, I believe they are called. In Indonesia.'

'And we are concerned for them?'

'I was asked to present a plaque to the charity worker who had brought in the largest number of contributions this year.' And because he was obliged to attend, he'd thought to ask if she would like to go.

When requested by a friend to 'keep an eye on her', he'd arranged for her to have a room in the residential hotel in which he himself lived when he came to London. It was in a former stately home in Surrey, a rather dull situation for a Parisienne. Marzelina had jumped at the chance of an evening's dancing.

On this occasion the prince would be known by his title. Generally he used a less noticeable name, which varied from country to country. In English-speaking territory he was

Mr Crowne. In France he was Monsieur Couronne; in Germany he was Herr Krone. He never enjoyed these formal occasions, because photographers were generally present and if there was one thing Mr Crowne hated, it was having his picture in the papers. A quiet life was what he wanted.

But now they were entering the borough of Kensington, and His Highness was rather regretting his good-hearted invitation. Because Liz Blair had been the love of his life until last year, when a sudden quarrel – short and disastrous as a whirlwind – had broken them up. If she was there this evening, he didn't know how he would react.

He confided none of this to Marzelina. She would soon finish the business matter that had brought her to Britain, after which he would probably never see her again. He gave her a momentary glance. Pretty, yes. Well brought up. Of ancient lineage – in fact, much more likely to please the hyper-royalist grandmother who had caused Liz Blair to walk out on him. The ex-Queen Mother of Hirtenstein had called Liz bad and wicked, claiming that she plotted to marry him because it would be good publicity for the clothes she sold.

It wasn't upon Grossmutti that his thoughts were fixed. He was wondering if Liz would in fact be there tonight and, if so, if she would smile at him.

He'd arranged to get to the hotel just before the supper break, so as to be greeted by and to shake hands with those who thought it important to shake hands with a prince. Then he and his guest would be invited to toast the enterprise in champagne, after which he would present the plaque. On such occasions he was sometimes expected to kiss the recipient, but luckily this time the recipient proved to be a tubby, middle-aged man, who was quite happy with a handshake.

Now Mr Crowne and his friend were allowed to eat, if they wished and, when the band recommenced, to dance. The prince wasn't a good dancer, but in days gone by Liz had taught him the rudiments of salsa.

He was extending his arm so as to sway his partner outwards when he saw Liz. It caused him to falter, and the countess had to clutch at his hand to keep her balance. He murmured an apology. She smiled. They got back into rhythm, and she glanced back at the cause of his mistake.

Liz was wearing a close-fitting short dress of some silvery

fabric. It made her look like a fine Italian rapier – slender and elegant and rather frightening.

'You know her?' Marzelina enquired softly and in French, the language in which she felt most comfortable.

'Somewhat.'

'*Hélas*,' she sighed in intuitive understanding.

It was his duty to dance with others, but of course not with Liz Blair. Ms Blair was unimportant – except to Mr Crowne; but he couldn't prevent himself from looking for her in the crowded ballroom. She was with a handsome, polished sort of man, in a dinner jacket considerably more fashionable than the one the prince was wearing. She danced with a few others too, but this seemed to be her partner. He had a possessive air.

Unfortunately at one point his glance collided with hers. There she was with this rich-looking type; here he was with a pretty blonde young woman in his arms. They froze each other with a look.

Worse still, as he and Marzelina were waiting, on departure, for his car to be brought, he saw Liz and her escort drive off in the very latest Porsche.

He was very downcast.

Next day he took the countess to the Museum of Musical Heritage, a small establishment, difficult to find, in a Georgian building in Mayfair. He knew it well, for he sometimes did research there when choosing works to make a programme for a concert. It contained manuscripts, books and portraits of composers born in Britain or who had visited Britain. Here she was to do some research on the Polish composer Chopin, who had made quite a lengthy stay in both England and Scotland in 1848.

'Shall I show you where to find the Chopin Collection?' he suggested as she paused in the entrance hall to glance around.

'No, thank you; I already wrote to the librarian so it's all arranged already, Gregory.'

'Well then, I've written down my mobile number for you, you see? When you feel like lunch just give me a call, and I'll collect you . . .'

'No, no, I'm sure you have other things you'd rather—'

'Nonsense. It's true I have a few bits of business but nothing important. And round here you wouldn't know where to find a place to eat – my dear, most of the buildings have got exclusive men's clubs in them!'

'Oh, well then . . . in that case . . . I don't know quite how long I'll be . . .'

'Doesn't matter. I'll be around and about all day.'

They exchanged formal handshakes. Mr Crowne took himself off to Spitalfields, where at the next festival his musicians would be performing. The great old building of Christ Church was always undergoing improvement, so he wanted to inspect it and ask what more might be done to it before next year. He went on to one of London's southern suburbs, where an instrument-maker was repairing a valuable oboe belonging to an orchestral player on tour in Brazil. By then it was lunch-time.

He rather wondered why Marzelina hadn't been in touch but decided not to call her mobile, because the museum wouldn't be pleased at having ring-tones disturbing its tranquillity. He found himself an agreeable pub, had a sandwich and a Budweiser, then returned to the city. In Soho he bought sheet music for a forthcoming performance of a work by Palestrina. He had it parcelled up and despatched to the group who needed it for rehearsal. He dropped in on a choirmaster who wanted him to arrange a summer tour of Canada for his amateur singers in the following year. Here he was trapped into listening to tapes, which kept him tied up for over an hour.

His watch told him it was close to five o'clock. The Museum of Musical Heritage closed at five. He decided the best thing to do was to go there and collect Marzelina. They might have a drink together so as to let the rush hour die down before they set out for Surrey.

As he went into the museum's entrance hall, a warning bell was ringing to let visitors know the place would soon be closing. The librarian at the enquiry desk greeted him with a smile.

'Good evening, Mr Crowne. You're too late to do any research today.'

'I'm meeting a friend who's been busy here all day, poor thing,' he explained.

'You know those songs by Elgar you wanted to look at? They've come back from the binder.'

'Oh, great, I'll come by and take a look as soon as I can. I've got a contralto who wants to put on an Elgar recital.'

They chatted for a while on musical matters. One or two

people came down the stairs, reclaimed coats and jackets from the cloakroom, said goodnight and hurried off.

Marzelina never appeared. The final announcement was played – a warning that the museum would be closed in five minutes. The desk librarian looked quite concerned. 'Which collection was he looking at, your friend?' he enquired.

'It's a lady, Taylor. You weren't at the desk when she came – she's doing some research on Chopin.'

'Hm . . . Well, that's quite an extensive collection, so she may have got immersed in her work; but all the same . . .' He looked anxiously at the hall clock. Its hands ticked remorselessly on. At the figure five the heavy front door swung shut and there was the click of locks engaging.

Taylor rose from his seat. 'Is she elderly, your friend? Might she have been taken ill upstairs?'

Greg Crowne started towards the staircase. 'On the contrary: she's young and fit.'

The Chopin Collection was housed on the second floor along with those of other foreign musicians and composers who had been visitors. They took the two flights at a run. They pushed open the fire door, which had automatically swung shut at five. There were no lights on – which was alarming, for it was five in the evening of a dull day in late March. The librarian switched on a light close to the entrance.

The room was equipped with rolling stacks which housed the books and scores. An area was set aside for those who wished to take notes – two or three tables with leather chairs, and swan-necked lamps to help read the crabbed writing on some of the works.

There was no one to be seen.

'She must have left earlier,' said Taylor, frowning.

'You've been on duty?'

'Since lunch.'

'Did you see her leave?'

'I wouldn't have noticed, Mr Crowne.'

'I think you would,' Greg replied. 'She's a very pretty blonde, in a fawn coat with a fake-fur collar and a long pink scarf.'

Mr Taylor smiled but shook his head. 'She might have left before I came on, because when you said she'd been busy all day, I take it you meant she came early?'

'That's true – I dropped her off soon after ten.'

'Well, that's it then – she must have gone while Joe was on.'

'Is Joe still here?'

'No, he left to take photocopies of Stainer's *Crucifixion* to Winchester Cathedral; they needed them urgently.'

They stood in perplexity.

'She was to ring me on my mobile,' Greg said. 'Of course, she could have gone off on her own, but she doesn't know London at all, and though she speaks English, I don't know whether she'd have ventured—'

'Speaks English? She's a foreigner?'

'From Paris, but Polish by birth. She speaks perfect French, but her English is a bit fractured.'

Taylor looked at his watch. 'Everybody else will have left by now, I should think . . . I mean office staff . . . We don't have a big staff and anyhow . . . they wouldn't see her, the office exit is at the back.'

'Of course!' Greg slapped himself on the forehead. 'If she took herself off, her coat will be gone.'

They ran downstairs again. The little cloakroom had four racks for hats and bags and hooks for coats.

A fawn cloth coat with a fake-fur collar hung on one of the hooks.

They went to look in the ladies' room, with much preliminary knocking on doors. All the facilities were empty. They looked in the first-floor room where the British-born composers were housed. No one was there. They searched the third floor, where photographs and copies of portraits were kept. They looked in the men's room, though they knew it was silly, because even though Marzelina's English was poor, she could have recognized the male figure on the door.

'This is weird,' Taylor said, looking rather scared.

Now they began opening every door they came to – cupboards, storerooms for cleaning materials, the staff cloakroom, the offices, where the desks were empty and the computers switched off. They turned on lights everywhere, peered in corners, looked behind open doors.

Taylor contacted his colleague Joe Packley on his mobile. The result was a negative. Joe had noticed Marzelina's arrival when Mr Crowne had brought her in. He hadn't seen her leave.

'She's here,' Greg said in bafflement. 'She wouldn't go without her coat; it's cold outside.'

'She isn't here,' Taylor said. 'We've looked everywhere.'

They made their way back to the second floor, thinking they might find some clue at the desk where she'd been working. There were no scraps of paper with scribbles or notes; no bound score; no book to give a clue to what she'd been working on.

'She's nipped out somewhere – like for a quick cup of coffee or something – and got lost,' Taylor suggested.

'Right,' Greg said. 'So let's find her.' He got out his mobile and dialled her number.

A trilling sound rose up on the air – there, in the room, from nowhere and no one.

The two men stared at each other. The librarian had gone white. Greg felt a shiver of apprehension. Slowly their heads turned in the direction of the sound.

It was coming from the rolling stacks.

Moveable stacks are big rows of shelves on wheels. They are heavy and cumbersome to move. A wheel built on to the outer upright must be turned to get the great weight to glide along to meet its neighbour. Generally a batch of rolling stacks is grouped together, with the row that's needed made open to access. To reach what you want, sometimes you have to turn the wheel on three or four stacks before you can get to the shelves you want to search.

Taylor hurried to the stacks. He paused at the first one, which was against the outer wall of the room. The next stack was stationed absolutely tight against the next one. So was the next, and the next. There was a slight gap between the fourth and fifth stacks, and a larger one between the fifth and the last. No one was in that gap. But the trilling of the mobile was coming from the narrow gap between the fourth and fifth.

Taylor desperately turned the handles on the stacks until the narrow gap was widened. And that was where they found Marzelina lying, crammed up against the fourth stack of shelves, with her pink silk scarf wound too tightly about her neck.

She had been strangled.

Two

It was late when Gregory Crowne signed his statement at the police station. Chief Inspector Glaston took it from him with a sigh.

'Chopin?' he muttered. 'She comes to London and gets strangled, and it's to do with research on Chopin?'

'So she said.'

'And you believed her?'

'I hardly knew her, Chief Inspector. An acquaintance of mine in Paris – a journalist, Arnold Lennard – rang and asked me to give her a bit of help because she'd never been to London. So I arranged for her to stay at Bicklesham – you know, just to be friendly . . .'

The Chief Inspector had complete faith in his evidence. Mr Crowne was known to the Metropolitan Police, but only in a good sense. He'd acquitted himself well in a case a couple of years ago, and was even said to be approved of by MI6 and the CIA. Gossip in police canteens occasionally referred to his helpful activities. So Glaston was satisfied there was nothing peculiar in the relationship between him and the dead woman – what he mentally categorized as 'hanky-panky'.

'You don't know of anyone who had a motive to kill her?' he ventured. 'It seems to have been something personal – I mean, not robbery or anything. Her wallet was still in her handbag, with a couple of hundred euros, and her credit card . . .'

'Her passport?'

'No, that wasn't there, but why should she carry it around? I've asked the Surrey police to have a look at her flat – it's probably locked up there in a drawer.'

Greg hesitated. 'She's not "known"?'

'Completely blameless, as far as we can see.' That had been his first thought – a Polish countess, perhaps with something of a reputation for – what? – dabbling in politics? A bit of a confidence trickster? But no. 'She's got this Polish title but she's French, really, by birth. The Sûreté have never heard of her; she works for this old lady . . .' He looked among his papers . . . 'Madame Wiaroz – Lord, what a name! Polish too, I gather.'

'Yes, but works in what way? Is Madame Wiaroz a musician – a concert pianist perhaps?'

'What makes you think that, sir?'

'Well . . . Chopin, you know.'

'Oh yes, of course.' Now that he'd been given the clue about playing the piano, Glaston's memory dredged up something about a film he'd seen, or perhaps a TV documentary, about some famous pianist who'd played Chopin. 'No, the countess seems to have been a sort of companion, or secretary or something. The local guys went to see the old lady when we let them know, and they say she's about ninety-nine and totters about with a stick.'

'The countess told me she was here in London doing something for Madame Wiaroz, but perhaps it was more than she wanted me to know?'

'Just looking up some stuff about Chopin, so the old lady says. She seems to be a bit of a Chopin fan.'

Greg smiled and nodded. 'Oh yes. I can imagine.'

'How's that?'

'A lot of people adore Chopin – especially women. There's something tremendously romantic about him. The music, you see – full of melancholy and longing. And the love affair with George Sand.' Seeing the surprise on the detective's face, he added hastily, 'George Sand was a woman who wrote novels under a man's name.'

'Uh-huh,' said Glaston. Not his sort of case, this stuff. He looked at Mr Crowne appealingly. 'I suppose you couldn't have a look around her flat when you get home, eh? The Surrey force will be there – we asked them to investigate, but of course they're not clued up about the music thing.'

When he reached the front entrance of Bicklesham a couple of hours later, the manageress darted out of her office, still up and fully dressed. She was in general a capable and bright middle-aged woman, but tonight she was rattled.

'Mr Crowne, Mr Crowne, the police are here! They wanted

to look at the flat that your friend the countess is using! Oh, Mr Crowne, don't tell me she's an illegal immigrant?'

'Not at all, Ms Bryce.' He took her hand. 'It's worse than that, I'm afraid. Countess Zalfeda is dead.'

The manageress had some experience of dealing with death, because there were elderly tenants and in the normal course of events there had to be funerals; but to meet a healthy young woman one morning and learn next evening that she had died was a shock. She stifled a cry of distress.

'An accident? I always think it's so *dangerous* for Continentals; they never expect traffic coming from the left.'

He told her the facts as gently but as briefly as he could. 'I have to speak to the police,' he said, 'so if you don't mind . . .?'

'Of course. I'm so sorry, Mr Crowne. Anything I can do . . .' She was longing to help.

'It's been a long day,' he sighed. 'If you could supply a cup of coffee, it would make a lot of difference.'

'Of course, of course.' She dashed off towards her own quarters. Mr Crowne took the lift up to the third floor.

The door to the studio flat was closed but not fastened. He knocked then stepped inside. A plain-clothes detective was sitting at the bureau looking through some papers. Sounds of activity in the bathroom suggested that a search was going on there.

The detective rose, was about to make some complaint at Greg's arrival, then checked himself. 'Mr Crowne? I'm Sergeant Connors. I was told to expect you. Look, sir, these things in this document case – one or two of them are in French and the others in some other language. Can you give us an idea of what they're about?'

Greg took the magazine that the sergeant was holding out. The prince could get by in most European languages, because the musicians with whom he dealt came from many different countries. He knew enough Polish to recognize that this had been published in Warsaw and appeared to be for nurses.

'Nurses? This so-called countess was a nurse?'

'Well, she was a real countess, but the title was mostly complimentary. And I can only suppose that part of her job with the old lady in Paris had to do with looking after her health. Can't say whether she was a qualified nurse; that never came up.'

Sergeant Connors frowned a little. He didn't care for the implied reprimand in the man's tone. Ex-crown prince, was he? Some tinpot kingdom nobody'd ever heard of. But the powers that be had told him to listen to what this so-called royal had to say, so he took back the magazine, set it aside, and offered a handwritten list. 'So what's that about, please?'

This was in French, in the fine slanting hand of someone schooled many years ago. 'Rose-verbena talcum powder from Gioia of Knightsbridge, Orange Pekoe tea from Fortnum's – it's a shopping list.'

'A shopping list? Some kind of code, maybe?'

The man's a fool, thought Mr Crowne, but patiently translated the rest. They were all the kind of thing an old lady would like to buy for herself if she were able to visit London. If it was a code, that would astonish him.

He translated the French and made such suggestions as he could about the Polish items. These were photocopies of what he took to be articles from health-care magazines. Clearly Marzelina's supply of reading material for her London trip had been chosen for its usefulness, not its entertainment value.

'It seems to me that this stuff proves Countess Zalfeda was what you call a "carer" to Madame Wiaroz. The items in French seem to be shopping and some advice about people to contact if she had any problems.'

'And about the music side?' asked Connors. 'Inspector Glaston sent an instruction that we were to look at anything to do with the music and the research.'

'Of course. So what else did you find? A briefcase or anything?'

'No, sir, this is it.'

'But she's here to do research on Chopin. Where's her research plan, her notes?'

'We looked, sir; there's only the couple of things hanging in the wardrobe, underwear and so forth in one of the drawers, toilet stuff in the bathroom. No papers, no document case or anything of that kind. Nothing in her travel bag – it's empty.'

Greg glanced around. He could see it was true. Marzelina had come to spend two or three days in London, had brought what she needed for that, and these few papers to glance at while she had her morning coffee.

'That's odd. I understood that Madame Wiaroz had sent her here to do a specific piece of research about Chopin. I mean, why else was she at the museum?'

'That's where she was killed?'

'Yes, upstairs in the department given over to foreign visitors to the UK. That's where the information about Chopin is housed. And she told me . . . more or less . . . that she was looking up something . . .'

'Well, there's nothing here, sir, and that's a fact.'

'No passport?'

'No.'

'It wasn't in her handbag at the museum. You're sure it's not here?'

The uniformed policeman who was hovering at the bathroom door shook his head. 'We been here a coupla hours, sir, and it's not exactly a huge area, is it? Looked everywhere – nothing squirrelled away such as in the toilet or anything.'

The studio flat was essentially one room, with a kitchenette and a bathroom partitioned off along one side. There was a single bed discreetly arranged so that in the daytime it could be a sofa, a writing bureau which doubled as a dressing table, a built-in wardrobe, a couple of chairs – all quite elegantly contrived and comfortable enough. These quarters were intended for short-term occupation. The one available to the prince was only a little larger. He understood that an efficient search would soon reveal any secrets.

Sergeant Connors was looking thoughtful. 'Seems the killer got her passport. Could he have taken whatever work she was doing?'

'Oh, don't say that!' Greg exclaimed. 'Killed for some notes on the life of Chopin?'

The sergeant didn't notice the distress in his voice. He said, 'Hardly seems likely. Well, we've done what we came for. You'll verify, sir? We found nothing about the music or the museum or anything of that.'

'Certainly, Sergeant.'

They shook hands; he accompanied the policemen to the lift, to be met by Ms Bryce emerging with a tray of coffee.

'Oh, you've finished? I thought you'd like a cup of—'

'No thanks, ma'am. It's really very late; we'd rather shove off, if you don't mind.'

'Of course.'

They entered the lift; she handed the tray without ceremony to Greg and got in after them to show them off the premises. He, parched and weary, sat down on the upholstered bench opposite the lift and took a hearty swallow of coffee. He had started on the second cup when Ms Bryce came sailing up again, contrite and embarrassed.

'What must you think of me! What a thing to do – I just wasn't thinking!'

'That's all right; I was dying for this. There's one cup left: sit down and drink it.'

'Oh, I shouldn't – it'll keep me awake; but then I don't think I shall sleep anyway.' She sank down on the bench, and picked up the remaining cup of coffee.

'Did they . . . Can I ask . . . Did they find anything helpful?' she ventured.

'Not a thing.'

'What were they looking for?' she burst out. 'Drugs?'

'Well, they didn't find anything.' Drugs? Cannabis? Was that on the shopping list for Mme Wiaroz? He'd heard that cannabis was believed to help in certain very serious ailments, and it was clear that Madame was ailing in some way. . .

Had the death in the museum been brought about by a quarrel over the buying of drugs?

But why on earth come to London to buy cannabis? His friend Arnie Lennard could probably name a dozen locations in Paris where it could be bought with no trouble.

No, poor Marzelina hadn't been killed over a drugs buy. He was sure of that.

But if not that, what?

He finished his coffee and escorted Ms Bryce to her own little nook on the ground floor, to help reassure her that all was well in the gentle world of Bicklesham. Then he went to his own apartment on the second floor, fell into bed, and was asleep within seconds.

Despite his late night, he was up very early next morning. He wanted to ring his family in Switzerland, before any slight hint of the museum event could reach them from some other source. By ringing very early he would find his father, ex-King Anton, alone in his little office next to the stables.

Ex-King Anton made a reasonable living by teaching dressage and advanced horsemanship. When politics had made it essential to leave Hirtenstein with his young pregnant wife and his mother, the Queen Mother Nicoletta, he had settled first in Geneva. Here King Anton's wife had died in giving birth to their son.

Later he had found a little farmhouse some slight distance up into the mountains to make a home for himself, his son, and the ex-queen mother. Here on the three or four flat pieces of terrain he schooled his pupils, youngsters from rich families who could afford to take on this difficult discipline in hopes of competing in the Olympics.

There were only two horses in the stables at Bredoux. Pupils brought their own mounts; but the ex-king was always up early, attending to the horses, cleaning out the stables, catching up with office work. Thankfully, the ex-Queen Mother of Hirtenstein wouldn't be around at that hour.

This was important to Gregory von Hirtenstein. He had scarcely spoken a word to his grandmother in the last twelve months. She and her idiotic monarchical ideas had broken up his relationship with Liz Blair.

All the same, he wanted to prevent any worry. Nicoletta was always in fear of something happening to her grandson. Some wild republican fanatic might take a shot at him. Some scheming tycoon might persuade him to join the board of his conglomerate. Some diplomat might trap him into saying something anti-American, or anti-Russian.

His father's gentle, placid voice greeted him. 'Ah, you're early, my boy. Are you going up a mountain for some skiing?'

'No, Papa; I'm in London, remember? For next year's Spitalfields.'

The king never could keep track of these strange places where his son arranged musical celebrations. He reported that his latest pupil showed promise, that the upland lane had been reopened after a heavy snow, and that ex-Queen Nicoletta was about to leave for an interior-decorating job in Turin. She was somewhat in demand by those who wanted a Biedermeier or a Louis Quatorze look.

Greg delicately introduced the story of Marzelina's death. His father was greatly distressed. 'Dear me, dear me, what a tragedy! My son, you won't get involved in this, now will you?'

'Of course not, Papa.'

Which proved to be extremely incorrect, because less than an hour later, when he was sitting with his second cup of breakfast coffee and the morning paper, Chief Inspector Glaston called.

'Good morning, sir, I hope I didn't wake you?'

'Not at all. Good morning to you, Chief Inspector.'

'Mr Crowne, the Paris force has been in touch with me overnight with a series of emails and telephone messages. It seems very little is known about the late Countess Zalfeda, and Madame Wiaroz gets very upset and weepy when they try to talk to her.'

'Good heavens, they haven't been talking to her all night?'

'No, no, but they went with a woman officer as soon as we got in touch yesterday evening, and Ribonet – that's the woman officer – stayed overnight in the flat because she was a bit concerned about her, and the long and the short of it is, she thinks she's doing more harm than good.'

'Yes?'

'This old dear seems to be tremendously concerned about whatever it was that the countess was to do in London, but they can't quite fathom what the task was.'

'Yes?'

'So . . . the long and the short of it is, sir . . . It's been suggested by my super that *you* might . . . er . . . you know . . .'

'Go to Paris and speak to her? What good would that do? If she won't speak to an experienced questioner such as Mademoiselle Ribonet, why should she—'

'Well, you see, sir, she knows you.'

'Me? I don't recall ever meeting anyone called Wiaroz.'

'Well, no, she hasn't met you; but you're a pal of this journalist Arnold Lennard who put the countess in touch with you, and she knows of you because she's interested in music, and so you see . . .'

It took some further discussion and persuasion, for the prince wasn't keen to deal with a weepy elderly lady; but Glaston promised all travel arrangements would be made and expenses paid.

'OK,' Greg sighed. 'So when do you want me to go?'

'Well, in fact we've booked you on Eurostar at ten-thirty.'

'*Today?*'

'No sense in hanging about.'

'But I . . .' Engagements at various London concert halls to discuss future plans weren't urgent, and in fact he felt guilty in some way. The countess had been put into his care, and she had died. It was his duty to do what he could to help find her killer.

'I think I can make it if the traffic isn't too bad,' he said. 'I've got to change and so forth, though.'

'No problem. Surrey are sending a police car for you—'

'Good Lord, no flashing lights, *please*!'

'No need: drivers always give way to police cars anyway. So you're on for this, right? And you'll let us know anything useful as soon as you get it?'

'Yes, but what's the Paris crowd going to say about this?'

'Oh, they're co-operating fine. Seems you're not unknown to them – for reasons that do you credit, of course. So you won't meet any problems with them.'

'Very well, then,' he sighed.

He dressed in a suit and tie, packed for overnight. It took a little while to explain to Ms Bryce and reassure her. He found it rather enjoyable to be whisked along the motorway in the fast lane.

He was set down at Waterloo station with time to spare. A plain-clothes officer was waiting with his rail ticket and a few passes and telephone numbers to ensure he was given attention. He made his way down the escalator to the Eurostar platform. It wasn't a very busy day – a few ski enthusiasts, a few holidaymakers, a few business types.

Among the passengers on the platform he espied a figure that he thought he knew.

No, it couldn't be her.

But as he came closer, she turned, and there she was – Liz Blair in close-fitting black jeans and a short jacket, and bearing an enormous shoulder bag of bright-green leather.

He stopped. They were only a few yards apart.

'You infuriating man!' she cried. 'Can't let you out of my sight for ten minutes! What have you got yourself into *now*?'

And they flew into each other's arms.

Three

They were still clinging together when announcements began to be heard about boarding the train. Reluctantly Greg tried to detach himself, but Liz clung on and went on board with him.

'Watch out or you'll get carried away to Paris,' he warned.

'I intend to get carried away. I'm going with you.'

He looked puzzled. 'How on earth did you know I was going to Paris?'

'Nitwit! I read about you in the morning paper so of course I rang Bicklesham to ask you how you were doing, and the boss-type lady told me you'd just left to catch Eurostar. So,' she said in triumph, 'since I live in London, I knew I'd get here before you!'

'But . . . but . . . no luggage?'

She patted the enormous shoulder bag. 'Overnight things in here. If I need more – after all, it's *Paris*. I'll buy what I need.'

He laughed. This was one of the things he loved about her: her instant reaction to problem-solving.

They went in search of his seat. The attendant took him in charge and, when informed he'd like to have his companion with him, instantly found him another place with an empty one alongside.

They sat with an arm around each other's shoulders, still half-smiling at their reconciliation. He was happy in a way that had been foreign to him ever since they had parted. She nestled against him with a feeling that she had come home again.

Eventually she asked, 'That was her, the blonde you were dancing with on Tuesday night – that was the Polish girl?'

He nodded.

'In the paper it called you a "colleague in the musical world".'

'Yes.'

'Not anything more?'

'Good heavens, Liz, I only met her on Monday!'

'So only a colleague, then.'

'Of course.' Now it was his turn. 'Who was that well-groomed fellow you were with at the dance?'

'Oh, my secret lover of many years.'

'No, really.' He knew it was a joke, but he still wanted to know.

'Just a bloke in the rag trade – owns a chain of high-street stores.'

'So . . . strictly business.'

'Absolutely.' Though, if she'd been strictly accurate, Reno Pargano might have had other ideas. But that had never really been likely from her point of view.

She wanted to pursue her own line of questioning. He'd been missing from her life so long . . .

'How are things back on the ranch? How's Rousseau?' Rousseau was Greg's loveable red setter, whom she regarded as a friend.

'Oh, he's living with Amabelle and her family now.'

Amabelle, his office assistant, was a young widow with two children who worked part-time except during school holidays. Liz didn't regard her as any competition in Greg's affections. But she was astonished at the news.

'With Amabelle? What's he doing there?'

'Well, you know . . . After what happened last year . . . with Grossmutti, you know . . .'

She said nothing, and they were both silent for a moment of sorrowful recollection. Grossmutti had staged a terrible and public quarrel in a fashionable Geneva hotel. Her aim – which she had successfully accomplished – had been to separate her grandson from a grasping, mercenary girl.

Liz had thrown his ring at him and stormed out. He'd tried to get in touch afterwards to apologize but she'd changed her telephone numbers and ignored his letters. She was sorry now. She might have heard news that pleased her.

'You're not saying you've moved out of Bredoux?' she ventured.

Sighing, he pulled her closer. 'I should have done it years ago,' he admitted. 'But you know, the money that Papa and Grossmutti earn is a bit uncertain, so what I contributed to the household expenses was important. And from time to time I helped Papa with his work – not the tuition, of course, just with the stables and so on. However . . .' He hesitated. 'It was impossible to stay on, unless I was going to . . . to let it seem that I thought Grossmutti was right in what she said.'

His grandmother – the Dragon Lady, Liz called her in her mind. That had been the first time they'd ever met, that occasion in the Hotel Belle Cascade, and she dearly hoped it would be the last.

'So where are you living now? With Amabelle and co?'

'No, no, good Lord, what an idea!' But he saw she was grinning, and gave her a hug. 'No, my angel – you remember Monsieur Guidon, the banker whose son I was supposed to help with his jazz band? He found me a place in a very good apartment block in Geneva.'

'He did, did he? That means he owns it, I imagine.'

'Well, perhaps he does, or the bank does. Anyway, it's old-fashioned but very comfortable. I think you'll like it. Lady friends allowed,' he added, grinning in his turn, 'but not dogs.'

She giggled. He found that astounding. She wasn't the giggling type. But there was so much delight in the sound that he forgave her.

They lunched on the train, though the food meant less to them than the feeling of sharing a meal together again. The train rolled into Paris not long afterwards. A room had been reserved for Mr Crowne at L'Ancienne Cloître not far from the station, so they set down their luggage there. They both changed into clothes more suitable for a house of mourning. Liz put on a slender wool skirt and laid aside the bright-green shoulder bag. The prince added a black tie to his dark suit.

He telephoned Mme Wiaroz to ask if he might drop in. Liz indicated she was ready to go out. He looked up ruefully. Putting a hand over the speaker, he whispered, 'She's dreadfully upset. No wonder the police couldn't get a word out of her.'

'Are we going?' she asked softly.

He nodded. 'Once I explained who I was, she was quite willing to see me. But she's in floods of tears.' He returned his attention to the telephone, saying in French, 'I understand completely, madame. Of course. Yes, of course. I can be there almost immediately . . . Yes, and if I may . . . I have a friend with me, a very sweet and gentle girl; may I bring her?'

Liz raised her eyebrows at this description but said nothing. He made lengthy farewells, then got up from his chair. 'OK then, you're to be sweet and gentle. It seems to me she needs a bit of . . . what do you call it? TLT?'

'I think you mean TLC. OK, I can supply that.'

Mme Wiaroz had an apartment near the Palais de Chaillot, which meant that she had money, a lot of it. They went there by Metro, walking the short distance from the station to the Rue St Cedde.

The hall porter in the marbled entrance was expecting them and murmured condolences in French to Greg, who nodded and murmured appreciation. They were conducted at once to the lift, a capacious modern affair in contrast with the metal cage at the Ancienne Cloître.

The door of the apartment was opened by a woman in something of a maid's uniform – not a lace cap and apron, but a wrap-around of dark blue with half-sleeves. She looked sombre and out of sorts.

'*Un moment.*' She left them in the vestibule while she announced them. When she returned to take their coats she muttered to Greg in French.

As they followed her to the drawing room, Liz enquired, 'What was that?'

'She said she hoped I wouldn't reduce her to yet another outburst of tears.'

'Hm.' It hardly sounded sympathetic. She nerved herself for the task of being sweet and gentle.

The drawing room was furnished in very fine art deco with lustrous surfaces only slightly dimmed by the lowered venetian blinds. Mme Wiaroz was in a leather armchair of the kind that could be turned into a recliner, but in the upright position, and close to a fireplace fitted with an electric fire giving out heat additional to the central heating. A walking stick leaned against one of the arms.

She was a very thin old lady, in a black dress and a delicate black-wool shawl. White hair beautifully styled shone above a lined face, the eyes red-rimmed from weeping.

'*Bonjour,*' she said, '*je vous remercie mille fois pour votre gentillesse, monsieur. Et mademoiselle aussi.*' She gestured to chairs set around the fireplace.

Greg explained that Liz could only speak a limited amount of French. 'Oh, in that case, of course, we speak English. I learned it many years ago at school, as we all did in Poland in those days, you know.'

'This is a hard time for you,' Greg said. 'I'm glad you feel able to talk to us.'

'Of course, anything to help in the matter of ... of ... the death of my dear Marzelina.' She faltered. 'No, I will not shed tears,' she said, after clearing her throat. 'We are trying to help find out what happened to my companion. I will be firm.'

Liz felt it was time to be useful. 'You are very brave, madame. Greg and I will do anything we can. If you feel you can speak to us about her, we'd love to learn more about Marzelina.'

'Ah, my little angel ... She has been with me almost two years. I need someone, you know, to write letters and open the pill boxes. My hands ...' She held one out. It was deformed, with the knotted joints of arthritis. She nodded towards the door.

'Doranne is a good worker and can cook, but music to her means pop songs and Madonna.'

'Marzelina was something like a nurse to you?' asked Greg.

'Oh, only to a slight extent, although she is very keen – was very keen to find ways to help me. Such things as tisanes and essential oils, and gadgets like extended scissors to reach for things. No, Marzie is more to me than that.' The faded-blue eyes began to fill with tears.

'A companion.'

'Yes, a lover of music, and like so many young people, expert with that.' She nodded towards a closed lap-top computer on a desk by the window. She moved her knotted hands a little. 'I, of course, cannot use it.'

'She loved music,' Liz said. 'So she went to London on some task to do with music?'

'Yes, and of course it seemed a very simple thing . . .' Some hint of reluctance came into her voice. She hesitated, then went on in quite a different tone, bright and social. 'What must you think of me? A poor hostess! You have come so far and I offer you no refreshments.' With her closed fist she pressed a button on the table next to her chair. 'Tea? Coffee? Sherry, perhaps, or I have some very good Madeira.'

Greg was about to say they didn't want anything, but a frown from Liz halted him. She said, 'Oh, you know the English: they always think there should be tea in the afternoon.'

Doranne appeared. 'English tea, Doranne,' she commanded in French. 'You make it with the tin labelled Orange Pekoe, remember?'

'And with what?' Doranne said rather testily. 'Lemon? Milk?'

'Milk and sugar,' Greg said. 'If you please.'

Doranne gave him a sulky look and went out.

'Oh dear. She's in such a bad mood,' sighed Mme Wiaroz. 'I must find someone . . .' She faltered. 'Someone to . . .'

'To replace Marzelina,' Liz said, bringing their hostess back to the subject on a note of sympathy. 'But it's too soon to think about that.'

'Yes, yes – Oh, *you* understand! Everyone else has been so official, so . . . so *unfeeling!*'

'But your friends, your relatives?'

'My dear, I've outlived all my friends, except for those I meet when I can get to a concert. And as for relatives: I never had

children and those few members of my family that I still hear
from – ah, they are scattered. Some still in Warsaw, the rest on
the other side of the world – Australia, Canada. And so Marzie
was so precious to me . . .'

'But not a relative.'

'No, no, we met at a piano recital. I have difficulty settling
myself in a seat at a concert hall, you see. And she sprang up
to help me, and then sat next to me and turned the pages of
the programme for me. Such a sweet nature – convent educated,
you know.'

'I think I can guess the recital was of Chopin's music,' Greg
suggested, smiling a little.

'Indeed it was! And so we met again from time to time,
and I invited her here to show her my collection. She was so
interested! And willing to spend time with me because she is
alone in the world – was alone, I mean. Her parents were
lost to her in the tsunami while holidaying in Thailand.'

'Oh, that's very sad,' Liz sighed. 'That took so many lives,
and without warning . . . So it was wonderful that you and
Marzie should find each other, through the music.'

Doranne came marching in with the tea tray. She set it down
and was about to begin pouring, but Liz made a little gesture
of help. Doranne looked at her, shrugged, and walked out. Liz
set about pouring the tea, thinking that before she left the apartment she might hit Doranne hard on the head.

'You mentioned a collection,' Greg said. 'Recordings of
Chopin?'

Mme Wiaroz smiled and swayed her head a little, almost
like a child saying, 'Wouldn't you like to know!' Liz brought
her her tea and set it down, at a nod of instruction, on the little
table. She came back to hover with the milk and sugar. The
blend achieved to the old lady's satisfaction, she was about to
go back to the tea tray.

'The table . . . turns . . . comes round . . .'

'Swivels?' Greg suggested.

Liz tried the idea. The table moved round so that it was
directly in front of Mme Wiaroz.

'Thank you. You are so kind. You know, I would have had
to recall Doranne to do that for me – she never stops to think
what more needs to be done. Marzie always . . .' She let the
words die away.

When they had settled with their teacups, she seemed to make a decision. 'I have been unwilling to speak of this,' she said, 'because I have enemies who would take advantage . . .'

'Enemies?' Liz echoed in astonishment.

'Oh yes. We collectors are by no means friendly towards each other. Items come up so seldom, and we are in fierce competition.'

'But what do you compete for, madame?' Greg asked, with the feeling that at last they were going to learn something to the point.

'They call it "memorabilia" these days. That seems to me a trivial term for what is so dear to us.' She drew in a deep breath. 'I collect whatever I can find that brings me close to my hero, my beloved Chopin.'

Horrid visions of death masks and locks of dead men's hair danced in Greg's head for a moment. Not just CDs or precious vinyl recordings, but clearly something less easily available. Letters, perhaps, or published programmes of his recitals? Diaries of his friends with intimate details – of the composer's love life? Some item of clothing – a glove, a cravat?

Liz, who was less aware of the fanaticism of some of the groupies of the musical world, asked innocently, 'So Marzie was in London to pick up something on your behalf?'

'Something so precious . . .' The old eyes filled with tears again.

Greg said gently, 'Can you tell us about it?'

She blinked and straightened her shoulders. After a few moments to collect her thoughts she began. 'A few weeks ago, I was made aware of the existence of a music manuscript by Chopin that was for sale.'

He frowned. Everything to do with Chopin's compositions was in museums or well-known private collections – and private collectors didn't offer their treasures for sale privately. They consulted experts, they used intermediaries, because great sums of money might be involved. He waited.

'It was Marzie who brought it to my attention. To please me she would visit what I think are called in English "chat-rooms", and it was in one of them she saw the suggestion that such a thing existed.'

'Oh, I sometimes look at that kind of thing, only about fashion,' said Liz, to keep the conversation going, because Greg was frowning even more emphatically.

He was telling himself that serious collectors would never talk about selling anything in a chat room.

'Marzie contacted the sender of the message. After some negotiation he asked us to write to him if we were seriously interested. Marzelina wrote to the address he provided—'

'But, dear lady!' Greg broke out, 'surely you must have been aware—'

'Yes, yes, you are going to say we were being hoaxed. Of course, we thought of that. Marzie – so intelligent, so careful always on my behalf – she wrote. She asked for proof that the manuscript existed. And in return we received something convincing.' She dragged open a little drawer in the chair-side table and nodded to him. 'The key there – it fits that cabinet over by the window. Please open it and bring the blue velvet box.'

The key he picked up was a pretty little thing, the cabinet a twenties secretaire in satinwood. He unlocked it. A blue velvet box, once containing chocolates, lay on the writing surface. He carried it to Madame Wiaroz.

She took it and, with great care and effort, she opened it. 'Look!' she said.

Sure enough, the scrap of manuscript inside was part of a musical score. But only a photocopy.

It dashed through his mind that anyone could make a photo-copy of one of Chopin's music manuscripts. There were books showing examples of his work; he wrote in an almost indeci-pherable scribble and with many crossings out, so that his works had to be copied for the printers by someone who could produce something readable.

'May I pick it up?'

'Of course. It's a copy – we know that.'

'So then you have remembered, madame, that there are many book illustrations showing—'

'But this is something that has never been published!'

'Ah, that isn't likely . . .'

'I tell you, I know every note he ever wrote! I have lived with his music all my life! When my dear husband and I had to flee from Poland because of the Communists, we settled here in Paris; and we kept alive the spirit of our country by playing the music of Chopin to other exiles. He played well, and I too played then . . . Ah, I sold my piano twenty years ago, alas, because I couldn't make music with these hands. But I go to concerts and recitals, I listen to broadcasts, I have hundreds of recordings, and I tell you – this has never been published. It is an unknown work!'

He read through the few bars that were shown on the scrap of paper. 'It's a mazurka,' he remarked. Typically Chopin.

'Yes, and it is known – suspected – that Chopin began on a mazurka while he was in London, shortly before his death. That was the belief of his friends and admirers. It has never been found.'

Greg was silent.

Liz had risen from her seat to come and look at the paper. To her it was a set of uneven rows with little dots and lines and some spidery writing. She could make out '*con espressione*' and a crossing-out that looked like '*vif*'. The photocopied score was shown in the middle of a sheet of paper that was otherwise blank. The score paper had irregular edges, as if torn long ago from a full page.

The prince was no expert on Chopin. Himself a pianist, he'd had to play his work during childhood lessons, but had never found it greatly to his taste. What he was looking at was certainly a mazurka; even in these few lines the rhythm of the Polish national dance was unmistakeable: triple time with an emphasis on the second beat of the measure.

He had an idea that Frederic Chopin had written perhaps sixty mazurkas during his life. He seemed to remember that he was known to be very careless of his manuscripts and that several of them had been lost.

Was this one of them? Was it a genuine excerpt from an unknown work?

Liz put the question in a more forceful form. 'Could it be a forgery?' she asked him quietly.

Mme Wiaroz caught the words. 'No!' she cried. 'I tell you that is his handwriting! Do you think I wouldn't know it, after having looked at his manuscripts in libraries and museums – his many, many letters to friends, his agreements with music publishers?'

'What was the name of the man offering it for sale?'

'Charles Hampton, at an address in London, but once we were in contact he told me that it was only an accommodation address: he shared my fears about the unscrupulousness of collectors. He felt someone might rob him of the manuscript if he let his real address be known.'

'But madame . . .' How could you be so foolish? he was thinking. A false address? Surely alarm bells should have been ringing.

And yet . . . The scrap of manuscript shown on the photocopy had the look . . .

'You are going to tell me I was a fool,' she said, with a hint of annoyance. 'But Marzie was very level-headed and we talked about it for hours. And she thought, like me, that the manuscript was genuine.'

'So you went ahead with the purchase.'

'Yes. Mr Hampton told me I had first refusal, so we made an agreement. I sent Marzie to London with a letter of credit to be honoured at the London branch of my private bank. The asking price was fifty thousand pounds.' She raised her crippled hands to hide her face. 'I sent her to her death.'

Four

This was the moment when Liz realized she must really be a comforter. She knelt by the chair and drew the silvery head to her shoulder. For a time there was no sound except the quiet sobs.

Greg waited for Mme Wiaroz to recover from her burst of tears; then, drawing a deep breath, took up the conversation again.

'Madame,' he said quietly, 'no letter of credit was found among the belongings of Marzelina.'

'Of that I am aware,' she said, lifting her head. 'The police when they came described to me the scene where she was found. No letter of credit. And no Chopin manuscript.' She seemed to shrivel away to nothing against the dark-brown leather.

'Shall I pour you more tea, madame?' Liz suggested. 'Or do you need something stronger?'

'Nothing, thank you. You are so kind, my dear. A tissue so that I can dry my eyes.' She mopped away her tears, then said to Greg, 'I must suppose that the whole intention was to get money from me. I am a fool – I know that now.' She hesitated. 'In a way, I somehow felt . . . I wondered if I was going to be defrauded . . . But I never imagined that Marzie would die.'

'No,' he agreed, his tone neutral. 'And probably that wasn't meant to happen. But if she resisted when he tried to take the letter? And then, she was wearing a long silk scarf – perhaps he only intended to silence any cry she might be making. Perhaps he dragged it too tight.'

'You think so?' she asked, eager for any release from the burden of total guilt.

'It's possible. I think I heard that con men are not usually violent.'

'Con men?'

'Confidence tricksters. *Les voleurs a l'américaine.* What was planned was what you half-suspected: a confidence trick, simply to get money from you.'

'This madness of mine!' she groaned. 'Anything to have some memento of my darling Chopin! And to prevent Armand Gestoupe from getting it first!'

'He is one of the "enemies" you spoke of?'

'A rival, yes. He got one of the candles that was burning in Chopin's room when he died. Yet he is not a true devotee – I heard that he sold it again.' She was indignant at the memory.

Greg said nothing, and Liz looked down so as not to show her surprise at this outburst.

To change the subject, Greg said, 'Marzelina's passport has not been found. I take it that if the letter of credit was presented, the bank would insist on seeing identification?'

'Of course.'

'Have you enquired whether the money has been withdrawn?'

She shook her head, quite vigorously, despite the fact that it must have hurt the withered neck muscles. 'Oh, no! My only thoughts have been for Marzelina! What do I care about the money? If it's gone, it serves me right. If I could pay a million pounds and bring Marzie back, I would do it!'

'Perhaps you could telephone now, madame, and find out whether the letter of credit has been honoured?'

She looked at the gilded mantel clock. 'No, it's too late; the bank is closed now.'

'Which bank?'

'Banque Léonide.'

'Perhaps you could enquire tomorrow?'

'Oh, I don't care!'

He didn't say that it would be helpful to know a fact like that. Instead, he left it to Liz to say comforting words, and after half an hour of kindness and consolation, they left.

Back at the hotel he telephoned Chief Inspector Glaston. The detective grunted in disbelief. 'She doesn't care whether this joker has got away with fifty thousand of her money?'

'She's still trying to come to terms with her grief, Chief Inspector.'

'It's not good, about the letter of credit *and* the missing pass-port. Means the doer knew what he was doing – got himself equipped to go and claim the money.'

'Yes.'

'Well, your poor old lady may think it's too late in the day to get in touch with the bank, but I'll rustle somebody up at the London branch to check.' He sighed. 'If the money's gone, so is the perpetrator. With a load like that, he could take himself off anywhere in the world.'

'I'm afraid so.'

'But, you know, there's something so *specialized* about this. Mme Wiaroz was targeted.' A pause. 'What about these enemies she was talking about? Other collectors?'

'Oh, I . . . No, that seems extreme – I mean, of course these enthusiasts will sometimes play hard tricks; but that's to get hold of something rare, you see. Nobody got anything this time except money.'

'You mean they're not interested in money? To me, that would be "rare"!' He chuckled. 'But let's say this was to do with getting this Chopin thing, and it all went wrong . . .?'

Greg thought about it. 'Well, she mentioned one man. Wait a bit while I try to remember.' He tried to recall what Madame had said. He had an excellent aural memory and after a minute or so it came to him. 'Gestoupe. Albert or Alphonse Gestoupe. He seems to be her greatest rival. And she implied he was a bit mercenary.'

'Well, there's an avenue there. How about you go and see Gestoupe while I chase up somebody at the London branch of Bank Léonide.'

'But I don't know where he lives – and anyhow, what reason could I give for visiting? I can't exactly present myself at his door saying, "Are you responsible for the death of Countess Zalfeda?"'

'You'll think of something,' the Chief Inspector said. 'Stay in touch.' He hung up.

The prince was taken aback, but shrugged to himself.

Liz, having listened to his end of the conversation, asked, 'Are you going to take on the Gestoupe idea?'

'It would be good to know something about him. I don't like to ask Madame Wiaroz in case it gives her ideas – after all, the poor man may have nothing to do with all this.'

Liz gave him an ironic glance. 'Come on! He's interested in music, isn't he? You always call on the Music Mafia in times like this.'

It was true that, through his career as a concert entrepreneur, Greg knew a great many people all over the world who shared his enthusiasms. Liz called them the Music Mafia, but had some respect for them nevertheless. They always seemed full of information and willingness to help.

He began to look thoughtful. Then he got his personal organizer out of his overnight bag and switched on.

'What are you doing?'

'Looking up my contacts among record dealers.'

'What for?'

'If you love Chopin, you want to hear his music played. So it's a good wager – is that what you say?'

'I think you mean a safe bet.'

'Whatever it is, I think Monsieur Gestoupe would collect recordings of Chopin, and not just CDs but vinyl – one of the great specialists in the music of Chopin in the days of long-play records was Horowitz – there are others . . .'

He paused to write down a name, went on for a moment or two, and at last had four possibles on the hotel notepad.

'So these are goodies?' Liz enquired, looking over his shoulder.

'They're dealers I've bought things from myself. I've got their addresses and telephone numbers here. I want somebody I can have a chat with.'

'I'll leave you to it. I'll just dash out and buy some decent soap,' she said.

He nodded and was dialling as she went out. His first attempt yielded an answering machine. Shaking his head, he tried the next one, a shop in Bonn, and got a response in angry German.

'So what's the idea of ringing me at this time of the day? The shop's closed,' said the irate dealer on the other end of the line.

'Berti? I apologize. It's Grego.'

'*Ah, ich freue mich sehr!* Listen, I went to hear your Swiss friend, the baritone, when he was here at Christmas – *ein wirkliche Singvogel*. But if you're ringing about the Hermann Prey, I still haven't found a copy.'

'No, I'm wondering if you have a Chopin fan called Albert Gestoupe on your list?'

'Oh, him! Armand Gestoupe – that's his name. No, haven't heard from him in quite a while. I'm trying to get a nineteen-sixties Ashkenazy for him: Four Ballades. You don't happen to know anyone who has it, I suppose? Give you a good price for it.'

'No, sorry, but I'm thinking of calling on him about something, and I wondered if you could give me some clues. What's he like?'

'Never met him, dearie.'

'But what's he like to deal with? Is he one of those fanatic Chopin enthusiasts – pay anything for what he wants? Offer half as much again to get something that somebody else wants?'

'Why are you bothered about him? I never thought you were a great Chopin fan.'

'No, well, I'm not – never could learn to play him quite right, somehow.'

'You want me to say I'm sure you played him divinely. Well, never heard you play so I can't tell, but you've never shown the slightest interest in him before. What's the buzz? You know something really great is around somewhere?' A pause, then in a reverent whisper, 'Not Paderewski?'

'Oh, good Lord, he probably recorded on wax cylinders! No, no, it's not a recording . . . I've got a clue about something that Gestoupe might be interested in.'

'Such as what?

'A . . . er . . . a letter.'

'A letter? Can't think why people bother with bits of paper. Music's about what you hear, not what you see. You sure Armand would want that? I've never heard him say he was into letters.'

'I was told he'd be interested. But if I put him in touch with the owner, it's going to cost him a bit.'

Berti grunted. 'In that case, I shouldn't bother if I were you, old friend. I got the impression our Armand has fallen on hard times these days. Now if you had that Ashkenazy recording of four of the ballades, he might fork out quite a lot – though not a fortune, you understand. But I never heard him gloating over letters or autographs or anything like that. Still, as I say, I haven't been in touch for months and months.'

'Right. Thanks. I think I ought to let him know about this letter thing but . . .'

'Well, if you see him, give him my regards, won't you, *Liebling*?' He supplied the address in Paris.

They disconnected with friendly words. Greg felt he had learned quite a lot. M. Gestoupe didn't sound like the fierce pursuer of memorabilia that Mme Wiaroz had portrayed. If she really did have 'enemies', M. Gestoupe didn't sound very frightening.

The Paris phone book supplied the telephone number. He rang, and was greeted by a rather sleepy voice. *"Allo?"* it murmured. *'C'est Laurent?'*

'No, monsieur, this is Grégoire Couronne; I'm a concert manager who—'

'Eh . . . Wait . . . Couronne, yes, I've heard of you, I believe. Forgive me, I thought you were my nephew Laurent. Yes, Monsieur Couronne, what can I do for you?'

'Forgive me if I'm disturbing you, but my friend Berti Fiergrunden tells me that you're a great expert on the music of Chopin . . .'

'Ah! So it's that! A concert manager – you want to put on a lecture-recital, yes? At last! Someone shows an interest in having a real discussion about his teaching methods! My dear young man, of course I will do anything I can to further your project – you may rely on that. People forget that Chopin taught the piano as well as playing it in the most masterly and original style.'

'That is a forgotten aspect,' Greg agreed. Forgotten by himself, if truth be told. It was nothing unusual, of course. Beethoven gave lessons, so did Mozart, and so did many others. In the case of Chopin, he said to himself, there would have been a difference: no one else would have been able to teach the method by which he played his works, because at the time it was absolutely unique to the composer.

'Might I come and discuss it with you?' he suggested, hoping that he wasn't raising hopes that might involve him in work he didn't want to do.

'Of course, of course, delighted! My dear sir, please, know that you will be welcome at any time.'

'This evening?'

'Ah . . . well, no; I'm not so fit and young any more, and it will soon be my bedtime, ha ha! But tomorrow, in the morning if you wish?'

'That would be great.'

'Let's say . . . ten thirty? Not earlier, because my nephew has to come and help me get myself up and about, you know. But by ten thirty I should be up and dressed and fit for battle, eh? So ten thirty, then. You have my address?'

Greg repeated it to him over the phone: a little street in the old quarter known as the Marais. 'Yes, you have it right. Until then, Monsieur Couronne.'

Liz had come back while the conversation was going on. 'Was that a dealer, or who?'

'That was Monsieur Gestoupe. I'm going to see him tomorrow morning. Want to come?'

'Ah, now, does he speak English?'

'I never thought to ask him.' He paused. 'No, I'd guess that he doesn't. He doesn't sound as if he's in quite the same class as Madame Wiaroz – probably no lessons in foreign languages when he was being educated.'

'Oh, well then, in that case, how about I go and see Madame Wiaroz? She seemed to me as if she needed kind words and a few cuddles. I'll take her some flowers and chat to her about her "enemies", to see how real they are. I was a bit worried about the way she went on about that.'

'That's a plan,' he agreed.

They turned their minds to their own affairs. They wanted to have a special meal to celebrate their making-up, and after that they had the whole night before them. Time to think of happier things than death and loss.

Next morning Greg found the apartment of M. Gestoupe in an old building in a little street off the Rue St Croix de la Bretonnaise. The concierge, an officious man, checked his name and gestured him onwards. He pushed the correct button according to instructions in the lift and found a door on the second floor being opened by a soberly clad young man as he arrived.

'Good morning,' he said. 'I am Laurent Morgilet, nephew to Monsieur Gestoupe. And you are . . .?'

'Grégoire Couronne.' He produced a card with the correct name. The nephew examined it but didn't take it. He stepped outside to speak in a low voice. 'My apologies, but my uncle wanted to be sure you were who you say you are. He has many very rare recordings and it sometimes happens that . . . er . . . dealers . . . or unscrupulous collectors . . . try to gain access.'

'I understand.'

'This way, then.' He escorted Greg into the apartment, which had lofty ceilings and vast windows, though in need of some redecoration. 'Uncle Armand, here is Monsieur Couronne.'

An elderly man, pale and wearing dark glasses, rose from an armchair to shake hands. And it then became absolutely clear why Berti Fiergrunden had said he wouldn't be interested in letters or programmes: M. Gestoupe was blind.

'I'll leave you then, if I may, Uncle?' To Greg he said in apology, 'I'm needed at my office. You must excuse me.'

'Of course.'

The uncle was still standing very close to Greg and holding his sleeve. 'Please, sit down.' He gestured towards a chair, and Greg obeyed. 'Now, with regard to the lecture: you may well imagine I have had it in mind for quite some time. I have here . . .' He took his own seat and expertly found a folder on a table beside it. 'Here is the outline of how I think it should be organized. You are aware, no doubt, that Chopin only set down a few notes of his teaching method in his last months, before he died.'

'No, I wasn't aware—'

M. Gestoupe swept on in an eager, almost challenging voice. 'Despite what some critics say, there was nothing effeminate in his playing! Those who heard him during his lifetime testified to the power and drama of his touch. Take for instance, the ending of the C sharp minor Etude – you know the one I mean: in Opus Ten; no one could ever judge that to be intended as weak.' He pointed towards shelves on the side of the room against the door. 'If you look at the record labelled "Rubinstein – Etudes and Waltzes", you will see the cover makes special mention of the power of Rubinstein's rendering of the last four bars.'

Greg rose to inspect the shelves. They had wooden slots built on them, upright, so as to contain old long-playing records. Each slot was labelled by means of some machine that gave raised lettering, so that by placing his fingers on them M. Gestoupe would know he had found what he wanted.

Greg didn't take out the old record to read its sleeve. He

was prepared to take his host's word for what it said. The man was clearly an expert on interpretation and in any case had gone on to something else by now.

'We should invite directors of music schools and orchestral conductors to the lecture. It's time they understood that teaching piano in general and teaching the music of Chopin are two entirely different things. I went to a performance of the E minor concerto with the Aquitaine Orchestra last month, and it was shocking, truly shocking!'

And so on. Greg wasn't bored, but he was quite at a loss. This enthusiast was almost obsessive about changing the method by which pianists learned to play Chopin, and that was by no means what interested him. He wanted to know if Armand Gestoupe was an 'enemy' of Mme Wiaroz.

By and by Gestoupe ran out of breath. Seizing the moment, Greg said, 'We could perhaps get Madame Wiaroz to help promote the lecture. She could probably summon up many Polish friends.'

'Ah, Madame Wiaroz,' Gestoupe echoed. 'I heard something very shocking yesterday – is it true, do you know? – that the little girl died, the girl who acted as companion to Madame?'

'I'm afraid so.'

'How very sad.' And the man seemed truly affected. 'Although Madame dislikes me, we have much in common. Not only our love of Chopin, but we each have a disability. I am, of course, very lucky: I have relatives to help me here in Paris, but not Madame, alas. I think I ought to send a message of condolence, but you know I can't write, and it's no use sending Braille, now is it?'

'I got the impression from Berti that you and she were often in competition for recordings?'

'Oh, not for years. Ah, I used to spend almost every penny I earned on that, but . . . well . . . I had my own business – gloves and scarves from Italy and Romania – but I had to sell up when my sight finally went. So now I have to be careful, and I don't collect any more.' He sighed then chuckled. 'Why should I? Look at what I already have!' He gestured to the shelves along his walls. Recordings – old singles, long-players, modern CDs. Not a sign of anything needing eyesight.

'True, Monsieur Gestoupe. You seem to have a fine collection.'

'Worth quite a lot. Laurent will get it when I die, and of

course he'll sell it because he thinks my interest in Chopin is mere folly. But he's a good lad, a good lad.'

They chatted for another hour. The prince began to think there really would be some interest in a lecture-recital but said he would have to think about it. He left when a young woman arrived, a voluntary carer who would cook lunch for M. Gestoupe.

As he walked towards the Pompidou Centre for the Metro, he was deciding that M. Gestoupe had played no part in the confidence trick about the Chopin manuscript. In the first place, he seemed not to feel any great enmity towards Mme Wiaroz. In the second, he wasn't interested in things you merely looked at – there had been nothing of that kind in his living room. And lastly, he didn't have the money to finance a set-up like the trick played on the old lady.

He had arranged to meet Liz at a favourite restaurant near the Miromesil station. She was already there, sipping Badoit. She leapt up to hug him when he appeared.

'*Juste ciel!*' he remarked, returning the hug but surprised at this public display of affection. 'What has brought this about?'

'Oh, Greg, it's just so *sad*! She's totally lost without Marzie. And that dreadful woman Doranne bounces about, huffing and pouting whenever she has to do anything – I could kick her!'

They sat down next to each other on the leather bench. She pressed close to him for comfort. Greg said, 'We'll find someone to take over in Marzie's place.'

'We will?' She stared at him. 'You in on a domestic-service mafia as well as the musical one?'

'My dear angel, there are musical students who are very hard on.'

She laughed. 'I think you mean hard up!'

'Very likely.' He sometimes let himself make mistakes so that she could correct him – he loved the grin of amusement when she did. 'There are students who would be very willing to help Madame Wiaroz for a little pocket money. I'm sure I can find one for her. That's if she would like it? Perhaps she couldn't bear to have anyone take Marzie's place?'

'Oh, I think she knows she needs someone, Greg. Oh, you are a darling! Get on to it at once, will you?'

'As soon as I've reported to Chief Inspector Glaston that Armand Gestoupe can be ruled out.'

'You sure?'

He gave her a brief description of his meeting. She was
astonished at the subject matter. 'You mean you think people
would actually pay money to be lectured at about how Chopin
taught his piano students?'

'Not many, perhaps. It would be small-scale. But I'll do a bit
of research. The Museum of Musical Heritage will help me –
they might have names of people who go there to look up Chopin.'

'Gee, you're a glutton for punishment. Well, right, we feel
Monsieur Gestoupe doesn't sound a likely criminal; so where
does Glaston look next?'

'It will depend on the money. If that letter of credit has been
presented and honoured, then it's a pointer – I mean, a *woman*
would have to present that, using Marzie's passport. So that means
a . . . Wait . . . a confederate – that's the word. So it's not just
some single person trying a trick on Madame Wiaroz; it's a plot.'

'Greg . . .'

'What?'

'Madame Wiaroz and I got talking . . . and I was saying
how clever you are, and how you know people everywhere
in the musical world and that if this man, whoever he is,
goes around tricking other collectors who want to buy music
memorabilia . . .' She faltered into silence.

'Tricking other collectors – yes, I get that. What else?'

'I more or less promised her that you'd find the man who
killed Marzie.'

Five

A fter this announcement there was a silence. She tried to
see whether he was vexed, but he'd turned to order his
drink from the waiter.

When he spoke, it was in a tone of deliberation. 'Glaston
may have somebody in custody already.'

'You think so?'

'Who knows? I think I heard that a con man has his own

style – for all I know there may be somebody that specializes in real or forged music scores. Glaston may have put his finger on him by now.'

'Does that sound likely to you?' she challenged.

'Well . . .'

'Here's this guy; he sets up a big temptation for a particular old lady in Paris who is fanatical about Chopin. How many criminal types do you think there are who can zoom in on a target like that? And, excuse me if this sounds like a put-down on them, but how many policemen do you think you'd find who know much about highbrow music?'

'Well . . . I really have no idea.'

'Don't bother looking. When you speak to him, you ask Mr Glaston who he has in mind as Marzie's killer, and if he says he knows exactly who he's looking for, I'll donate my new Paul Smith to a charity shop.'

'You may be right, but Glaston isn't going to want me meddling in his inquiries.'

'Meddling? You're not going to meddle. You're going to offer him some useful hints on where to look for the louse that tricked poor Madame Wiaroz and took away her best friend. You must know you've got more idea where to look than he has.'

'Well . . .'

'Stop saying "well . . .", because it doesn't get us anywhere.' She finished her glass of mineral water then picked up the menu. 'Let's eat,' she commanded, 'and then you'll telephone Glaston.'

'Not here. I can't have a conversation like that on a mobile in a busy restaurant.'

'Right, then, we'll go back to the Ancient Monastery, or whatever it's called. And afterwards,' she said, in a much more sweet-natured way, 'who knows? – we may go in for a little relaxation.'

Chief Inspector Glaston, when contacted, sounded downcast. 'No luck here,' he admitted. 'We checked the accommodation address that Madame Wiaroz wrote to, but the owner doesn't remember who hired the box. Dozens of clients, he says; can't be expected to remember one particular one. That's bad enough, but there's more.'

'What?'

'The letter of credit. It was cashed on the same day that the countess was killed. Late afternoon. A woman came in, presented it, had an authentic passport as identification.'

'A woman.'

'Yeah, had to be, didn't it? – because the passport was Marzelina's. The bank clerk gives a description: blonde, medium height, speaking with a foreign accent; 'sfar as he's concerned it was the countess.'

'But if he was going to hand over bundles of banknotes, surely he'd . . . I don't know . . . consult a colleague?'

'He wasn't handing over cash. The money was transferred immediately to an authenticated account in the Cayman Islands. The bank there is being less than helpful. We can't find out whether the money stayed there or went on somewhere after that.'

Greg accepted this in silence.

'Hello?' said Glaston. 'Did you get that?'

'He's well organized, isn't he?'

'You've said it! The thing is, I don't know where to go next, unless your old lady's "enemies" are turning out to be important.'

'Not in the least. My friend Ms Blair spent all morning with Madame Wiaroz and she tells me she's sure there's really nothing in all that – they're just very ordinary people who've beaten her to the purchase of some item.'

'That's a pity.'

'*I* spent the morning with the chief suspect, Monsieur Gestoupe, and he turns out to be a blind man in rather poor health who's living on his pension.'

'Oh, Lord.'

'Yes, the criminal isn't going to be found here in Paris among Madame's so-called "enemies" – I think I can say that for certain. It seems more likely that it's in London, or somewhere in the UK, that the criminal set it up.'

'Yes,' agreed Glaston on a sigh, 'because he arranged a London address as a meeting place and asked for the money in pounds, not euros.'

'Exactly.' Greg paused before going on. 'The main theme of the plot is Chopin. The trickster gets to know Madame through a chat room devoted to Chopin; he offers a piece of a Chopin score as bait; he arranges to receive the money in a room in a museum where Chopin's visit to Britain is chronicled.'

'And that leaves *me* more or less in the dark. I've got nowhere to go and no groundwork to depend on. My super is saying this has to be put on the back burner.'

'Where?'

'It has to be set aside while I deal with other cases – those where I'm getting results.'

'I see.'

'I'm really sorry, Mr Crowne. I wish I could offer more optimism. And I'd like to thank you very much for handling the Paris end of this for me. I've told the Sûreté people that I regard the case as on hold, and they agreed. So that's that.'

Liz heard a repeat of this conversation with muted indignation. 'Great! He's going to do nothing – is that it?'

'He's got nothing he can do, Liz.'

'Oh, so he sent some great clod-hopping constable to ask at the postal shop if he remembered a customer and the owner said no he didn't. What do you bet it was some little place where they sell bus passes and cigarettes and can send money home to Tashkent or Timbuctoo?'

'I think that's probably right, but what point are you making?'

'If some sweet, well-mannered person had come into the shop and asked the man nicely, don't you think something might have been remembered?'

'Some sweet well-mannered person being you?'

'Well, I'm quite ready to give it a try. And as for you: what about all the Chopin stuff? What about the people at the museum? Can't you wangle some information out of them?'

'It might be a good starting point.'

'There you are. Let's ring the airport to get on the next flight.'

'No, something else comes before that.'

She laughed. 'You mean that promise about a little relaxation?'

He shook a finger at her. 'You have a frivolous mind. No, no. Before we leave, I have to find someone to take Marzelina's place with Madame Wiaroz.'

The laughter left her face. 'Oh. Yes. And we have to go and see Madame, don't we? – to say goodbye and tell her we're going to help.'

'And also to recommend the person who will replace Marzelina; but first I have to find her. And for that I need the phone book.'

An afternoon of conversations with various teachers at conservatoires, friends with student daughters and rich people fostering the careers of budding opera stars left him with two possibles as companion to Mme Wiaroz. He telephoned them to ask if they might be willing to undertake the role of companion to an elderly Chopin fanatic. One seemed quite keen, the other less so but needed the money.

Mme Wiaroz agreed to see them in the evening. It would leave Greg and Liz time to catch a nine o'clock flight to London. She was distressed to hear they were leaving, but took it heroically. 'And you will, as dear Liz has suggested, pursue this villain who took Marzie from us?'

'I will, madame, so long as the London police have no objection. But to do so . . .'

'Yes?'

'The photocopy of the supposed Chopin manuscript – may I borrow it?'

She shuddered a little and sighed but indicated the drawer with the key to the cabinet. He took out the chocolate box and extracted the sheet of copier paper. 'You'll find an envelope in the escritoire,' she directed. She watched intently as he inserted the copy into the envelope, shaking her head. 'I know it's foolish; it may be a sham, yet it *might* be by his own hand.' She managed a little, foolish smile. 'I believed I would know his writing with absolute certainty. And I still think . . . I still can't persuade myself . . .'

'You think it's genuine.'

'Yes . . . You'll say I'm a silly old fool. But you know, Grégoire, it *is* possible.'

'Because some of his manuscripts are known to be missing?'

'Because this offer came from *London*. The score, if it exists, might be one of those he had with him in London.' She was setting the information in order so as to convey it with conviction. 'He went there in 1848, you know – very ill, but at the insistence of the terrible Jane Stirling.'

'And who is Jane Stirling?' Liz enquired, looking to Greg for the information. He, however, shrugged and looked as puzzled as she did.

'Ah, who is Jane Stirling! The bane of his life at that time!' She made an angry gesture with one of her little gnarled hands. 'Jane Stirling! Music lover, piano student, rich middle-aged Scottish lady who became passionately attached to my poor dear Chopin! There were others who came to learn under his tuition – many women – and I cannot blame them if they felt devotion but *she* . . .!'

'What did she do?' Liz asked, quite alarmed at the ferocity of her dislike.

'She persuaded him to go to London. He needed the money so he went. That was bad enough: he was ill, he should have stayed at home and been nursed carefully; but no, she tempted him with tales of how much he would be paid, and so he went, and then *she* persuaded him to go to Scotland – to Scotland!' There was incredulity in her tone. 'I have never been there but everyone knows: in Scotland it is cold, it rains and snows, the castles and stone houses are draughty and uncomfortable; and he was desperately unhappy – you cannot know how unhappy he was, in his letters to his friends here in Paris he laments ever having agreed to . . .' Her energy failed; her voiced died away.

Liz, who had been in charge of coffee brought in earlier, now poured a fresh cup for Madame and stayed by her as a comforting presence. By and by she looked up, summoning a tremulous smile.

'You think I am mad. But I love him. I believe that if I had been in London when he visited there, I would have prevented him from going north. I would have saved him.' She blinked away tears. 'However, setting aside my imaginary world, I believe that my poor beloved Chopin was writing this mazurka of mine while he was being dragged around Britain. He was always working, though he was often dissatisfied with what he wrote, and I believe that the manuscript might have been left . . . *might have been left!*'

She stopped for a moment to see if they were listening intently enough. 'He was writing wherever he was staying – in other people's homes. And when he eventually escaped from his so-called friends and came home to die, the mazurka offered to me by Mr Hampton was left behind.' She nodded at the envelope that contained the photocopy.

Her listeners were startled. Her belief in the possibility was fervent. That explained why she'd let herself be convinced into sending her companion to London to buy the manuscript: there *was* actually a chance that the composer had left papers of some kind behind him.

She accepted the coffee that Liz was offering again and, holding it between her two hands, sipped a reviving mouthful. Then she said, 'He was careless, my poor Chopin. He was also a perfectionist. He rewrote and scribbled over everything. When his servant was packing to go home, there might well have been paper that Chopin regarded as litter. "Throw it away" – I can imagine him saying it. But someone might have saved it.'

Greg allowed a moment or two to pass while she had another sip or two. She returned the cup to Liz, who placed it on her chair-side table and hovered, in case she was needed again.

'Madame,' said Greg, tapping the envelope, 'let me take this with me to London. The Museum of Musical Heritage should be able to recommend an expert who can look at the writing and make a judgement on its authenticity.'

She looked away. Liz felt she could almost hear the sound of her heart strengthening itself for this farewell. Then she said, 'Yes, of course. It must be examined, I understand that. But you will take care of it?'

'Of course. And thank you for letting me take it.'

'Oh, well . . . I trust you. But looking at it with logic, what is it? A sheet of paper with a photocopy – absurd to treasure it!'

He put the envelope aside, taking care not to bend it carelessly or put it in his pocket, because he knew it would hurt her to see that. 'I'm afraid we must be going soon. But before we leave – may I offer you some possible replacements for Marzelina?'

'What?'

'No one can be the same, I know that, madame. But Liz and I . . . we would be worried about you if we left you with no one to . . . to . . .' He'd been going to say, 'intervene between you and your servant', but let it drop.

She smiled. 'How kind. But I couldn't bear to have some stranger who didn't share my interests . . .'

'I can't guarantee that either of them will love Chopin as you do, but they are both musicians.'

'Really?' The blue eyes brightened a little. 'Polish, perhaps?'

'Ah, no, that was beyond my reach. But they are both pleasant young ladies, so far as I could gather by telephone, and were recommended by friends of mine.'

'That is so good of you! There are two?'

'Yes.'

'But I don't know if I would care to summon them here and interview them – I'm not good at that kind of thing. You see I was mistaken when I hired Doranne.'

He smiled in commiseration. 'Speak to my two nominees on the phone. Then you might know whether you want to see them in person.'

'Ah.' A long hesitation. 'Which one had the sweeter voice?'

Liz, unseen by the old lady, raised her eyebrows at him and grinned at the question.

He laughed. 'This is your process of elimination?'

'Oh, my dear boy, I'm so old and it's so hard for me to meet strangers . . . Tell me which one you think had the gentlest heart.'

'Well, I would say Céleste Plagiet . . .'

'Then I'd like to speak to her. Will you dial the number for me?'

Mlle Plagiet had been hoping for the call and replied eagerly when he asked if she would speak to Mme Wiaroz.

He and Liz fetched their coats. When they were ready to leave, Madame was awkwardly replacing the receiver. 'Well, she sounded nice. She is coming tomorrow morning to see if she would like to work for me.'

'I hope it will turn out well. If not, telephone me, and if you like, I'll try again.' He laid a sheet from the hotel pad on her table, with the number of his mobile and of the phone where he would be staying in London – with Liz, of course.

They reached her North London flat in late evening. She rushed around switching on lights and heating, tidying away discarded shoes and the fashion sketches she'd abandoned on reading the newspaper with the story of Marzelina's death.

'We'll want to eat. Shall we go out now, while the place is getting itself revived, or order some pizza or something?'

'"A jug of wine, a volume of verse, and thou,"' he quoted.

'You what?'

'It's an invitation by a Persian poet to his beloved.' He took her in his arms. 'I may have got the words a bit wrong, because I only know it in French, but I hope you get the message.'

She giggled. 'Don't have any volumes of verse. But wine, yes . . . and as for the rest: let's find out.'

Before they finally settled down to sleep, he telephoned Chief Inspector Glaston. The detective was off duty, as he had expected. He left a message saying he intended to consult a musicologist in the morning in hopes of learning something

about the handwriting on the scrap of music manuscript, and
if Glaston disapproved, would he please telephone first thing.

To his surprise, Liz had kept some of the clothes he'd left
in the flat in times past. 'I thought you'd have cut everything
up with those great scissors you use for dressmaking,' he
murmured.

'I was going to give it all to Oxfam. But somehow I didn't.'

He was therefore able to dress respectably before he set out
for the meeting with Professor McDavis at the museum. Liz
had elected to try her luck at the place where the so-called
Charles Hampton collected his mail.

It turned out to be in a busy little street in Shepherd's Bush
alongside the railway track. As she'd prophesied, the shop had
several lines of business: it sold cigarettes and lottery tickets,
it had a fridge with cold drinks and sandwiches for the lunch-
time crowd, and on the wall further into the premises there
was a shelf with locked boxes; but, contrary to her hopes, her
chances of bewitching the proprietor with her blonde charms
and pretty clothes were nil, for she found a portly middle-aged
Asian lady in charge today.

'Ach, you aren't the police, are you? – the police already ask
all this,' she said irritably when Liz began with an enquiry after
Mr Hampton. 'Mr Hampton, Mr Hampton – I don't remember.'

'I'm a friend of Charlie's,' Liz invented wildly. 'I only get
his answering machine when I ring, and when I dropped by
yesterday, he wasn't at his flat.' The rest of this lie had to be
suspended while the shop-lady served a customer. Since it was
Saturday, there was a brisk sale in lottery tickets.

When she turned back from dealing with the sale, she looked
vexed at finding Liz still there. 'Yes?' she said in a cross voice.

'Do you know if Charlie's moved?' Liz asked.

'Already I told all this. I don't know him – nothing about him.
He rented box. One month. He came in some time, and he went
– I don't remember. When he finished with the box, he leave
the key in the lock; this is before the time runs out, a month.'

'Are we talking about the same man?' Liz persevered. 'Tall,
thin, has a moustache?'

'I don't remember.' A man came in asking for cigarettes. She
gave him her attention. Finding Liz still at the counter afterwards, she said with a sigh, 'I don't think he had moustache.'

'But tall and thin?'

She was shaking her head. 'I don't remember.' Two children came in for fizzy drinks. When she had served them, she said slowly to Liz, 'Nice soap.'

'What?'

'I remember he smell of nice soap.'

Fifteen minutes of intermittent coaxing produced nothing more. No moustache and smelled of nice soap. Easy to identify him from that.

Greg was meanwhile greeting Professor McDavis, recommended by the curator-in-chief of the museum, who performed introductions and led them up to the second floor. The professor, a portly man in his early sixties, panted a little as they went.

'You'll find the specimens of Chopin's work, such as we have, in this display cabinet.' He tapped it. 'Here is the key.' He produced it and also some cotton gloves. 'If you pick up the score or the autographed programmes, please wear these. There are some photographs of a page or two of various scores in "Collected Works" – Paderewski's editions – and a letter is reproduced facsimile in Hedley. I've had the stacks rolled open at the Chopin bookshelves, to save you from having to manipulate the rollers.'

'Thank you,' the professor said. 'Will other people be coming in?'

'No, no, I've arranged for you to have the room to yourself for as long as you wish. Please call me if you need anything.' He nodded at the wall telephone. 'Press ten for my office.'

The professor put on the gloves before gently lifting the page of music from the display cabinet. He carried it to a table, where they sat side by side. He switched on a swan-necked lamp, then sat, quietly staring at the page.

The work was by no means as chaotic as the prince had been led to expect. The writing was spindly but quite legible and with only two alterations, both smudged but neat.

'We see that this was written in 1839,' said McDavis, referring to the card that had lain beside it in the case. 'I'm no expert on the career of Frederic Chopin, but I gather that what you have to show me was supposedly written some ten years later.'

'Yes. And when he was in very poor health.' Greg opened the document case lent by Liz, and took out the envelope with the photocopy. He'd already explained the circumstances to

McDavis on the phone, to be greeted with snorts of protest at being asked to examine a photocopy.

'Mm-m,' said the expert, eyeing it as it was laid on the table alongside the genuine manuscript. 'It isn't good science, you know, trying to say anything useful from a photocopy.'

'I understand. But anything you can tell us would be very helpful.'

'Well . . . Can't say anything about the original paper, although you can see for yourself from the copy that it's several shades darker than the A4 sheet it's copied on. The tear looks rather fresh – see – its edges aren't frayed or crumpled, as they would be if the paper had been torn a long time ago. So I'd say that whatever this scrap is, it's from a sheet of old paper but freshly torn.'

Old paper. Greg felt divided emotions : a little surge of optimism that the paper was old and sadness that the trickster had torn it. Because if it, by any chance, was really by Chopin, to have torn it was vandalism.

'However . . .' said McDavis.

His heart sank at the word.

'The writing on the *original* from which it's copied is faint. Very little pressure on the pen. The single alteration on the bottom line of the stave . . . I don't know . . . You see the semiquaver – I don't know if that's done by the same pen. But then . . .' He wagged a gloved finger. 'We could expect a piece of music to be composed over a period of time – Chopin might easily have made the alteration with a different pen.'

'Does "faintness" imply a forgery?'

'Not necessarily. A forger is likely to press rather heavily because he needs to work quickly. *Hesitation* is one of the most important signals that writing is being copied. In this case, if we consider that the composer was in poor health, the faintness may be due to fatigue.' He made the little snorting sound that seemed to be his way of conveying disbelief. 'We are accepting, of course, that Chopin was in very poor health at this time. So, my good friend, the forger might take that into account when he set to work.'

'Only if he knew much about the life of Chopin,' Greg objected.

'But, surely – if a man was going to undertake a fraud based on a piece of music by Chopin, he'd do some background research?'

'Yes, of course he would.' A sigh of frustration. 'It would be so much better if we had the real piece of paper.'

'It would be better, but not conclusive. Forgers can easily find paper from the Victorian era. Remember that in those days there was no recorded music. If you wanted entertainment, you had to have real people there. So there were millions of pianists, and probably thousands of composers or would-be composers, scribbling away on music manuscript. There's plenty of paper in old piano stools and books and folders. The ink too – now that we know so much more about the ingredients of ink, it's not so difficult to make a very good replica.'

'You're not being very constructive, Professor,' Greg groaned.

'Well, we can't tell very much from the mechanics. Let's see if we can find out anything by making a strict comparison of the handwriting.'

He laid the photocopy close to the genuine specimen from the showcase. To Greg's untrained eye, the writing looked identical.

McDavis sat alongside, whistling softly to himself – to his hearer's irritation, whistling not the music on the Chopin score but what sounded like something by Rossini.

'Well?' he asked at last.

The professor eased his head backwards and did a few shakes, to let it be known he'd been under a strain. 'Could be,' he murmured. 'Could be. Yes, the similarities – you see how he writes the G clef. That swirl of the curve – that would be difficult to do with certainty if you're forging it. And you see how the notes are grouped for a *trilleto* in the genuine score – that's very like the run-up here on the photocopy, though that's shorter.'

'Please tell me – are you saying you think the photocopy is a piece from a genuine Chopin composition?'

'Let's look at a few other examples of the real thing.' He strolled off to the shelves where the Chopin reference books were housed, leaving Greg to stare in glum depression at the manuscript already examined and the photocopy. The expert returned with three books. The reproductions he wanted to examine were at the front. He laid them all out in a row and stooped over them.

The examination and the intermittent debate went on for an hour and a half. Since the professor spent a lot of time staring in silence at the illustrations and the manuscripts, Greg amused himself by reading one of the books – a life of the composer.

In the end, with the manuscript and the letter returned to their case and the books to their shelves, McDavis delivered his verdict.

'I can't say,' he announced.

'*Might* it be from a genuine piano score by Chopin?'

The reply went into a lengthy weighing-up of the pros and cons, ending with an almost equally lengthy defence for being so indefinite.

Greg gave up. Depressed, he called the curator, who locked up the display case and collected the cotton gloves for laundering. They made their way downstairs, making polite noises to each other. He was glad to get away, to ring Glaston on his mobile and report on the morning's work.

'So, to put it bluntly, your professor was no help.'

'I can't quite say that, Chief Inspector. In a way it justifies Madame Wiaroz. She swore to me that that was Chopin's handwriting, and it turns out my professor couldn't swear it wasn't.'

A deep sigh came over the phone. 'Look, could we meet for a drink and a chat? I don't mind admitting I'm totally out of my depth here.'

'Well, I'd arranged to meet someone for lunch . . .'

'Your young lady? Well, why don't you bring her along, eh?'

'Where to, exactly?'

'How about the Dragon, in Clove Street?'

'Where on earth is that? Liz and I are meeting in a place just off Shaftesbury Avenue.'

'OK, I'll meet you there.'

Greg gave him the address of the wine bar, hailed a taxi, and set off to meet Liz, who arrived with carrier bags and packages.

'Dropped in on a fabric supplier on my way,' she explained. 'I'm doing a mock-up of a spring spencer for Barbatar; they're thinking of going ethnic.'

'Was that in the English language?' He seldom understood her references to the fashion world. He knew she had a talent for copying whatever appeared on the catwalks – her designs were never exactly illegal but they always seemed to catch the right note. He also knew that she made a good living out of that talent. But that was as far as his understanding went.

He explained that the Chief Inspector would be joining them.

'What's that for?' she rejoined. 'To tell you to clear off and let him get on with it?'

'Quite the opposite. I think he wants to pick my brains . . .'

'Which may take some time because you have so many, sweetheart.'

'Thank you. And you have too, and moreover you're very beautiful, which is what you wanted me to say.'

'Yes, well, don't let's tell Mr Glaston that I went to the shop where the letters were sent. I don't think he'd like that.'

'Probably not. What did you find out?'

'Charles Hampton didn't have a moustache and used scented soap.'

He laughed. 'Very useful.'

'The lady didn't remember him at all, really. The shop's busy. She said he rented the box for a month and left his key in the lock before the month was up. So that seems to mean he just had it long enough to receive the letter saying Madame Wiaroz was going to pay.'

'Upon which he telephoned, giving time and place for delivery of the money.'

'Seems so.'

'Scented soap?' he said, going back to her first remark.

'Her exact words were, "He smell of nice soap."'

The arrival of Mr Glaston put at end to this discussion. He settled himself at their table, picked up the menu, summoned a waitress with a wave of one finger, and ordered a sandwich and a glass of Chardonnay.

They followed his example. That done, Glaston turned at once to business.

'This supposed piece of Chopin's work may actually exist, then?'

'Professor McDavis didn't rule it out. And you know, Madame Wiaroz put up a good case for it. She said he might have been working on it while he was on a visit to Britain and could have thrown it away as – I don't know – not good enough.'

'Do composers do that? – throw stuff away?'

'Well, these days I think they may be more organized. They do use computers, and modern business methods have pushed them into keeping better records, because there are royalties to be considered, contracts with record companies, that kind of thing. But in the past . . .'

'And what I'm told is that there actually was a – what was it? – a mazurka that got lost?'

'Oh, good heavens, there were several. I was just reading about his work this morning, while the professor was see-sawing about the photocopy. There are at least ten of Chopin's works that never got to publication stage – *at least*. So there could quite easily have been a mazurka he was writing while he was in London or'– he paused to recollect – 'Manchester or Edinburgh.'

'Well, I don't think I'll get the manpower to go on a round-Britain tour over this. It would mean asking other forces to take over bits of the inquiry, and I can imagine how enthusiastic they'd be about that – going round museums and libraries asking if Chopin left a piece of his music there.' His tone mimicked what he thought the response would be.

They all accepted their food and wine, and for a moment or two concentrated on that.

Then the chief inspector said, 'It needs someone who knows something about this bloke and his compositions.'

Liz gave Greg a dig in the ribs. 'Volunteer!' she urged.

'But ...'

'If you're worrying about treading on police toes, sir, I can sort that out for you.'

'And if you're thinking about the cost,' Liz said, 'Madame Wiaroz told me she'd give anything – money or information or whatever was needed – to help you find Charles Hampton.'

He quibbled for some minutes, trying to put forward reasons why it wouldn't work. But his heart wasn't in it. So it became a certified project. He was going to look for the man who was offering for sale a lost and unknown work by a great composer – because the man was perhaps a forger, and certainly a fraudster and a murderer.

Six

Liz cleared away all the artist's paraphernalia in her living room so as to make room at a table for a planning session. She made coffee, brought it to the table, drew up two chairs, and said, 'Well now, where do we begin?'

'I've been thinking,' Greg said. 'First of all, we learned that a woman cashed in the letter of credit. So far I've only been thinking of one man doing all this; but now we know he's got an accomplice. I think I have to go back to the museum and ask whether a woman has been showing an unusual interest in the section with the Chopin material.'

'You'll get as much joy out of that as I did in the letter-collection place. Without a description, it's hopeless.'

'But we do have a description of the woman.'

'No we don't!'

'Yes. She must have looked something like Marzelina, mustn't she?'

'Ah.' Liz was taken aback, but thought about it. 'Well, yes. If the bank clerk checked the photograph in the passport which was used for authentication, the woman must have looked like Marzelina.'

'Exactly.'

'No, wait – I mean, Greg, any woman can put on a blonde wig and – well, I suppose she'd have to buy contact lenses if her eyes weren't the right colour, but for so much money, she'd do it. So I don't think you can put too much reliance on the description.'

He wasn't prepared to let the idea be dismissed. 'Look here, it had to be someone about the right height – it couldn't have been a great big Amazon because Marzelina was slim and about a hundred and sixty-five centimetres. And the height is given on the passport.'

'That's about five foot six,' she murmured. In dress design, she was used to working in both measurements but found it easier to picture a human being in the old familiar terms. 'Right, a woman about medium height, blonde, fair complexion – what colour of eyes?'

'Blue.'

She gave him a frown of mock reproof. 'You needn't go on as if you've got her imprinted on your memory for ever,' she said.

'Sorry. But in fact, my memory of her will begin to fade quite soon, won't it? I only knew her for a couple of days.' He sighed. '*So leben wir, und nehmen immer Abschied.*'

'That sounds as if it's something sad,' she said, remorseful. 'What does it mean?'

'"This is how we live, always taking our leave" – a sort of continual goodbye.' He shook off the moment. 'We need a proper photograph.' He made a note on the pad she had provided. 'Telephone Madame Wiaroz for a photograph.'

'Right. You're going to ask at the museum if anyone, either a man that we can't describe—'

'But who uses nice soap,' Greg supplied rather mournfully.

'Yes, and no moustache – either him, or a young woman who looked something like Marzie but wasn't – were they showing a lot of interest in Chopin?' She paused. 'How will they know? I mean, people just walk into a museum and look at what they want to.'

'Not this one. You have to sign the visitors' book.'

'And say which part you're going to visit?'

'Well, no. You don't *have* to. But I think it would be common practice for the reception person to ask if they could help.'

'And this guy, who's no fool, wouldn't say anything abut Chopin. He'd tell him he was going to look at something completely different – to do with Gilbert and Sullivan or someone.'

He sighed. 'We have to ask if they noticed either of them having a look around, even if it seems a waste of time.'

They sat in thought for a moment; then she said, 'This man's a crook. I suppose there is such a thing as a crook who loves Chopin, but thinking about . . . well, you know, someone who happened on an idea for a swindle but didn't know much about composers – how would he go about finding out?'

'The Museum of Musical Heritage . . .' His voice died away.

'No, of course not. That's not the first place you'd look. It's quite a small specialist museum, tucked away in a Mayfair square.'

Liz held up a hand for attention. 'Remember how he contacted Madame Wiaroz! By internet. I bet he looked up Chopin on the internet.'

He made a second note: 'Look up on the internet.' He began to doodle musical staves on the pad. 'He wants to get some musical fan to hand over money, and he looks up Chopin, and he finds out that the poor man came to Britain in the year before he died, and so . . . and so he finds out about the specialist museum in Mayfair for composers who lived in Britain or came visiting, and . . . what?'

'Decides it's a good place to choose for the delivery of the money? Because it sort of reinforces his story about being a Chopin enthusiast, doesn't it?'

'Yes, and it sounds safe and respectable for Marzelina.'

'Reassuring, yes.' She looked at him with serious enquiry. 'Do you think he actually did have a manuscript to hand over? I mean, not a genuine one probably, but at least something – a forgery or something?'

'You mean a couple of pages of music composition that would *look* like Chopin? Something by John Field, perhaps.'

'Who on earth is John Field?'

'An Irish composer who was writing that sort of thing before Chopin arrived on the scene. Oh, no, never mind, sweetheart; the idea's silly. Whoever had a John Field score would have to copy it out in the handwriting style of Chopin, wouldn't he? Because Madame Wiaroz would know if it wasn't in Chopin's hand. No, it's too difficult for some trickster to do that.'

'But look here: if it's so difficult, Greg, you're saying that Charles Hampton actually had something that looked genuine to start with . . .'

'Or at least had enough of a page to tear off that corner . . .'

'So he made a photocopy of a genuine page – but how would he get access to a genuine page?'

'Well, he couldn't, in my opinion. But he might get something pretty close to genuine. There are publishers who publish facsimile editions. And yet . . .' He paused to think about it. 'Those are mostly for the works of the more modern composers. At least I think so. I'm not into using autograph manuscripts for anything, so I don't know.'

'I didn't understand any of that,' Liz said, huffing a little.

He smiled. 'I apologize. There are publishers who produce books of reproductions of the scores written by the composers in their actual handwriting.'

'Right, I've got that.'

'But I can't believe there are any books of facsimile scores by Chopin,' he went on, thinking it through. 'The originals are in museums in various parts of the world, and perhaps a few in private collections. None of those people would let modern technology anywhere near them.'

'Then does it mean he actually has a piece of music in Chopin's handwriting?'

'Of course not, Liz. He must have managed this in some other way.' He crumpled up the piece of paper on which he'd been doodling, frowning fiercely. Then he said, 'Well now, I was reading a life of Chopin in the museum. It had a photograph of a page from one of his *études*. What if he borrowed a book like that from a public library and photocopied that?'

'But would it look *genuine*? – a photocopy of a photograph?'

'I don't know. I think you can do a lot with computer enhancement and so forth these days. Isn't there some process that produces banknotes that fool everybody?'

'Oh, yes,' she agreed. When she went to discuss future fashion requirements at department-store headquarters, she often heard about the problem. 'I think they put them through a sort of washing machine after they print them, to make them look used.'

'Mm . . . McDavis said the torn piece on the photocopy looked as if it really came from something old. So does that mean it could be done? And he just borrowed a book, copied something out of it, and aged it by dipping it in weak coffee or something like that?'

'Well, what if he did borrow a book? It's not a lot of help. We can't go round asking public libraries if somebody's borrowed a book with an illustration of something by Chopin.'

'No. And you know . . . It can't be something that's already published, can it?'

She was baffled again. 'Why not?'

Greg was surprised that she hadn't thought of it. 'Because Madame, who adores Chopin, thought it was a genuine *unpublished* work.'

'She couldn't possibly tell from those few notes on a torn piece!'

'Yes she could. It's recognizable as a mazurka, even though there are only a few bars, and I would take a bet she knows every note of every mazurka he ever wrote.'

'That's impossible,' she protested, frowning and shaking her head at him.

He laughed and gave her a hug. 'You don't know anything about musical devotees! There are people who can sing you every single note Verdi ever wrote. I've got a friend who doesn't need a score in front of him if he's conducting anything by Brahms.'

This declaration caused an argument, which ended with the decision to take a break and refill the coffee cups. As they were doing so, she stopped with the cafetière held aloft to say, 'You know . . . he *could* copy something from a book and then alter it a little bit so that it looked like something never published before.'

'So that it looked like Chopin? Impossible.'

'Why not?'

'It would have to be someone who actually knows something about music.' This was in a tone of reproachful protest.

'Well, maybe he *does* – I mean, perhaps he's a music teacher who's hard up, or perhaps he plays the piano – you know, like in the posh department stores: they sometimes have a pianist tinkling away in the afternoons, and it seems to me . . . Yes, I do think I've heard something that could be Chopin.' She began to sing, waving a hand to keep time.

'No,' Greg said, trying not to grin. 'That's the Moonlight Sonata, and it's by Beethoven.'

'It is?'

This caused him to go off into gales of laughter, ending in hugs and kisses. It took them a few minutes to remember they were supposed to be getting fresh coffee. That done, they settled down to work again.

'All the same,' she resumed, as if there had been no interruption, 'it proves what I mean. He could be one of those guys who plays in Palm Court sort of places, or does work in backing groups for recording studios.'

'He wouldn't be playing Chopin in a backing group.'

'No, but he might know a lot about music all the same.'

'A composer *manqué*?' He was being made to face a thought that he disliked. 'It's possible.'

'You know people in musical academies and such. You could ask. And do you know anybody in the recording industry that you could ask?'

He shook his head. 'I'm not on that sort of wavelength, Liz. It's true I know professors and teachers, but . . . it's such a wide field . . .' He fell into silence, then murmured, 'I've had a dreadful thought. What if it's a student? What if it's something that started as a student prank in some conservatoire?'

'Oh, dear!'

'No, it can't be that.' He was dismissive, suddenly more sure of the thought process.

'Why not?'

'Because a music student or anybody in the musical world wouldn't bother wasting time with an old lady like Madame Wiaroz. He'd offer it to one of the big collectors and make a lot more money – that's if he brought it off.'

'A lot more than fifty thousand pounds?'

He shrugged. 'A rediscovered score by Beethoven sold at auction for more than two million dollars two or three years ago.'

She stared at him in astonishment. 'Really?'

'But of course,' he went on, ignoring her surprise, 'offering anything to a rich collector is a lot more risky than targeting an old lady.' He was shaking his head. 'No, let's not go down that avenue. This man took all kinds of precautions, knew how to go about it. Let's stay with the idea that he's a con man who had an idea about playing a trick on a gullible old lady, only it went wrong.'

'The so-called Charles Hampton and his wife or girlfriend. And – hang on – he's got some know-how about finance, because he'd got a bank in the Cayman Islands all ready to receive the money.'

'So he's clever, he's got some education, he's probably British, he had some reason to use music for his crime, specifically Chopin.'

'But why Chopin? Was it just because he knew there were a lot of devotees, or because he had some – I don't know – some smattering of knowledge about him, some reason to choose him?'

Greg threw up his hands in frustration. 'I think we're going in for – what's it called? – psychological portrayal?'

'Psychological profiling,' she corrected him, grimacing at the idea. 'And as we aren't trained for it, we should stop. Let's do some of the practical things, Greg.' She was rising from her chair as she spoke.

It was silently acknowledged that Liz, although no great expert, was better with computers than Greg. She sat down at her desk, while Greg went into the bedroom to call up the people on the telephone list.

A lively voice speaking in French greeted him when he was connected: 'Apartment of Madame Wiaroz, good evening.'

'This is Grégoire Couronne. Who is that speaking?'

'Oh, Monsieur Couronne! This is Céleste. Thank you so much for recommending me to Madame. I'm "on duty" for the first time; it looks like being a very pleasant arrangement.'

'Glad to hear it, Céleste. Is Madame available?'

'She is nodding at me. One moment while I take the telephone to her.'

Madame spoke a moment later. 'As you heard, monsieur, I have found myself a friend, thanks to you. How wonderful to be so much at ease with someone new. Thank you a million times.'

'I'm very glad, madame. Now I'm ringing with a special request. We need a good photograph of Marzelina. Do you have one?'

She gave a muffled little sound of mourning at the words but said at once, 'Indeed I do! I asked her to sit for a portrait photograph as my Christmas present. But . . . my dear friend . . . is it urgent? I don't want to part with it. I would have to have a copy made to send to you.'

'I believe not,' he said in reassurance. 'Is Céleste able to use your computer?'

There was a moment's conversation off the microphone, the fresh young voice quite clearly saying she could do most things. Madame resumed: 'She says she can "transmit" the photograph. Is that correct?'

'I think so.'

'It will not damage it?' Céleste was heard laughingly protesting at that. 'What a wonderful thing,' sighed Madame. 'She says she will do it at once. Let me return the phone to

her so that she can know where to send it. No, wait – before
I go, what have you to tell me about the search for the monster
who killed my Marzie?'

He replied with reluctance: 'Nothing, sad to say. My friend
Liz went to the shop where the letters were collected but learned
nothing useful. Chief Inspector Glaston told us that your letter
of credit was presented at the bank by a woman.' He explained
why it was essential that the woman resembled Marzelina's
passport photograph. 'So you see, a photograph might be useful.
I plan to go to the museum to see if someone rather like the
girl in the photo ever came to the museum before Marzelina's
visit.'

'Ah.' She understood it wasn't a very good chance. 'And
besides that, have you anything to report?'

'We are trying to work out how Hampton came across the
idea of using the work of Chopin for a fraud. Liz is at the
computer as I speak – we think it was probably on the internet
that he found the information he needed.'

'Well, my dear, you know more about these things than I
do. I wish you good luck, and I hope you will keep me in
touch with your progress.'

They wished each other cordial goodnights. He went back into
the living room to tell Liz she should expect the photograph.

By and by she finished her search on the internet, printed
out two or three copies of the photograph, then swivelled her
chair round to address him with a teacher-like air.

'There are thousands of sites dealing with Frederic Chopin,'
she announced. 'It would take ages to look at them all, but as
far as I've got, you can buy books about Chopin that have
paintings as illustrations and an actual photograph—'

'A photograph? As early as that?'

'Oh yes. I remember from my art-college days that there
were early versions of photography – daguerrotypes – so it's
probably something like that they're talking about. You can
also buy prints of a painting by Delacroix – let's get a copy
of that: I have a good opinion of Delacroix – and you can have
portrait busts in various sizes, large and small.' She paused.
'Who on earth wants portrait busts?'

'Oh, lots of musicians have them in the room where they
practise or compose. Handel, Beethoven – you must have seen
them; they unfortunately feature in some interior-decoration

schemes.' He was remembering for a fact that his grandmother had sometimes used Roman busts in some of her more grandiose decorating.

'I'd hate to have a solid face glowering at me while I worked. But people seem to want not only busts but posters, medallions, reproductions of the death mask . . .'

'You're making this up!'

'No, I'm not; there are postage stamps with Chopin on them, and there's at least one chess game . . .'

'How can they make a chess game using Chopin? Who is he on the board? – the king? – the white knight?'

'How should I know! What I'm trying to tell you is that there's quite a little industry in items commemorating the man. Some of them seem to be things you can carry around with you – lockets and pendants, and for instance one of the busts is only about four or five inches—'

'But are there facsimile reproductions of his piano scores?'

'Ah.' She shook her head. 'Not so far as I've got. Some of the advertisements list the book illustrations, and one or two say they have photographs of various bits – usually the opening passages.' She was glancing through her notes.

'Well, what we have on the photocopy is *not* an opening passage.'

'It isn't? No, of course not, it would have those squiggles at the beginning if it was.'

'You mean the clef and the key signature.'

'I expect I do. So if in general they illustrate the books using the front page of a score, our musical trickster probably didn't copy from a book.'

'It's interesting about the other things,' he mused. 'It certainly tells you that you could sell almost anything if you could link it to Chopin.'

'Have they got things like that on sale at the museum?'

'Certainly not!' he said, quite shocked. 'It's a place for serious students. Things like that would only be sold in – what do you call it? – *una tienda de regalos*?'

'No idea.'

'*Boutique touristique?*'

'Oh, a gift shop!'

'That's it. But the museum does sell books. We need to buy some, to see what this man Hampton might have learned from a book.'

'Well, let's go there tomorrow and buy one with the painting by Delacroix in it.'

'It's closed on Sundays.'

'What? But Sunday is a main museum-visiting day!'

'This is a privately maintained museum. It has its own rules.'

'That's very autocratic! Well, we could go instead to the letter-collection shop in Shepherd's Bush and try out the photograph on the shop-lady.'

'Yes.' He looked interested. 'I have never been to a part of London called Shepherd's Bush. It sounds nice; I look forward to it.'

'Boy, are you in for a disappointment!' She was thoughtful for a while. 'Greg, listen . . . We've spent a lot of time arguing the pros and cons about how this chap managed to fake a piece of musical score. But remember? – Madame Wiaroz was convinced the bit on the photocopy was genuine.'

'She was, indeed.'

'Well, then, let's suppose – just *suppose* – that it's genuine.'

He gave her his attention. She'd expected him to protest, but when he simply waited, she went on: 'So if it's genuine, somebody got hold of it – happened on it, perhaps, do you think?'

'That would be great good luck. But what if he happened on it?'

'*Where* did he find it? Madame said she thought it was something Chopin might have thrown away as rubbish, while he was staying with friends in London. And you know, things do turn up – people are always appearing on the TV shows about antiques, looking pleased and saying, "I found it in the attic." So what about these places where he was living while he was in London? They probably all had attics – servants lived in them.'

He was unconvinced. 'Your suggestion is that someone living in one of those houses *now* is the criminal?'

'Well, why not?'

'But Chopin was here in the eighteen-forties. Those houses probably don't even exist any more.'

'We don't know that!' she protested. 'It's worth a thought, isn't it?'

'Yes it is.' He said it without conviction, but was willing to consider the idea. 'I was looking at a life of Chopin while McDavis was studying the handwriting. And I do seem to recall that he lived in Piccadilly – or perhaps St James's? And Bentinck Something-or-other.'

'Write that down.' He obeyed. 'And think about it, and write down any more you remember. Because, you see, if we can't go to the snobby Museum of Musical Heritage tomorrow, we can have a look at those places to see who's living there now.'

Perhaps it was worth doing. He knew she would be upset if he refused. So that became the plan. They would go house-hunting in Mayfair.

Seven

As Liz had foretold, Mr Crowne was not greatly taken with Shepherd's Bush. But it was a popular place, with a flea market going on nearby and attracting a big crowd.

The little shop was busy once more. This time the counter was being looked after by a middle-aged man, who looked pleased enough when Liz approached but became annoyed when Greg produced the photograph.

'Why you asking if I see this lady? This is she here,' he said, nodding at Liz.

True, Liz was fair-haired and fair-complexioned. Her eyes weren't blue, but that didn't seem to matter. She was dressed in outdoor clothes, bright checked coat and emerald-green scarf – to Greg's eyes entirely and delightfully different from the portrait. But the shopkeeper was shaking his head in irritation.

They could only thank him and retire defeated.

They set off for Mayfair. Greg had remembered one of the addresses from the biography: number 4 St James's Place, which turned out to be a little cul-de-sac off the main thoroughfare of St James's Street. One look was enough to tell them that the building had been restored and refurbished many times, so that the chance of anything having been left undisturbed in an attic was slight indeed. Moreover, it was now being used as a suite of offices, with a plaque on the wall to commemorate Chopin's connection with the place.

'So they're totally clued up about him,' Liz sighed, 'and if anything had been lying around that belonged to him, they'd have found it years ago.'

'I'm afraid so.'

'What was that you mentioned about Bentinck?' she asked, determined not to give up.

'Bentinck Street, I think. Is that a place?'

'Yes, of course; it's in Marylebone. Come on; it's not far.' She was feeling in need of exercise. Three days had gone by and she'd not been out for her usual morning run. She set off briskly, but was forced to stop when Greg discovered they were coming into Wigmore Street. The Wigmore Hall was one of his most dearly loved venues, where he'd sent many performers to launch themselves on the discerning London public. There was a little crowd there, going in to hear a morning programme of Mozart.

'Mozart,' he murmured, inspecting the placard outside. There was some slight longing in the word. But a moment's thought reminded him that the queue he was looking at was waiting for returned tickets, meaning that the performance was booked out.

She dragged him onward. But in Bentinck Street they could only sigh and turn away. Once again the area was given over to business, and the whole scene had been modernized.

'The addresses do seem to exist still,' he commented, 'but I don't think there is much chance of anything being suddenly found today that was lost a hundred years ago. Every building has been cleaned and polished and remodelled.'

'I'm afraid so.' She was vexed, because she'd thought it was a good idea. 'Why didn't you make a list of the other places he lived, when you were reading that book?'

'My angel, I didn't know I was going to be asked to go visiting. Besides, I was only reading it for ten or fifteen minutes. We'll get a copy of the book tomorrow at the museum.'

'So what are we going to do now?'

He looked around. The day was blustery with a last traditional March wind holding off the milder days of April. They had got up in a hurry and come out after only a glass of orange juice. Not far off was a friendly-looking restaurant. 'Let's have lunch,' he suggested.

They stoked up on carbohydrates, starting with panini and

coffee then going on to pasta and wine. Liz chose options without meat: she was always trying to be a good vegetarian. Altogether it was an odd meal, but it helped get their thinking process started again.

'I think another place that was mentioned in the book was Great Poultry Street,' he offered.

'Poultry? That's in the City.' Liz knew London well. She'd worked in or visited dress shops in almost every district.

He knew that the City was the commercial area. He looked dubious. Would Chopin have stayed among the money-makers? The feeling he'd had, while glancing through the biography, was that the composer had loved the nobility. Almost all his friends were either dukes and duchesses or their near equivalent.

He ate some tortellini while he thought about it. 'Wait. I think it was the home of a piano-maker. Broadwood – yes, of course. But did Chopin stay there? Or only give a recital there?'

'Well, even if he only went there for one evening, he could easily have taken musical scores with him. We'll go out and catch a bus to the City . . .'

'Poultry Street,' he mused. 'No, it's not poultry. Poultry is chickens and geese, no? If the name had really been Great Poultry Street, I would have thought that more odd. It conjures up a mental picture rather in contrast with my idea of Chopin.' He was grinning a little.

Hearing him say it again made her understand the meaning. 'It's Great Pulteney Street,' she declared, throwing up a hand in triumph.

'Ah, I believe that's it! Excellent. Where is Great Pulteney Street?'

'It's near Piccadilly Circus. And,' she added with a shake of the head, 'it's no more likely to have the house in its original state than the others we've looked at.'

'But we have to look.'

She sighed yet again. 'I suppose you can't recall the number of the house?'

'No.'

'Look here ' – and she was glancing about – 'there are plenty of bookshops around here. Let's get a copy of the book you were reading.'

'But I don't think it would be available in an ordinary book-shop. It was old, and you know – very specialized.'

'Well, lover, I'm sure you know all the places to buy musical stuff; let's go to one of those shops.'

'Musical scores, yes; if we wanted the score of a mazurka I could lead you straight from here to a shop that would have what we want – or, no' – he was sighing as he said it – 'it probably wouldn't be open on a Sunday; it's in an out-of-the-way little street where there isn't much going on on a Sunday.'

'Stop muttering to yourself,' she scolded. 'You're saying we have to wait till tomorrow to buy the book at the museum and verify addresses?'

'I'm afraid so.'

To his surprise, she was quite unperturbed. 'Perhaps that's just as well, really,' she said. 'You know I bought all that stuff to get started on my ideas for the spencer.'

'The what?'

'Spencer. It's a kind of vest,' she began, keen to talk about the subject in which she was totally expert. 'Used to be worn under your dress for extra warmth, but now it's a loose vest that you wear on top when you're layering.'

'Layering.' He said it with bewilderment but without wanting an explanation and, accepting the fact, she let it go.

'Anyhow, it would help me if I could get something down on paper so that I can take it to Herol at Barbatar tomorrow.'

'So you want to go home and do some sketching.'

'Would that be all right? I think we came out just too keen to be *doing* something today.'

'Perhaps,' he agreed. 'And I ought to call up the answering machine back in my office to see if there's anything urgent. And ' – with less enthusiasm – 'I ought to ring home to let them know what I'm doing.'

He meant he ought to ring his grandmother. Even though they weren't on cordial terms since her quarrel with Liz, his sense of duty required him to keep in touch. She understood, and smiled in sympathy.

So they went back to her flat instead of journeying further around London. She was soon lost in her work. He found that once he'd listened to his messages, he needed to talk to Amabelle, his assistant back in Geneva. She reminded him that he had to finalize the programme for the Spitalfields Festival.

One thing led to another. The afternoon sped by; soon it was mid-evening. They went out to eat and told each other they would start next day, bright and early, on the serious matter of the Chopin trail.

Liz was out for her morning run in the dawn of a murky April day when His Highness rose. They kept to their agreement for an early start. Liz went off to her clothing store in Edgware while he presented himself at the Museum of Musical Heritage.

The doors had scarcely opened. The receptionist was Joe Packley, junior attendant, who had been off delivering choral scores in Winchester when Marzelina had died. But he'd been on duty when she'd first arrived, so Greg produced the photograph.

'Oh . . .' Joe said on a lingering note of regret. 'That's the young lady who was killed.'

'Yes, it is: Countess Marzelina Zalfeda. But do you remember anyone rather *like* her – someone who came before Marzelina arrived?'

Joe thought about it but was soon shaking his head. 'In fact, I can say pretty firmly that when the countess first appeared, I was really . . . you know . . . struck by her looks. No one anywhere near that standard had been on the scene – at least, not while I was on duty.'

'The man that was with me when we found her – Taylor? – is he here today?'

'Oh, yes, but he's in the office. He does afternoons, mostly. Shall I give him a buzz and ask him to come through?'

Christopher Taylor remembered Marzelina only too well. Not with the same enthusiasm as his colleague, yet with enough clarity to say he didn't remember anyone like her visiting the museum. 'Of course we have young ladies as visitors,' he remarked: 'students, amateurs studying with an amateur orchestra, older ladies who are perhaps teachers – all kinds.' He gave the photograph another long scrutiny. 'Who knows? I can't say I pay a lot of attention unless they enquire for something a bit special – Early Music, something like that.'

'Would it be any good to ask your boss?'

They both smiled. 'He only comes out of the office for someone special, and if it was someone special we'd remember her.'

So he went on to ask if they had noticed a man asking particularly for the Chopin collection. They looked put out.

Of course men came to look at the Chopin collection – over a month they probably had about a dozen, usually wanting to sit down with one of the volumes of the Paderewski editions. These were the most-often-asked-for volumes of the scores.

'No one who seemed – you know – perhaps not much of a musician?'

That was met with blank dismissal. People asked silly questions all the time – nothing unusual in that.

'Thank you.' He put the photograph of Marzelina into his document case. 'Now I'd like to buy some books, please.'

The museum shop was a screened area alongside the enquiry desk. Taylor led the way and put Greg's purchases into a carrier bag with the museum's logo: a stave of music from Purcell's *Faerie Queen*. Armed now with a biography and the collected letters of Frederic Chopin, Greg thanked him and took himself off.

Liz was to meet him at a favourite Indian restaurant near Oxford Circus station.

'How did the dress design go?' he asked as she walked with her bright vigour into the quiet, shaded restaurant.

'It's a spencer. Herol likes it but wants it multicoloured.' She made a face. 'Spoils the presentation, but the boss is the boss. I'll get to that when I can.' She sat down, picked up the menu, and without further conversation set about ordering. A friendly waiter hovered nearby but she seemed disinclined to smile at him.

She poured from the bottle of mineral water Greg had already started, and demanded, 'At the museum – had they seen our woman?'

He shook his head. 'And as to the man, he was even less on the scene.' He quoted: '"People ask silly questions all the time."'

'It was a long shot,' she said with an impatient shrug. 'I see you bought books. A little page of notes is sticking out of one of them. What's the verdict?'

'Chopin wrote letters like a man who had nothing else to do,' he complained. 'And I've found out, to my surprise, that he was in London in 1837.'

'No, you mean 1847,' she corrected

'No, I mean 1837.' He consulted his notes. 'And the later date is 1848.'

'Stop showing off!'

'I apologize.' He let a moment go by then went on, 'I was a bit bothered. Is that right – bothered? Or do I mean dithered?'

'No, bothered.' Generally when she had to correct his English, she was amused. But today there was no smile to go with the correction.

'I thought we might have to start looking at the places he'd stayed on that first visit. But no; in 1837 he was here gadding about, mainly. Music didn't seem to come into it at all.'

'No piano-playing?'

'I think it was because he was trying to pass the time while he waited for a decision. He'd asked someone to marry him and he was waiting to see if the parents would allow it.'

'And did they?'

'No, afraid not. So he went back to Paris to nurse his broken heart, and never came back to London until Jane Stirling talked him into it in 1848.'

'Oh yes.' Now he had said something that pleased her because she recognized the name. 'The hated Jane Stirling. Mme Wiaroz sounded as if she'd have liked to suffocate her.'

'A Mrs Erskine arranged for him to say in Bentinck Street – that was one of our attempts yesterday. But our friend Chopin didn't like it, only stayed one night.'

'Who's this Mrs Erskine?''

'I don't know. I've only skimmed through for addresses.'

'Are you sure you're not missing any, just *skimming* through?'

'No, skimming is enough to collect the addresses.'

'I don't see how that can be efficient.'

'Sweetheart, Chopin wrote letters like the rest of us – he put his address at the top of the first page.'

'Oh,' she said, chastened, and was glad to turn her attention to the plates and dishes the waiter was setting before her. Then she said, very repentant, 'Sorry if I've been snappy. It's because I lost the argument with Herol.'

'Is Herol a he or a she?'

'Herol is a visionary, and I should know better than to quarrel with her over fashion trends. So go on with the list of places we should look at.' Now she was more herself, relaxing in her chair, shaking her head at her ill temper.

'*C'est dure, haute couture,*' he quoted to comfort her.

'You can say that again.'

'I won't make the mistake of doing so, because I recognize

that as a "saying". To return to our quest, I read that our Frederic played at Guildhall.'

'Guildhall!' She looked alarmed at the prospect of dealing with one of the main venues of the City of London.

'But only once,' he said in reassurance, 'and I can't imagine he'd be scribbling down the score of a new mazurka while he was there.'

'Why not? If inspiration struck?'

'Because he'd be done up in evening dress, and he wouldn't have carried notebooks and pens around with him on an occasion like that. He seems from what I've gathered to have been rather spruce in his appearance. Spruce is a tree, but it is also a word for neat, elegant – am I right?'

'You're always right, Mr Music.' She knew she was being coaxed into a good mood, and let him know by her smile that she'd quite recovered. With a more thoughtful air she went on, 'Well, you know the Guildhall is a very big place. If we were to have grounds for thinking someone on the staff had dreamed up some scheme about Chopin . . .'

'What?'

'How could we deal with that? We couldn't ask to interview the entire personnel. They'd tell us to get lost.'

'Aha. Well perceived.' He ate some of his food, thinking it over. 'How about this: we don't attempt the difficult places, but try the more likely ones. And if it turns out we think the villain is someone at a place like Guildhall, for instance, we hand it on to Scotland Yard.'

'Right.'

'Manchester,' he mused, offering her his list across the table. 'He went to Manchester en route to Scotland, stayed with a Mr Schwabe and performed at what seems to have been called a "Gentleman's Concert".'

'No, really?' She laughed. 'How sweet.' She began on her vegetarian *passanda* with one hand while holding up the list with the other. 'So shall we be going to Manchester in quest for Mr Schwabe's home?'

'Well, it's not so much Mr Schwabe; it's the Royal Northern College of Music.'

She looked at him, waiting for an explanation.

'A very well-known school. And I know for a fact there's a statue of Chopin there.'

'Which means . . .?'

'Well, you remember before . . . I had a horrid idea that a music student might be involved. But after all – a statue – anyone could see it. A student, a professor, a visitor, even just a cleaner or someone on the library staff – anyone going in or out.'

'What you mean is, some crook might happen to see the statue. And if he had a pal who could forge things, he might be struck with the idea that Chopin was a good theme for a confidence trick.'

Greg was silent for a moment or two, thinking about it. 'You know,' he said at length, 'a score for piano is much easier to forge than, say, one for a string quartet, or a full orchestra.'

'Easy to forge. But not what forgers usually get up to.'

'That's perhaps the charm of the idea,' he argued. 'It's not likely to attract attention. If Marzelina hadn't died, Madame Wiaroz would probably never have said anything to anybody about buying a Chopin score. She might just have kept it to herself, to gloat over.'

She frowned for a moment. 'Wouldn't she have made a fuss about it – to triumph over poor Mr Gestoupe?'

'If she'd made it public, she might have had pressure put on her – to donate it to a museum, something like that. Madame Wiaroz isn't an important *personage*, with up-to-date security and so on.'

'I see.' She nodded in approval. 'Mr Glaston was right to turn this over to you. It wouldn't occur to him that this might never have been known about if our villain had just got his money and pushed off.' She smiled at a sudden thought. 'I bet he hasn't any idea what an orchestral score even looks like.'

Greg shrugged. He was accustomed to the fact that the reading of music was something of a lost art. On many occasions he'd read or been told that members of successful boy bands or sexy girl groups couldn't read a note.

Liz took up the discussion again. 'Well, now that it's occurred to us that a statue might have been the impulse for this fraud, what about Manchester? Are we going to go there and question the people at the Northern Royal What's-its-name?'

'Oh, asking questions at the music school . . . I think that might be a big undertaking: it's a busy place. I know a couple of people there; I could get them on their own, perhaps. But it might be worth checking out Mr Schwabe. He must have been someone of local importance to have played host to Chopin. His house seems to have been quite a big place.' He was looking uncertain. 'Schwabe . . . I never heard of him in the music world, but then he might just have been a Chopin admirer.'

'Of whom there were many.'

'Oh, thousands.'

'Crumpsall House,' she read from the list.

'Crumpsall . . .?'

'Don't you know it? It's a bit north of the city centre.' She had helped to put on fashion shows in many big cities, Manchester among them.

He shook his head. 'I only know the places where music takes me. You'd be surprised how little I know about, for instance, Tokyo. Concert halls, opera houses, offices of people who engage performers – those are the places I know in most cities.'

'We'll look it up. If Crumpsall House was an important place, it might be there still.'

'So our plan will be . . . what?'

'Go round looking at the rest of the London addresses to see if anyone's living there now. I think it needs someone actually using the place as living quarters, don't you?' She made dusting motions. 'Tidying up things in the attic, or in the cellar, so that they might happen on a manuscript in an old desk or something.'

'We could perhaps look up maps – there must be archives. Is there a library nearby?'

'Sure, Holborn Library – or Westminster. And if that's no go, we could do some research on the internet.'

'*You* can do the internet, *querida*.'

She chuckled. It always amused her that he found technology so forbidding.

'OK, that's the plan for today. Then, when we've done that, we head for Manchester to see if we can track down Mr Schwabe's house. If that's no go, it's off to the Wild North, where – according to poor Madame Wiaroz – her beloved Chopin was dragged by the wicked Jane Stirling.'

'You know,' Greg said thoughtfully, 'Jane Stirling sounds like the kind of woman who would have treasured anything that belonged to him. Maybe that's where the manuscript came from? Maybe someone found something in what used to be her home?'

'If there *is* a manuscript,' she replied.

Eight

Manchester was in one of its grimmer moods when they reached it late that Monday evening. They had booked a room at a city-centre hotel with plentiful computer facilities and good room service. They settled in; but after only a few minutes work on the web, Liz was yawning.

That afternoon her work had yielded nothing very useful about the London sites. Greg, among the printed archives, had ascertained that the house in St James's Square where Chopin had given his second London recital was gone, a victim of the air raids of World War Two. An address in Dover Street was still there but occupied by businesses.

As to Guildhall, he'd telephoned the chief inspector's office, saying that if all else failed, he might be asking for some inquiries at that historic edifice. This was greeted with a distinct lack of enthusiasm.

However, Mr Glaston had given him a name in Manchester's police force. 'Just in case you need it.'

'I think we'll be heading north to Edinburgh after Manchester, Chief Inspector.'

'Let me know when you get there and I'll rustle up a contact for you.'

Their first day in Manchester was to be two separate efforts. Greg was going to look up some musical friends. Liz was going to the suburb of Crumpsall, for despite a determined effort among the websites she'd learned almost nothing about Crumpsall House.

It had existed, so far as she could make out, until the death of its then owner, Salis Schwabe, a few years after the visit of Chopin. His widow, Julia, had been left with seven children, all of them too young to take over the family business, which was textile bleaching. Nevertheless Mrs Schwabe had thrown herself into good works, rushing to the aid of the revolutionary

leader Garibaldi in Italy and later helping to found the Froebel
School in Kensington.

Liz took the tram to Crumpsall. When she alighted, she was
pleased with the outlook. While she had been doing her early-
morning run the day had been drizzly and cold but had brightened now, so that she gazed around on an attractive scene.

The district wasn't entirely unknown to her. She'd been there
some years ago, to put on a fashion show for charity in the
Abraham Moss Centre. But she'd spent all day scene-setting
and rehearsing, with only brief moments to get a breath of fresh
air. All she really remembered was that many nurses from the
nearby General Hospital had been in the audience for the show.

Crumpsall was displayed this morning as a rather appealing
collection of old houses, in poor condition now and clearly
offering cheap accommodation to nurses and junior doctors. She
turned away from them and walked down the road, stopping
after a minute or two to recognize the fact that she was looking
at an expanse of council housing.

She certainly wasn't going to find Crumpsall House there.
Her researches had told her that it had been a fine Georgian
house 'with extensive grounds and an ornamental pond'. So
she took the next turning to the right and right again, so as to
head towards the older buildings.

She walked along residential roads where some of the houses
had names: Grange Villa, Park View, and one or two grandiose
claims such as Maison Richelieu. But these were Victorian
houses. No sign of anything Georgian.

She'd given up on researching the house on various websites
when she was advised to have recourse to Probate Records and
other scary sections. That meant legal documents, and she was
fairly sure she wouldn't be able to understand a word.

She'd then decided it would be easier to find out something
about the place if she went there in person. But now she was
here, and the house was not. Certainly not.

After an hour's tour of the residential roads, she bought herself
a carton of coffee at a little shop, then went into the local park
– a pleasant place, with a children's playground, fine trees beginning to show green buds, and plenty of benches. She settled on
one of the benches, sipped her coffee and looked about.

An elderly man with a portly dog was sauntering along the
path. Liz in her bright-pink padded jacket and slim jeans made

an attractive picture. 'Nice enough day,' he remarked, smiling at her from a round, rosy face.

'Not bad,' she agreed. She studied the dog. 'Pomeranian?'

'Ah, tha's kept-at!' he cried, seating himself beside her with relief. 'Hardly anybody recognizes her. They ask if she's a mongrel o' some sort. This is Garnet. Say "'Ow do," Garnet.'

Garnet gave two little short barks.

'There y'are!' cried her owner. 'No mongrel could do that, now could it?'

'Of course not.' She offered her hand to Garnet, who sniffed it then allowed herself to be patted on the head. 'Lived here long?'

'Afore them council things went up. But *you're* not from around here, lass, I can tell.'

'No, I'm here looking for Crumpsall House – a big place that was quite important in the eighteen-forties. Are you into local history? Does that ring any bells with you?'

He shook his head, then took off his trilby to rub hard on a bald patch. 'Everything here's been built and rebuilt till you can't tell owt from nowt. ICI building changed the place. Everything changed a lot in the nineteen-sixties, when this area was all included into Greater Manchester, as I seem to recall.' He drew two or three chesty breaths. 'Cold air,' he sighed. 'Doesn't do me any good, but Garnet needs her walk.'

'This house I'm talking about had land around it – had a pond and a fountain.'

'Ah?' He thought it over then glanced at the scene. 'Happen this park was made from the land around the house, then? I think there used to be a pond here but they filled it in – or was that Herristone Park?'

'Oh.' That made sense. She sat staring at the obelisk that created a focal point in an expanse of lawn before her. 'I've been walking around for ages. I'm wasting my time, it seems.' She sipped her coffee, and the dog, with a sigh, put her head up to be stroked again.

'One thing's certain,' said the man: 'there's no house here with a big garden and a pond – not no more. Only thing that's got a story is that.' He nodded at the obelisk. '*That* used to stand in Market Street in the shopping area – moved it to let the traffic flow better. I tell you, lass: nothing ever stays the same for more than two minutes at a time.'

Garnet, as if sensing that this was the end of the conversation, tugged gently on her leash. Her owner got to his feet with some difficulty, made a gesture of goodbye with his hat before putting it on, and moved away.

She sat long enough to finish her coffee, then, duty bound, made another inspection of some of the avenues. But she found no trace of Crumpsall House. Defeated, she headed for Middleton Road to catch a bus.

She was meeting Greg in what she regarded as 'veggie heaven': the Eighth Day Café near the university. She arrived in Oxford Road to see the tall, lean figure of Mr Crowne walking ahead of her towards the café.

She trotted to catch up with him. 'Hello, stranger,' she said, taking his arm.

'Ah, a damsel in distress.'

'Am I in distress?'

'Well, you're hungry, no?'

'Yes. And to tell the truth, I am a bit fed up. Nothing doing at Crumpsall. The great house has vanished.'

'And with it any memorabilia that might have been there, about Chopin or anyone else.'

They stopped to look at the chalked menu outside the café. 'I'm feeling the cold so I'm going to have the ragout,' she announced.

'Then so shall I.' The interior was lively with the chatter of students and a music centre playing something difficult by a guitarist. They found a seat in a corner and, once the food was ordered, began to exchange news.

She gave him a brief summary of her morning. 'And how did you make out, chatting up the music students?'

He shrugged. 'I've quite a lot of contacts here, some of them pianists. Sometimes I hire someone local as accompanist to a singer, you know.' She nodded, and he went on ruefully, 'I started with some of them, then dropped in at the college. But I began to feel a bit of a fool, asking tutors and instructors if any of their students had seemed to come into a lot of money recently.'

'Would they know about that?'

'Only if they had been showing off with Tagheuer watches or Louis Vuitton handbags. The general response was: students are always short of cash and no one's been buying any Porsches or Chanel clothes.'

'No,' she agreed, studying the garb of the girls in the room. Her thoughts drifted away to her own affairs for a moment. 'Mm . . . I begin to think Herol may be right about going ethnic. There's a lot of flouncy skirts here.'

'Which particular nation or race is she thinking of?'

'Well, sort of Balkan, I think. Which colours do you think of as being Balkan?'

'*Verde este foarte frumos,*' he responded.

'What does that mean?'

'"Green is very beautiful", in Rumanian. At least I think that's what it means. I had a Rumanian contralto under my wing who was always asking if her dress was suitable for the concert platform, so I learned a few phrases just to say something tactful.'

'So do you think I ought to put green into the multicolour mix for my spencer?'

'"Green is very beautiful,"' he said, and addressed himself to his vegetable stew.

Taking out a notebook, Liz made a hasty note for her proposed spencer and drew a dark line under it to mark its importance.

Greg's thoughts too had gone elsewhere, but still on the quest that had brought them here. 'I'll tell you something that *was* a little bit interesting,' he remarked.

'About what? – Rumanian singers?'

'No, about the music students. I was agreeing that life was hard what with student debt and so on, and Eduardo – that's Eduardo Colinelli, teaches voice production – he said some of them play in nightclubs for a little money, and some do sing in backing groups, though I thought that was unlikely, didn't I? There's quite a recording industry in Manchester.'

'Oh, I know *that*! But not your kind of stuff.'

'No, I gather not. Anyway, Eddie went on to say that one of the girls had found another way to make a little money – what he called "a nice little earner": she sells jewellery, not gems or gold or anything – what do you call it when it's fake?'

'Costume jewellery.' She frowned at him. 'What women wear is always important to me, but where is this chat about fake jewellery going to take us?'

'What she sells, my love, is little miniatures of Chopin.'

'No!'

'Yes,' he said with some satisfaction at having surprised her. 'Someone has had the clever idea of making a pen-and-ink sketch of the head of Chopin from the statue at the school, and this girl has it for sale on pendants and on brooches and things.'

Reaching in his inside jacket pocket, he produced a little item wrapped in tissue paper. Liz took and unwrapped it, to find a bracelet consisting of two pseudo-gold chains holding in place a piece of pseudo-ivory about the size of a penny. On it was imprinted a profile of Frederic Chopin.

'Oh.' She put it on her wrist without fastening it. She tilted her hand back and forth. 'Can't say I can ever see myself wearing this.'

'But I did see one or two of the girls here and there in the building wearing the pendant.'

She ate in silence for a moment or two. Then she asked, 'You bought it from the girl who sells these things?'

'Yes.'

'And . . . you're thinking she's a Chopin aficionado, and might be . . . might be the female part of the fraud partnership?'

'That was a sort of idea I had until I met her. But it doesn't work; she couldn't be the one who played the part of Marzelina in the bank: she's small and plump.'

'But she *is* someone who's thought of using Chopin as a money-making ploy.'

'Well, not only Chopin. She has a miniature of Mahler conducting, and on a letter-opener she has a violinist whom she says is Paganini.'

Liz was disappointed. 'Catering for all branches of the music-learning market. She buys this stuff from those sites on the internet, I take it.'

'No, that's the rather interesting point. I asked her where she got them, and she said from a shop in the city centre called – and please don't blame me – Music Hath Charms.'

'Oh dear.'

'She was telling me that the man who runs it got the idea from one or two little shops he saw in and around Edinburgh. I quote, more or less: "Some lady lived there and had this crush on Chopin and made a big fuss of wearing a lock of his hair in a locket after he died, so there's quite a lot of Chopin things for sale up there." So Music Hath Charms, selling a range of music kitsch, was inspired by other shops.'

She shook her head in mock reproach. 'Jane Stirling – what have you done!'

'Apparently it's supplied my little friend Louella with a way of earning some spending money. And it's given a livelihood to a few shopkeepers.'

She let the information settle into her mind. Then she said, 'And perhaps it's given rise to other, more grasping ideas? Supply a locket, make a fiver. Supply a manuscript, make fifty thousand?'

'It's a possibility, Liz.'

'We'd better go to the shop and have a look at this man,' she said, reinvigorated at the idea of a target. 'After all, there's no reason why our criminal should be a Londoner just because he used a London mailing address.'

Music Hath Charms was in a turning off Deansgate, in company with an old-style barber's with a red-and-white pole, an umbrella specialist, and a teddy-bear shop. Its window held a display of music boxes, reproductions of songbooks from the Edwardian music-hall era, and miniature busts of Handel, Beethoven and Liszt. In the front row was a little shelf covered in blue velvet. On this rested three or four pieces of jewellery.

Liz paused to examine the jewellery. Only one item showed any connection with the composer that interested them. It had the name 'Chopin' in letters of gold, or something like gold, strung out on a necklace.

With a sigh she followed Greg into the shop. The proprietor was sitting on a high stool reading a newspaper, but set it aside as he rose to attend to them.

'Good afternoon, fellow music-lovers,' he greeted them.

He was in his late forties, with something of a beer belly, which was emphasized by the fact that he was wearing a grey sweatshirt with the logo: 'Face the Music'.

'Good afternoon,' said Greg. 'I was just talking to a friend of mine at the Royal Northern, and she told me that her very pretty pendant with a Chopin picture on it was on sale here.'

'Oh, the profile by George Sand?' He moved along his counter, the top of which consisted of glass showcases. 'This is it here.' He put his finger on a spot on the glass. They bent over it to see an ivory-coloured oval on a fine chain. 'I've got it with a gold border too – just let me show you.' He turned to the shelves behind him, selected a small box, and opened it to reveal a different version. 'This one's eight, the other's five.'

'It's not ivory, is it?' Liz asked. 'I'm against ivory.'

'Oh, I couldn't do it so cheap if it was ivory. No, that's a very nice man-made background for the portrait, which you may know is from a drawing by his lady friend, George Sand. Probably drawn when they were off on their romantic jaunt to Majorca.'

He had a ready flow of talk. Liz, who knew a lot about city-centre trading, thought he felt a need to chat, to be involved with perhaps infrequent customers. It was her task to lead the conversation towards the things they wanted to know. 'It's very pretty,' she said, picking up the gold-rimmed pendant and holding it aloft to study it. Then, with something of a sigh, 'I *adore* Chopin's music, you know . . .'

'Yes, I find he pleases a lot of the ladies. Very tuneful, and of course he's got the looks.'

'How ever did you come to think of stocking a pretty thing like this?'

'Oh, well, you see,' he said, settling his elbows on the glass top so as to be comfortable, 'I was up north two or three years ago, on the Fringe at the Edinburgh Festival.' He broke off, a fond smile spreading across his rather jowly features. 'I handled a folk group then – part-time, you know. My name's Jemmy Salter, but you probably wouldn't have heard of me. The old ticker started to play me up, so I had to pack it in.'

'Oh, what a shame! Did you do well at the Fringe, Mr Salter?'

'So-so. A bit too much competition; Scotland's full of good folk groups. But we enjoyed it – a lovely atmosphere. Ever been there?'

'Yes, I love it; Princes Street is great, isn't it?'

'Well, and those little side streets around the Royal Mile – they're fascinating. I came across this shop selling all this memo-rabilia stuff – about Chopin and Jane Stirling and so on – and I thought that would just do fine for Music Hath Charms.' Another pause while he decided which angle might interest them. 'I like to keep up with trends. Did a lot of business with stuff to do with Rachmaninov, after that film – you know: *Shine.*'

Liz was unable to follow this, never having seen the film. Greg was nodding in acceptance. 'Rachmaninov's not so romantic as Chopin, though,' he commented.

'No, you have to agree Chopin's got more appeal, with the love affairs and all. And it hasn't died off, like the Rachmaninov thing. I have to keep an eye on the profits. My shop's my main income, you see.'

'It's a lovely place, Mr Salter,' Liz said admiringly, glancing about at the array of miniature busts and framed programmes and gilded miniature pianos.

He smiled at her. 'Call me Jemmy. I do a few things on the side as well,' he told her, leaning more towards her in fellow feeling. 'A bit of talent-spotting, arranging gigs in pubs for amateurs; but I always keep my eye out for new notions for the shop. When I saw this line in Edinburgh, about this romance with Jane Stirling that actually happened here in the UK, it seemed like a winner.'

'Jane Stirling?' Liz asked, in an innocent, puzzled tone.

'Oh, yeah; she was nuts about Chopin, you know. She lived around there, the Edinburgh region, her and her family – quite the nobs, they were, and some people say they were more than just friends.'

Liz obliged by saying, 'I'm not very well up on the history side, Jemmy. I think I knew he went to Scotland, though.'

'Yeah, that's how come there's quite a bit of interest there. One of the last concerts he ever played was in Edinburgh. Was quite a wow, as you can imagine, although what Jane's family thought about it I don't know – they were kind of strict in those days, I imagine.'

'Oh!' Liz sighed, looking sad. 'Poor girl, I never knew she existed; I thought George Sand was the big love of his life.'

'We could find out about her if you're interested, sweetheart,' Greg said. 'Where was this shop that features Jane Stirling, if I might ask?'

'In a little side alley. But I came across a couple more, selling tartan things as well – you know: for the tourists.'

'Oh, of course. There are a lot of musically minded tourists like us in Edinburgh during the festival.'

'Right. So the Jane Stirling thing goes quite well up there, but nobody in Manchester's interested, so I've dropped that side. I just concentrate on him and a few other of the Romantics.' He smiled at Liz, shaking his head. 'You young ladies! Chopin and Berlioz . . . just because they were good-lookers!'

'What else have you got that's to do with Chopin?' Liz enquired. 'Any concert programmes? Letters?'

'Oh, one or two – framed reproductions, of course. No great call for those; they're more sort of bric-a-brac, things you'd have for interior decoration. They're in the back. Shall I fetch them?'

He didn't seem keen. 'What seems to go the best is something to show off – now am I right? Something you can wear so as to let your pals know you're a fan.'

'It's quite a specialized line, though,' she said, holding the pendant against the front of her pink jacket and gazing down at it in consideration. 'I'm in the fashion trade, Jemmy, so I know how difficult it is to find just the right thing for a niche market like this.'

'Well, I'm lucky there. There's a chap drops by a couple of times a year – let's me see the new products. The necklace in the window, with the name spelt out? – that only came into his stock this year.' He glanced about. 'Would you like to look at that? Here it is, in the blue presentation box.' He opened the lid of the showcase. He was eager to make a sale.

'Which one would you like, sweetheart?' Greg asked.

'Oh, the one with the portrait, of course.' She dangled the gold-rimmed pendant before him. To the shopkeeper she said, 'If you ever get earrings to match, I'd like to see them.'

'Earrings?' he said, surprised. 'I don't think Jim has ever thought of earrings. Next time he comes by, I'll ask him.'

'When will that be?' she asked coaxingly.

'Oh, not till June, July. He gets new stock in time for the various festivals and the Proms, you see.'

'Perhaps we could ring him?' Greg suggested.

This was received with some slight irritation. 'I'll speak to him about it next time I see him.'

'But couldn't we get in touch before that, Jemmy?' Liz pleaded. 'Have you got his number handy?'

'No, I haven't, as it happens. And after all, I've got a shop to run, you know, miss,' he said. 'Can't waste time rummaging about for things like that.'

'I'm sorry. It's just that I'd really like to have matching earrings.' She turned mischievously to Greg. 'It would be nice to have a set, wouldn't it, dear?'

Greg managed an approving nod.

'Oh . . . well . . . I'll see what I can do for you when I see Jim again.' Jemmy was unwilling to pass up the chance of a profit. 'If earrings are going to be made, I'll get in touch. If you'll just write down your name and address for me . . .' He pushed towards her a flier with his shop name on it, and turned it over so that she could write on the blank side. 'In the meantime,' he went on, 'what about the pendant – would you like it in its box?'

Understanding that she'd stepped on his entrepreneurial toes, Liz exclaimed enthusiastically that she must have the pendant and its box, wrote down her name and mobile number while Greg paid, and smiled a friendly goodbye as they left.

They walked a few paces away from the shop so as to be out of sight. Then Greg drew up short and stared in outrage at Liz. 'Earrings?' he challenged.

She giggled. 'Wouldn't it be awful? Little miniatures of a dead musician on fake ivory dangling from my ears! But all the same, love, you must admit it worked. I think he might ring the supplier and we could perhaps get a look at him.'

'Yes, it's the man who brings the rubbish that interests me.'

'Yet I can't see Music Hath Charms as a hotbed of inventive crime. Jemmy's not a doer; he's a lazybones.' She took his arm. They walked on to the corner of the street. 'There seems to be quite a little industry,' she remarked. 'When I looked on the websites, I could see there were people out there who wanted trinkets and tokens to do with Chopin, but I never expected to learn there were quite a few shops actually selling this stuff.'

'Not only about him. Jane Stirling seems to be something of an attraction.'

'Not in Manchester.'

'No.' He sighed in bewilderment. '*Someone* is greatly interested in Chopin as a money-making idea. Who's supplying all this stuff?'

'Well, it could be the same man who decided to produce a lost manuscript, couldn't it?'

'I don't know what to think. I'd really like to meet the man who is supplying the goods – just to see him, either to rule him out or list him as a suspect . . . Perhaps we should wait a day or two and go back to the shop – see if we can persuade Mr Salter to give us the address.'

She shook her head.

'No? Then perhaps we should ask for some help from the Manchester police. Mr Glaston gave me a number to call.'

'No, don't do that, Greg. I think there may be some slight tax fiddle attached to the business. Buy stock for cash, keep it off the books so he doesn't have to pay VAT – that sort of thing.'

'Really? That never occurred to me.'

'Well, it occurred to me. He was Mr Conviviality when we

first arrived, but did you notice how fast he took a dislike to us when we started asking for telephone numbers?'

He gave it some thought. 'Then that's a reason to let the police know, don't you think?'

'That's not my feeling about it, Greg. So far we're not scoring very high, so wouldn't it be better to keep him sort of on the files? So that we could come back to him if we don't get any other possibilities.'

'I suppose so.' He considered it in silence for a moment, then said, 'It's a good thought. For the fact is, we don't have any other possibilities here. The house where Chopin once stayed is gone, so there's no hope of anyone living in it and finding a missing mazurka. The people I spoke to at the music college didn't provide anything useful. Music Hath Charms is the only place where there's been the slightest hint of . . . double-doing?'

'Double-dealing. And I'm not convinced he's into anything big, Greg. All the same, we should keep him in mind.'

'For how long? What's your idea?'

'Well, I think we should press on. One of those shops in Edinburgh might be more willing to give us information about the Chopin trade. We could approach it more diplomatically.'

After some discussion, they decided to head north. Enquiries at Piccadilly Station provided them with train times, none of which was very convenient, and in any case they would have had to change at Preston. So instead they went back to the hotel where they booked on a morning commuter flight from Manchester Airport.

During the evening they both turned their attention to business. Liz had bought herself some pastels so as to set down on paper a few ideas about colours for the spencer design. Greg made telephone calls to confirm some upcoming concert engagements, and to let Chief Inspector Glaston know what they had been doing.

'You really think there's anything doing up in Edinburgh, then?' Glaston asked with some scepticism.

'We thought we ought to check it out. Do you think it's a wild-goose chase?'

'Who am I to say?' Greg heard a grunt of irritation. 'All this classical music is a mystery to me. No, I'm not going to say it's a wrong trail, Mr Crowne. Go for it – that's what I say.'

Greg's last call had to be to Geneva. He had, as he expected, a spiky conversation with his grandmother.

'Manchester? Why are you in Manchester?' she demanded. 'Unless of course you are hoping for business with the Hallé Orchestra?'

'There are one or two things I have to attend to here.'

'When are you coming home? You seem to have been all over Europe ever since the New Year, and now you are all over England.'

'I'll be in Scotland tomorrow.'

'Ah. You have something to arrange for the festival.'

'For next year, perhaps.'

'I don't know how you keep it all in control, planning so far ahead.'

'You know Amabelle does that for me. But tell me how your own work is progressing.'

'Oh, well enough. I'm doing a reading room and library for the Chenil Hotel next month. They're looking at paint charts now.'

'Excellent. And Papa is well?'

'Quite well; but you know, of course, he has much more to do on his own now that you have decided to live elsewhere. He misses your help.'

'I'm sorry. But you know, madame, the parting of the ways had become inevitable.'

He meant as a result of her public insults to Liz. He thought she ought to have learned by now that reproaching him for having moved out was foolish, because it was she herself who had driven him to it. They parted with polite farewells. The ex-Queen Mother of Hirtenstein knew how to extricate herself from a conversation she was no longer enjoying.

As he set down the receiver, Greg was a little depressed. He felt duty bound to keep in touch because he knew that his grandmother entertained foolish fears about him. She thought some anti-monarchist might physically attack him, or entrap him in some embarrassing scene such as had turned up to embarrass Prince Albert of Monaco. He did his best to keep in touch, but it was always a relief to say goodbye to her.

Liz, too, was a little downcast. Her colour sketches looked wan and uninspired. They decided to go down to the hotel restaurant for the comfort of food and wine.

'Are we achieving anything, Greg?' she asked as they waited for their food. 'Or is it all just chasing shadows?'

He didn't know how to reply, for he'd had the same thought. It was almost a week since Marzelina had died. They'd spent it in hurrying hither and thither with almost nothing to show for it.

'We're following the only path that seems open,' he pointed out.

The waiter came to pour their wine. They sat silent until he'd gone. Then he picked up his glass and held it out towards Liz. 'We're doing it for Marzelina,' he said.

At that the shadow of frustration disappeared from her face. She clinked her glass with his. 'For Marzelina,' she agreed.

Nine

The Hill House Hotel was an old haunt of Mr Crowne's. When he came to look after clients at the Edinburgh Festival, it was here he always stayed. He had reserved a room by telephone the previous night.

The owner, Hector McVay, was behind the desk in person when they arrived. 'So here's yourself and your lady!' he cried, offering them a visitor's form and a pen. 'Twice in the one year – that's grand. But there's nothing on in the way of your music at this time of year, sir?'

'No, not at the moment, Hector. This is Ms Blair –'

'Of course, how could I forget her? Only glimpsed the last time you were here, Ms Blair, but fondly remembered.'

McVay was inclined to gush, but he was a very good hotelier. Since the Scottish Parliament had taken up duty in Edinburgh, his business had flourished, as evidenced by the number of people strolling out from a hearty breakfast into the entrance hall.

McVay nodded greetings to one or two then relinquished the reception desk to an underling. He himself led the newcomers to their room, an elegant one on the first floor of what had once been a very fine Georgian house.

They unpacked enough extra clothing to protect them from

the boisterous wind that was shaking the trees outside. They walked to George Street to catch a bus, Liz heading for the National Library to see if she could find out more about the country houses visited by Frederic Chopin, Mr Crowne to hire a car for the forthcoming expeditions to visit them.

They arranged to meet in the restaurant of the Balmoral Hotel for lunch. 'Well now,' she said later when they were in the bar for a pre-lunch drink, 'I'm afraid I've had very little success. There's more about the subject in the library than I found on the internet, but it's sort of negative.'

He nodded, looking attentive. 'Calder House still exists, but it's a private residence,' she began, ticking items on a list. 'Milliken House was demolished in 1923. Strachur House still exists, but the estate seems to be run as a very efficient business, so I don't think there would be any Chopin mementoes lying around undiscovered.'

'Right.'

'Keir House still exists but . . . wait for it . . . was sold to the ambassador from one of the Middle Eastern states years ago.'

'Which means, I suppose, it's been thoroughly tidied up and refurbished. So once again no Chopin manuscripts waiting to be found.'

'I'm afraid not.' She ticked off that item. 'Now, Hamilton Palace, which sounds very grand and durable, was demolished in . . . let me see . . . 1919, and all the contents were sold off. I gather the interior was something wonderful. Bits of it – furniture and room settings – are in museums here and there throughout the world.'

'None of which are likely to have had Chopin mazurkas hidden in them. This isn't very helpful, my angel.'

'Well, the last one on your list of places visited by our musical traveller is Wishaw House, near Glasgow and, sad to say, that's named in an official list of "Scotland's Lost Houses". I don't know how it got lost. Perhaps it just got swallowed up when Glasgow was spreading out in the twentieth century.'

'Yes, that was another of Jane Stirling's grand relatives he stayed with. But there was a Polish friend somewhere in Edinburgh,' Greg insisted. 'What about that?'

'That just seems to have been an ordinary little house in . . . I can't read your writing . . . Warrior Crescent?'

'Warriston. Well, we can go and look at that. It's somewhere near the Botanic Gardens, I think.' He got out the volume of Chopin's letters. After a moment's page-turning, he said, 'He gave a performance in the Hopetoun Rooms, but that was in Queen Street and that's full of solicitors' offices and that sort of thing. There couldn't be any piano scores still to be found there.'

'The possibilities are growing a lot fewer, Greg.'

He read on. 'He says in a letter to Lady Bellhaven that he's only staying in Warriston Crescent for three days. That's hardly time to unpack, Liz! I don't think he'd be starting on any new mazurkas there.'

'So that's a no-go? Should we head for Calder House, then? See if we can chat up the owners about Chopin?'

Greg was still reading. 'Oh, *wie unartig*!' he exclaimed. 'He really was a naughty man. Says here his Scottish ladies are "so tiresome"!'

She smiled and shook her head. 'Poor Jane Stirling. She probably thought he liked her as much as she liked him.'

Greg let that go. After all his reading, he found the subject of Jane Stirling very painful. Unlike Mme Wiaroz, who hated her, Greg felt utterly sorry for her.

'Let's have lunch. It's getting late; the menu will be taken off if we don't go in soon.' He put the book in his briefcase. Liz stuffed her lists into her handbag.

They had a lot to discuss, so by the time they finished eating, afternoon tea was already being served in the hotel lounge.

Greg began: 'The car's in the parking area . . .'

'Oh, what did you get?'

'It's a Nissan, but look here: if we're going to go out to Mid-Calder we ought to ring the owners first and ask if it's OK.'

'Well . . . I suppose that's true.'

He was giving the matter more thought as he spoke. 'If I could, I'd like to do it through somebody that knows them, whoever they are.'

'Do you actually know anybody that could give us an introduction?'

'I could ask around. Look here, let's leave that for the moment. I was going to say, the car's on that parking slope near the station—'

'You mean Waverley Bridge. Are we heading back to the hotel?'

'No. I was going to say, we're on the doorstep of the Royal Mile and the High Street, and that's where all the gift shops are. How about having a look at what they have in stock, to see if they have the same supplier as Music Hath Charms?'

'Ah, now! That makes sense.'

While he paid the bill, Liz collected their coats. She was weaving her emerald scarf around her neck when he joined her. 'That's really a good colour for you,' he remarked, tucking her arm through his.

'Glad you like it. Black's very smart and all that, but I do feel always that it needs a sort of exclamation mark, you know?'

They came out into Princes Street, then walked around the corner and over the North Bridge to the old High Street, which crossed the modern shopping street at Hunter Square. The stretch with shops that were kept busy by tourists led on towards St Giles' Cathedral.

'How about I take one side of the street and you take the other?' she suggested.

'All right. Which side would you prefer?'

'I can see a dress shop over there, so that's my side. Meet you at the car, shall I? What colour's the Nissan?'

'It's a dark-red Sport; it's near the tour-of-the-city buses.'

'All right, let's say in about an hour or a bit more?' This was called over her shoulder as she hurried across the road towards the dress shop.

Liz always paid attention to clothes in shops. Most of her business was with big department stores or high-street chains, but there was a lot to be learned about presentation from boutiques. She studied the window display, an outfit clearly intended for the approaching Easter wedding season. Not bad, she decided. But she was supposed to be looking for gift items for Chopin devotees. She passed a sandwich shop, a kilt-maker, a sweater shop, and then came to one called Edina. This, she recalled, was the poetic name for Edinburgh.

The window contained the usual photographs of the castle and the spire of the Scott Monument. But there was a little group of books between marble bookends; and one of the books was called *Jane and Frederic: A Love Story*.

She went into the shop. There was a table with books and magazines. Most of the material was guides to the city. But *Jane and Frederic* was there. She picked it up.

The cover illustration, a black-and-white drawing, showed a young girl with centre-parted hair, ringlets framing a pensive, rather serious face. She wore a low-necked, tight-waisted dress and a pendant on a fine chain. The frontispiece inside the book was a black-and-white reproduction of the Delacroix portrait of Chopin, a semi-profile, his expression alert, lips slightly parted as if about to speak.

The first paragraph of text began: 'The romance between Jane Stirling and Frederic Chopin is one of the greatest untold love stories in the world. They met first in Paris, that city of romance . . .' Skimming through, she saw that the text only covered about ninety pages, generously filled out with grainy postcard views of Victorian Edinburgh and photographs of prominent citizens of the time.

From remarks made by Greg as he read Chopin's letters, Liz knew there had been only the most sedate meetings between teacher and pupil. Moreover, she'd just heard him read out Chopin's phrase about tiresome Scottish ladies. That hardly seemed to be the sort of words a lover would use.

It was a paperback and the price wasn't high. She bought a copy. As the assistant was about to ring it up, Liz enquired, 'Have you anything else to do with Chopin?'

'Well, madam, did you notice on the cover, the lady's wearing a locket? We have copies of that for sale.'

True enough. She produced a locket very similar in size and design to the pendant Greg had bought for Liz in Music Hath Charms of Manchester, but made in silver. One half contained a photographic copy of a profile of Chopin, identified by Jemmy Salter as being by George Sand. On the other side was a small reproduction of the head of Jane Stirling from the drawing on the book cover.

The implication was that in the drawing, Jane was wearing a locket commemorating her love affair with Chopin. But the drawing was of a young girl. Liz knew that when 'Jane and Frederic' had first met, Jane had been a plump lady of about forty.

She murmured that the cost of the locket was too high, paid for the paperback, and took her leave.

Another gift shop a few doors along was primarily a jeweller's, its window display showing items made from semi-precious stones associated with the Highlands. To one side, so as to make it easy to distinguish from the rest, was a little show of articles against a background of black velvet. There were Chopin pendants, the silver locket containing the two miniature portraits, and a cameo brooch with Jane Stirling's head. A small notice stood alongside: 'JANE STIRLING AND FREDERIC CHOPIN – OTHER ITEMS AVAILABLE.'

Inside there were copies of the paperback. This time she paused long enough to glance at the end. This was a tender farewell scene at Chopin's deathbed, with Jane vowing to be faithful for ever to his memory.

The shop assistant came to hover nearby. 'Can I help you, miss?'

He was a teenager, perhaps an after-school part-timer.

She smiled at him. 'What I'm really looking for', she said, 'is earrings.' She already knew from Music Hath Charms that there were no earrings available. 'To match the cameo brooch in the window. I've already got that; my boyfriend gave it to me for my birthday.'

'Ah, now, we've nothing in the way of earrings among the Chopin Collection,' he said. 'But if you'd care to look at the stand here – these earrings are Cairngorms – natural stones you see, with a silver setting?'

She parried his rehearsed sales talk while she examined the other items in what he called the Chopin Collection. 'Are these made locally? Couldn't you ask the person who made them to do matching earrings?'

He explained ruefully that their stock had just been refilled. 'Easter's coming, you know, and that's when visitors start to arrive, so I don't think any more will be coming in for quite a wee while yet.'

She tried for an address to which she could write. He shook his head, flustered. 'We don't particularly specialize in the Chopin items so much as some other shops. I'm sorry, miss, I can't help you there.'

She thanked him and was about to leave. The shop assistant, anxious to make a good impression on a visitor, said, as she was opening the door, 'There's a place hard by the Grassmarket that goes in for a lot more of the Jane Stirling items than we do. If you just go on for a bit past the cathedral – St Giles', you know, miss? – and then turn down the wee sloping lane and turn left, you'll see it. It's called Fond Memory.'

'Oh, that's very kind,' she exclaimed, rewarding him with a warm smile. 'Thank you so much.'

Fond Memory was trying to be tasteful. It had the lines from Thomas Moore's poem in gold letters on the plate glass of the window: 'Fond Memory brings the light / Of other days around me.'

The goods on sale ranged over quite a period of history – anything to do with famous people who could be connected to Scotland. Cartoons of Boswell with Dr. Johnson, Rob Roy tartan scarves, framed poems by Robert Burns, songs by Lady Nairne on disc, sketches of Robert Louis Stevenson's cottage in the Pentland Hills – an interesting enough selection.

One table held a range of portraits of Chopin and of the sketch of the young Jane Stirling. In front were items of jewellery, and two or three copies of the paperback.

As soon as Liz began to examine the jewellery, an assistant came from behind the counter to serve her. She was a pleasant, middle-aged lady in a dark silk blouse and a tartan skirt. 'Are you a devotee?' she enquired. 'We make quite a speciality of Chopin mementoes; I'm very fond of his music.'

'Oh, me too,' enthused Liz. 'And I'm ever so keen on learning more about Jane Stirling. Hardly any attention is paid to her – I knew almost nothing about her until I came to Edinburgh.'

'So sad,' said the shopkeeper. 'Let me show you this – it's new.' She picked up a small antiqued silver frame, holding a silhouette version of Jane Stirling's head.

'Oh, that's really pretty!' Liz cried, and in fact it was less tacky than some of the other offerings. 'Oh, I must have that! And there's a matching one for Chopin, of course?'

'Ah . . .Well, in fact, no . . . We just got our stock a few days ago,' she apologized, 'and I think this is the only version.' She went to the back door of the shop and called. 'Walter! Walter, can you come here a minute?'

After a slight delay Walter appeared, wiping his lips with the back of his hand. In his grey moustache lingered a few crumbs. 'What is it, Margo?' he said in a grumpy tones. 'I'm in the middle of my tea.'

'This lady is asking if there's a matching miniature for the Jane Stirling silhouette in silver?'

'If there was a matching one it'd be on the stand, would it no? I spent most of yesterday setting it all out.'

'But when you come to think of it, Walter,' she replied in a soothing voice, 'it would make sense if there was another to make it a set.'

'Well, if there had been, I'd have bought it, so there isn't, and if there's going to be one, we'll get it in due course.'

His wife was silenced by his manner.

Liz said, 'Could you get in touch and ask if there already is a partner? I'd really love to have them as a pair, you know.'

'We've bought in what we need for the season, miss,' Walter said with irritation.

'Well, let me have an address or a telephone number, would you? Then I could ask about it for myself.'

'It'd do you no good, miss,' he replied, turning away. 'He's a law unto himself, the maker of those things.'

'But we ought to do what we can to help the lady,' his wife protested, summoning up courage. 'She's an enthusiast like me, dear, and I'd really like it if we could help her.'

'And I'm telling you that it's not good business to waste any more time on it, Margo, so that's the end of it.' He turned to Liz with a pretence of civility. 'You'll forgive my wife, miss, but she thinks we run the shop for love. No business sense, I'm afraid. Sorry not to be able to be of assistance.'

'Oh, well,' said Liz, opening her handbag, 'I'll have the miniature of Jane, and then perhaps you could enquire for me about a partner to it, and I could come back in a day or two?'

Margo darted to the table. 'It is really pretty, isn't it? And I'm sure we can do something about one of Chopin.'

Liz watched as she picked it up. There was a leaflet folded under it to steady the back strut that held it upright. It seemed to be a price list. She reached for it and handed it to Margo, who popped it into a polythene bag with the portrait.

Walter moved forward unexpectedly. His wife looked at him in surprise. 'I can manage, dear. You go back to your tea; it'll be getting cold.'

He frowned, seemed uncertain for a moment, then withdrew.

Margo looked in apology at Liz. 'My husband isn't interested in the Chopin items, I'm afraid,' she sighed. 'He's not a sentimental man.'

Liz murmured a response about male shortcomings and waited for her credit card to be accepted. They parted with friendly goodbyes. She went out in triumph. She thought she had a price list, and a price list generally contained the name and address of the supplier. No matter that the Chopin-memorabilia business seemed to be one of those little tax dodges wanting to remain unnoticed – now she had a clue to its identity.

She set off at a quick pace. Greg would be waiting for her in the road by Waverley station. She hurried along little lanes into Market Street and then left for Waverley Bridge.

She saw Greg a few cars down, leaning on the roof of his Nissan and looking around for her. She was about to wave to him when something dragged her fiercely backwards. She lost her balance, and went tumbling down hard on the pavement.

She cried out as she hit the ground. A hand shoved her on to her side, her shoulder bag was dragged off, and her assailant fled.

Ten

Greg saw it happen. Among the bobbing heads of commuters on their way to the station he glimpsed the emerald-green scarf. One moment it was there, the next it suddenly dipped out of sight. He heard the faint cry.

He ran. Pedestrians tried to avoid him; he barged into one, dodged another, saw people stooping over a fallen figure, and was there.

She was on her left side, trying to get up. A young woman had her right arm, helping her. He knelt, put his arms under her and lifted her. She let him hold her steady, finding her feet again.

Her left temple was grazed; there was grit on her cheek.

'Sweetheart, are you all right?' She flinched as he tightened his grasp. 'Are your ribs hurt?' And he let her go a little.

She muttered something. He leaned down. 'What?'

She said it again. 'My dignity's hurt.'

'Let's get you to the car.'

'Just a minute.' She put up a hand to dust grit from her brow. 'Who was it?' she asked, blinking round at the group of bystanders.

'Some man,' said the young woman.

'I didna' get a real look,' said someone else.

'Och, it's been one of they youngsters that lounge about in the shopping centre,' suggested another voice.

People were hurrying around them, eager to get to their home-going trains. Liz said, 'My bag's gone.'

'Never mind that. Let's get you to hospital . . .'

'No, no, let's get to the Hill House.'

'But you've had a bad fall; you might have broken—'

'I'm all *right*. Let's go, Greg.'

At least he could get her to the car. 'Should we call the polis?' a bystander asked.

'Och, what good wad that be? He's away and off by now.'

'Can we go, Greg?' Liz was begging. 'I must look a mess.'

At this – her priority – he hardly knew whether to smile or sigh. He helped her to the Nissan. He put her gently into the passenger seat. Already the little group of supporters was disintegrating as they went about their own business. Another day, another mugging – nothing unusual.

As they drove to the hotel, Liz investigated the graze on her temple with a tentative finger. 'Does it look awful, Greg?'

'No, no, it's not too deep, nothing to need stitches –'

'No, I mean, am I a mess?'

He sighed and smiled. 'You could never be a mess, my precious. But we ought to go to the hospital just to check—'

'I'm all right. I just got a knock, and I'm a bit scared, that's all.'

'What happened?'

'He dragged me back by the strap of my handbag all of a sudden. Then he grabbed the bag. I never saw him.'

'We should call it in. Do you feel up to making the call on your mobile?'

'My mobile was in my handbag, Greg.'

'Oh, confound it. Mine's in my pocket. I can't try to reach for it in this traffic.' They were in Princes Street with the rush hour all around them. Traffic restrictions had to be carefully observed on this main thoroughfare. He waited for a permitted turning, eventually manoeuvring the car into a quiet side street on the north side of the city.

Chief Inspector Glaston had offered to get him a contact in the Edinburgh force, but the ex-Crown Prince of Hirtenstein wasn't unknown to them. In the first place, he'd done them a great favour a few years ago in helping to solve the mystery that had surrounded the missing Amati cello. And in the second place, he was an ex-royal, on their list of VIPs to be looked after. Not a very high-echelon VIP, and never causing any problems. They quite liked him.

He asked to be put through to a sergeant he knew. He reported the mugging. 'In the name of the Wee Man,' cried Sergeant Tulloch, 'those toe-rags in the Waverley shopping centre – they're always up to something. Is the young lady badly hurt?'

'She says not. But her handbag was taken.'

'Of course. Great value in it?'

Greg passed the mobile to Liz. 'He wants to know how much you've lost.'

Into the mobile she said, 'Just a minute.' Then to Greg she said, 'I haven't lost any priceless treasures. But listen, sweetie.' She paused, assembling her thoughts. 'All my notes about Chopin and some stuff I bought in the gift shops – they're gone.'

'Oh.'

She said, 'I think we ought to put your detective friend in the picture.'

'What is the picture, exactly?' There was no teasing in the question. He was genuinely puzzled.

'Now I'm using my head a bit, I feel . . . I feel the man who attacked me was probably from the last shop I visited.'

That startled him. He frowned at her.

'He was quite surly,' she said in explanation. 'And I managed to pick up what I feel sure was a price list. It could have had information about the supplier on it. He saw me do it, I'm sure. And I think that was what he was after.'

'OK. Tell Tulloch there's quite a lot to explain, and ask him if he can come to the Hill House.'

'Right.'

Before she could speak into the mobile he added, 'Ask him to send someone to the shop you were in. If you're right, we want another copy of that price list.'

'Good.' She passed on all this to Tulloch, who took it into consideration for a few minutes before saying, 'Will do. And I'll be round to see you at the hotel in about an hour.'

She guessed this high priority for a run-of-the-mill mugging was out of respect for the crown prince. She switched off, laid the instrument on the dashboard, and leaned back. She at once leaned forward again. Her left shoulder blade hurt. Luckily the rest of the drive was short.

Hector McVay, in conference with a departing guest, saw the signs of the damage on Liz's face as they went in. 'Excuse me,' he said to his customer, then hurried after them as they went to the lift. 'Ms Blair! You've been in the wars! Shall I call a doctor?'

'No, no, I'm all right – just a fall.' Seeing that wasn't enough to dissuade him, she said, 'I slipped on the Waverley Bridge.'

'Oh, that wee brae there is dangerous – I've always said so. Well, now, I'll send up a first-aid box; you should disinfect that scrape on your brow. Dear me, are you sure you wouldn't like the doctor just to look at it?'

'Thank you, Mr McVay, but I'll be fine.' Her tone told him all she longed for was the sanctuary of their room. He bowed and let them go.

She went immediately into the bathroom to set about examining her injuries. Her padded black jacket had protected her back when she went down, so that the skin on her shoulder blades was unbroken. Her jeans had protected her leg when her assailant had thrown her on her side, though her left knee ached a little. Her right arm, on which her handbag had hung, felt wrenched and sore, with rasped skin at the point where its strap had been pulled across.

Although none of the damage was life-threatening, the sight of it appalled Greg. 'Oh, Liz, my little gem . . .'

'It's all right. He just pulled me off balance so he could get the handbag. If I'd been wearing flatties, I might not have gone down.'

He was considering an alarming possibility: 'Liz, are you sure it was the man from the shop? Could it have been . . .' He let the question die away: it was a very bad idea.

She understood at once. She shivered. 'The man from the London museum? No – really – is that likely? That he would be here, in Edinburgh?'

'Perhaps not.'

'It's just a coincidence. He wanted to stop me, and my handbag was dangling down my back.' A pause. 'And yet . . .'

'What?'

'People in the shops told me that they'd just had new stock delivered, for the oncoming tourist season. That begins at Easter, it seems. So if the man at the Museum of Musical Heritage is the same man as is fostering a Chopin-and-Jane fad, he *could* be here, topping up supplies.'

There was a knock at the door. Greg went to answer. A maid offered a box showing the first-aid symbol. 'Is there anything else you'd be wanting, sir? Food or drink?'

'Tea,' Liz called, half-joking. 'Cups of sweet hot tea are supposed to be good for accident victims.'

The maid accepted this as a genuine order and left. Opening the first-aid box, Greg took it into the bathroom.

'What I need is a long, hot shower to clean away the grit. Then we'll have the tea, and you can anoint me.' She handed him the tube of disinfectant lotion. 'Then I'll slip into something comfortable for Sergeant Tulloch.' Her tone was light, jokey, but her voice trembled.

When she came out of the shower, he wrapped her gently in the Turkish bathrobe and held her close. She gave a little whimper of distress. Tears fell on the bathrobe.

'I was scared, Greg. I thought I'd be brave in a situation like that, but I felt I was absolutely . . . done for.'

'You were marvellous, *querida*,' he soothed. 'You've kept it together; you've held up perfectly –'

'Until now.'

'Well, there's only me to see you crying. And I won't tell.'

When the telephone rang to say that Mr Tulloch had arrived, Greg asked him to come up. Coincidentally the tea arrived at the same time, with iced biscuits and shortbread fingers. Liz, now in slacks and a fawn cashmere sweater and with her damp hair tied back, took up hostess duties. Mr Tulloch, who was broad and muscular, was pleased to accept tea and biscuits to help keep up his energy after a day that had already seemed long.

They explained the situation to him, taking turns to sort out the intricacies for him. When they'd finished, he frowned and nodded. 'I had a bit of a conversation with Inspector Glaston of Scotland Yard, so I know you're trying to find this man Hampton who killed the countess. You may have struck lucky with your angle of investigation – this mugging could well be linked to it. A thing based on the composer Chopin – who'd have thought it!'

Liz didn't say, 'Greg thought it.' Instead she murmured agreement, that a swindle based on music was probably unusual.

'You're right there, miss, but there's frauds to do with Old Masters and with antiques – why shouldn't there be frauds to do with music?' He sighed. 'It's just that it's never come up before.'

'The way I look at it', said Mr Crowne, 'is that Hampton is somebody who had a normal interest in Chopin. Then he hit on this money-making idea of fake jewellery and mementoes, a small business that needn't attract any attention from the Inland Revenue. But then somehow the idea came up of faking a music manuscript, which would make a *lot* more money.'

'You're saying now that it's a fake manuscript?' Liz intervened. 'I thought you felt there might actually be one.'

'Yes, why else were you looking at places where Chopin had actually stayed?' Tulloch agreed.

'Well, you know, Sergeant, lost compositions do turn up.' He told him the story of the reappearance of the Beethoven piano scores.

'Two million, eh?' gasped the sergeant. 'Oh, then it's easy to understand why this rascal might have had a go. Oh, aye, I see that.' He paused to assimilate this. 'So here we have a wee villain that has a go at the big time, makes a hash of it and kills a lady. So he makes himself scarce, gets off out of London on his delivery round to his customers.'

They viewed this résumé in silence for a moment.

'Yes, and what I think is this, Sergeant,' Liz said: 'I think two or three of the customers we've met are in on the fiddle. Not all of them – I think a couple of the shopkeepers I spoke to this afternoon were totally innocent. But I think Fond Memories was in on it – the husband, I'm pretty sure, although the wife perhaps not.'

'Did you go there?' Greg asked Tulloch. 'Did you get a price list?'

'Ha! The shop was closed, the shutter wound down. We had somebody look up the key-holder – you know we always have that, in case of fire or flood. The key-holder is a Walter Fairbairn, and there was no reply from his home address when we telephoned. I sent a man to enquire there, and a neighbour said they had gone away this evening – a family emergency, she'd been told.'

'And of course no forwarding address.'

'Exactly, miss. They've cleared off. And you know, to give up on a shop site in that area, where there's a good trade with the tourists – the man knows he's done something serious.'

'You mean you think *he's* the one that attacked Liz?'

'Yes, that's it – he mugged somebody – oh, no, of course, you're thinking he's Hampton, the man who was at the museum. And killed the countess.'

'No, Greg,' Liz declared, 'the man in Fond Memories is certainly not the same man who attacked Marzelina. Walter Fairbairn wouldn't know a Chopin portrait from a postage stamp. *He's* not the brains behind this thing. And his wife is a sweetie. No, that pair aren't involved in anything but a tax swindle – I'm sure of it.'

'So where's Himself: the big man? – the man who was calling himself Hampton?' Tulloch mused.

'I wish I knew,' said Greg. 'Let's suppose he's the man who went for Liz to get the price list out of her bag. *If* that was him, how did he know she'd got something that might be evidence? If he's off in London?'

'But we said he could be here, on his delivery round, and then Fairbairn telephones him,' Liz proposed, 'and says I walked in, Mrs Nosey-Parker, and walked out again taking a price list with his name and address on it—'

'And he dashes out to find you, Liz?' Greg put in. 'How could he possibly find you?'

'Walter tells him to look for a woman wearing a long bright-green scarf.'

'Yes, but . . . sweetheart . . . that's too much of a coincidence. We can't possibly say he was in Edinburgh and somewhere close by so that he could find you on a public street.'

'Unless . . .' said the sergeant, 'unless he was in the back-room of the shop.'

'No, no!' Liz protested.

'Why not?

'Walter was having his tea.'

'Well, this Mr Hampton could have been having a meal with him, could he no?'

'Oh, don't say that!' Liz cried.

Greg hastily repeated his view that it was all too coinci-dental and he didn't believe it, and after a moment the sergeant caught on. Nodding agreement, he began to plan out what the Edinburgh police should do next.

'We'll keep on after the Fairbairns. Of course it's likely they haven't gone to relatives, but we'll find out what their family ties may be. And we'll keep an eye on the shop, to see if anybody goes back there.'

'Could you get into the shop,' Greg asked, 'to look for a price list with the supplier's address?'

'It would need a warrant,' sighed Tulloch. 'And I don't think we've got enough grounds. But we'll see, we'll see.'

After some further consideration he rose to take his leave. Greg accompanied him out into the corridor. 'Do you think it's possible that Hampton really is here in Edinburgh?'

'I wish I could tell you, sir. All I'd like to say is: be a wee bit careful, because, you know, if Hampton was at the shop while your lady was buying the miniature, he's *seen* her. It wasn't the green scarf that found her for him; he followed her from the shop.'

'Yes.'

'But it's more likely that it was Fairbairn. And we'll be on the lookout for him, you can be sure.'

'Thank you.' They shook hands and Tulloch went for the lift.

Liz was sitting at the dressing table brushing her hair, now dry after the shower. Greg watched her in silence for a moment or two.

'What?' she asked, glancing round at him.

'You used to have little soft strands that came down on to your cheek in a sort of curl,' he recalled.

'Oh, straight hair is the thing these days.' She paused. 'Do you like it this way?'

'Whatever you do is perfect.'

'Except when I lose my handbag with all the important stuff in it. I've got to report my stolen credit cards, Greg – it's such a bore.'

She spent an hour or so over that chore. Then it was time for dinner. They went down to the restaurant, where McVay escorted them personally to their table, reserved for them although the place was busy.

'Are you feeling yourself again, Ms Blair?' he enquired with concern.

'Yes, yes, thanks, except that I'll have to buy a new handbag and a few other things. My favourite lipstick was in that handbag,' she mourned.

'Oh, a wee shopping expedition, then.'

'Listen, Hector,' said Greg, recalling that Hector was a fund of information, 'Liz lost a lot of stuff she bought this after-noon – little trinkets about Chopin, from a shop near the Grassmarket – things she'd like to replace.'

'Oh aye, one or two of my guests have come in with items like that. Guests during the festival season, mostly.' His atten-tion was on the tardy waiter hurrying towards them with the menus. 'The best place for that is Livingston, of course.'

'Livingston?' Greg, who wasn't a shopping fiend, had only barely heard of the place.

'Oh, yes, great,' cried Liz. 'I'll buy a new handbag there in the Designer Outlet Centre.'

'But the Chopin trinkets,' Greg urged. 'There's a shop?'

'Yes, people have mentioned it to me – a great stock of things to do with Edinburgh's olden days. I think it's in the main shop-ping mall; it wouldn't be the Designer Outlet, I fancy.'

'Thank you.'

Hector lingered to recommend the venison and the tropical fruits *à la reine*. When he'd gone Liz said, 'So it's off to Livingston in the morning, yes?'

'Ah ... well ...'

'What?'

'Don't you think ... You had a bad shock today ... Don't you think you ought to take it easy? Stay indoors, rest and recover?'

She stared at him. 'What brought that on?'

'Well, it would do you good to have a day in bed—'

'I never have days in bed. And I want to go with you to see this famous trinket shop in Livingston.'

'No, really, you could take it easy ...'

She frowned, nodded, then smiled. 'Oh I see. Wrap me up in cotton wool and keep me safe from the nasty man. Are you nuts?'

'Well, Liz, we ought to take that into account ...'

'Not on your life. I'm going to Livingston with you and that's that.'

Eleven

They allowed the morning rush hour to go by before they set out on Thursday morning. The day was fine but with that strange clarity that told of rain in the offing. It was cold, too, but Liz didn't put on her emerald-green scarf.

Greg watched her push it to the back of a drawer. He was glad. Probably Liz didn't like it any more because it reminded her of her scare. He didn't like it because it was too noticeable.

He drove conservatively. He didn't want to swing about from lane to lane on the A8 because it might jar her shoulder blades. He'd watched admiringly while Liz, with an expert hand, covered up the graze on her cheek and the bruise on her brow with make-up, but her back now showed the colouring of a bad bruise. The red mark on her arm from the handbag strap was diminishing.

They went out past the rugby ground at Murrayfield and the zoo at Corstorphine, past the airport, and then on to the M8 by means of a devilish intersection.

'That was fun,' Liz said with some sarcasm.

'There was a big shopping centre there. We could have stopped to buy you a new handbag.'

'No, no, I'm going to do that at Livingston.'

Past Ratho she began to notice signs announcing names with 'Calder' in them. 'Calder House must be somewhere near here,' she said, pointing off to her left.

'But we're not going there; we're going to Livingston.'

'You've given up the idea that there might have been a genuine piano score tucked away at Calder House?'

'I've put that on the . . . the back cooker.'

'The back burner. Why?'

'Because the shops with memorabilia are more interesting.'

'But it would be nice just to have a look at it.'

He shrugged. In the course of his life, attending weddings

and christenings among exiled royals, he'd seen lots of stately homes and castles. They had no great appeal.

'Come on, Greg; at least let's take a look. It would get us off this boring motorway.'

Well, why not? He looked out for a turn-off that signalled the correct names, led them left, then under a viaduct, down a straight road of country residences, right along a road that looked as if it would take them towards Mid-Calder – and that was where he got lost.

'*Ah, merde,*' he muttered as he came to a halt a little past a turning he'd intended to take. A glance had shown it to be a farm track leading to a barn. 'Never leave the *autoroute* without a map.'

'Drive on a bit.'

'I don't see the point of that. You can tell by the trees that the next turning bends off to the south.'

'And we don't want to go south?'

He smiled. Quite a lot of people had no sense of north and south. He had noticed it often when doing his yearly military stint as a Swiss citizen.

He began preparations for a three-point turn in the narrow road. 'I think we'll go back and find somebody to ask.'

'Yes, there's a guy hesitating back there, waiting for you to decide what to do.'

The vehicle was a white van. The driver got out, leaned on the open driver's door, and seemed to be studying them.

'Well,' thought Liz, 'there's no need to be so sarcastic. We'll only be a minute.' She turned to tell Greg there was someone about a hundred yards behind him waiting to pass.

The Nissan gave an abrupt lurch. The rear window cracked. There was a sudden sound, like a shot. The window crumbled in a tinkling of glass.

They both ducked instinctively. Greg shoved Liz down without care for her bruised back.

The white van came surging past, mounting the verge and crushing the thorn hedge as it went. Raising himself an inch or so, Greg saw something hurtling towards them from its driving window. He threw himself into the well of the passenger space, taking Liz with him. He held her fast, waiting for the explosion.

Ten seconds. Twenty. Nothing.

He loosened his grip on Liz, who was making muffled sounds of protest. Gingerly he put himself high enough – just high enough – to see the missile.

It was a narrow rectangular cardboard box.

He eyed this for a while. It simply lay there. He sat up.

Liz came with him, complaining. 'What on earth happened?'

'Somebody shot at us.'

'*What?*'

He turned his head to look at the shattered rear window. She did the same.

'Oh,' she said.

He took another long look past her at the cardboard box. It was still innocently lying on the rough road surface. He opened the driver's door and got out.

'What now?' cried Liz, grabbing at his jacket.

'He threw something.'

'Who did?'

'White-Van Man.'

'White-Van Man?'

'Didn't you hear him roar past?'

'Couldn't hear anything, with you practically smothering me!'

'Well, someone in a white van just took a shot at us – with a shotgun, I think – and then, as he drove away, he threw something. I, nitwit that I am, thought it was a bomb.'

She looked at him in contrition. She understood. This was his grandmother's constant nightmare: that someone would attack the exiled heir to the kingdom of Hirtenstein.

'So what do you think now?' she asked with something of a tremble in her voice.

'I don't know.'

She let go of his jacket.

He got out of the car and walked round to the passenger side. The little cardboard box still lay there. In the hedgerow were several thorn twigs torn off by the racing van. He selected the longest and, leaning away from the box, gave it a nudge with the twig.

It didn't explode. Nothing happened at all. But he learned that it was extremely light – too light to contain anything explosive. He stepped up to it. Liz, by this time out of the car and hovering there, gave a cry of alarm.

'Don't!'

'It's practically empty. It can't be harmful.' He leaned down to pick it up. Liz leapt to his side. 'Go away,' he said, straightening.

'If it's going to explode in our faces, we're going to go together.' She clung resolutely.

He put an arm round her for a moment of reassurance. Then, fairly convinced the thing would do no harm, he picked it up.

It was a slim box covered with faintly patterned paper, the kind that might contain a necklace or a bracelet. A small piece of sticky tape held it closed. He peeled it off.

Inside was a folded piece of paper. He unfolded it.

Printed in one of the largest typefaces offered by computers were the words: 'CLEAR OFF!'

Liz burst into laughter. Then she hid her face in his shoulder and began to cry. She muttered something.

'What was that?' he asked, somewhat shaken himself. He was holding her rather too tightly.

'Thank you for not saying "I told you so".'

'What do you mean?'

'You tried to leave me at the hotel, nice and safe. But I wouldn't be left. And now somebody's shooting at us and I'm scared again!'

'No, no,' he soothed.

The first thing was to make sure the assailant wasn't coming back. Over the hedgerows nothing could be seen – he was out of sight by now, probably along the road going south.

Liz holding his arm fiercely, he walked slowly back along the road, his gaze directed to the ground.

'What are you doing?'

'Looking for shotgun cartridges. Ah!' There it was, a cylinder a little over two inches long.

'That's what he was doing,' Liz exclaimed, remembering. 'Sighting his gun from behind his open door.'

'You saw him?'

'We-ell . . .'

'Did you get the number plate?'

'Oh, come on!'

'Ah well . . .' It was too much to expect. And probably not helpful anyway. He turned to look back at the Nissan. 'He was pretty lucky to hit the car at this distance – or perhaps he didn't particularly want to hit it, just scare us.'

'He succeeded, as far as I was concerned, pardner' – a shaky attempt at lightness.

'We'll have to let Tulloch know,' he said.

'Well, we can't drive on into any civilized place with a car covered in pock marks on its back and a broken rear window.'

'I'm sorry now that I picked up the box.' He still had it in his hand. 'There might be fingerprints on it.'

'Yes.'

'"Clear Off" – it really isn't very revealing.'

'No.'

'Are you all right, Liz?'

There was a little silence before she replied. She straightened her shoulders, patted her hair, then said, 'That's the second time this guy's made me feel chicken. I'm going to *get* him!'

He laughed and hugged her.

'Ouch,' she protested.

'Sorry.' He kissed the top of her head in apology. 'Do you agree the best way to "get" him is now to get in touch with Tulloch?'

'Yes, I agree. And I bet there aren't any fingerprints on the box. It's a brand-new box taken out of stock and probably handled with great care.'

'Taken out of stock. Then you think it's from the memorabilia shop in Edinburgh – what's its name? Fond Memory?'

'Looks very like the one my framed miniature was in, the one that was in my stolen handbag – different shape but the same kind of surface.'

'Ah well. It's the locals telling us they don't like our interference.'

'So go on, ring Tulloch and tell him, and then we ought to get on to Livingston. There will be a price list in this curio shop that Mr McVay recommended.'

He got out his mobile, made the call, and after a delay was put in touch with Tulloch. Liz then listened to quite a long one-sided conversation. It ended with Greg agreeing to stay where they were until the sergeant could get to them.

'He asked if we saw the number plates?' she asked.

'Yes.'

'Don't tell him we were cowering down out of his line of fire.'

'I think he probably guessed that, angel.' He smiled at her.

'But of course he needs to see the crime scene – to collect the cartridge case and see if there are tyre marks. He's thinking they might match the treads to something.'

'Some hopes. A white van? There must be millions of them.'

'Alas, yes.'

'And besides, it was probably stolen in the first place.'

'Could be.'

'But it's got to be Walter Fairbairn.' She thought for a moment. 'Would shopkeeper Walter Fairbairn own a gun?'

'It's possible. Did you get the impression that he spoke with a country accent? Ayrshire? Highland?'

'How would I know?' she groaned. 'I haven't got a trained musician's ear! All I know is, he was Scottish.'

'Sorry. What I'm saying is that he might come from a rural district. Country folk are used to going out after crows and pigeons and so on.'

'So Walter might own a gun.'

'Or borrow one. "Let me have your gun for a couple of days, I want to bag a rabbit or two."'

She hesitated then said, 'You said a minute ago he didn't want to kill us?'

'No, no, that wasn't his intention,' he said in reassurance. 'You don't bring a message in a cardboard box for somebody you intend to shoot dead.'

'Oh.' She gave a tremulous chuckle. 'Why didn't I think of that?'

They sat in the Nissan discussing the problem until Tulloch and a uniformed constable drove up behind them in an unmarked car. In the meantime the promised rain had come on quite hard. Any tyre tracks would be washed away on the uneven surface.

The only evidence of the car's passage was the torn hawthorn in the hedge. The shattered glass on the back seat had little pellets that would give information about the cartridge load. He arranged for a low-loader to collect the Nissan. But as to the cardboard box with its message, the sergeant was sceptical as he put it into an evidence bag.

'We'll have a look, and you never know – fingerprints – people aren't as clever as they think they are, particularly with sticky tape. But if he's not in the system, it's not going to help much.'

Greg nodded acceptance of this.

'What bothers me is: how did this sniper know where you were going to be?' asked the sergeant.

'Oh, that's easy,' Liz said, eager to show her mental processes had recovered from the shock. 'We were probably followed from the hotel. My notes were in the handbag that was stolen. And the notes were on paper with the hotel's name and logo.'

'Um-m. So you're saying this was the laddie from the Fond Memory shop, the same chap that mugged you? It's all to do with scaring you off the Chopin thing?'

Greg understood that his VIP status was in Tulloch's mind now. There always was just the faintest possibility that some ardent anti-monarchist would choose His Highness as a target.

'Well, it's not a very serious effort,' he said. 'The way I see it, there's a little group – a handful of people, perhaps – who keep in touch because they're involved in tax evasion. So Mr Fairbairn wants us to go away.'

'We ought to get to Livingston,' Liz urged, 'to pick up that sales list from the place in the shopping mall.'

'Aye, that would be helpful. Hop in; I'll take you there.'

The constable was left in charge of the crime scene. They drove off. Tulloch took them back to the motorway and they sped into Livingston.

The parking area showed that the shopping centre was doing good business. It was lunch-time, so the cafés and restaurants were full. Pausing only to consult a board with a map of the sales area, they made their way through the mall to the shop calling itself simply Bygones.

It was a larger enterprise than any of the other shops they'd seen – a double-fronted site. One window was given over to Scottish tartans and a map of clan territories. The other had jewellery, reproduction paintings, photographs of historical sites, antique silver and some crystal. But nothing at all about music. Nothing about Chopin, or Jane Stirling.

They went in. A smartly dressed young woman came at once to take her place behind the counter. 'Good afternoon; may I help you?'

By silent agreement Liz took the lead. She said in a tone of wistful enquiry, 'I was told you had a good selection of things here, in memory of the romance between the composer Chopin and Jane Stirling.'

The assistant stiffened just a little. Then she said, 'Oh, I'm so sorry, madam! We decided not to go on with that this season. There isn't a great demand for it.'

'But I understood you had a big range . . .'

'Yes, we did go in for it quite a bit.' The response was quick, ready at hand, almost rehearsed. 'But you see, we needed the space for other things that really do sell well all the time – the clan histories, that sort of thing.'

Liz was at a loss. Greg took it up. 'I expect you have a few things tucked away somewhere – anything, really – we'd just like to have a look.'

'I'm sorry, sir. We got rid of what was left of the Chopin Collection to another outlet.'

'Which one would that be?' asked Sergeant Tulloch.

Sergeant Tulloch made her nervous. He had all the looks of a policeman. She tried to smile at him but stammered a little. 'Er . . . to . . . er . . .to Fond Memories, in Edinburgh.'

'Was that recently?' Fond Memories had been locked and shuttered since yesterday.

'No . . . Well, not long ago.'

'Ah, that's too bad,' said Greg.

'Yes, I tried there,' Liz explained in a mournful tone, 'but it's closed down. Could you give us the name and address of the makers of the Chopin Collection? I could try contacting them myself.'

'I'm really sorry, miss, but we didn't bother to keep anything of that sort. We're not going to handle that kind of thing any more, you see, so we cleared out all the paperwork.' She was regaining confidence. 'We had some things about Mendelssohn too, you know – Fingal's Cave and all that. But the musical side never made much money, so we've given it up.'

The sergeant was gazing about the premises with a perceptive eye. 'What used to stand there?' he enquired, nodding towards a little round table with a soft blue cloth over it.

'Er . . . what? Oh, there. Oh, that was . . . er . . . a collection of items made from stag's horn, but we're going to put something more colourful in its place.'

'Uh-huh,' he said. He produced and showed his warrant card. 'Mind if I look around a little?'

'But . . . but . . .' Her suspicions confirmed, she was at a loss, but recovered with an effort that made her almost breathless. 'I can't see why you should want . . . but please yourself, Sergeant.'

That was disappointing. If she wasn't worried, then there was nothing to see. For form's sake Tulloch strolled into the back of the shop and was gone for a few minutes. Meanwhile the sales-lady had decided on the attitude she should take.

'I can't understand what this is about,' she said in indignation. 'This is a respectable business! What on earth brings you here causing trouble?'

'It's nothing serious,' Liz said, now adopting a slightly official mode. 'Just an inspection. We had complaints.'

'Who from? Who's trying to make trouble for us?'

Tulloch returned, shaking his head. 'Nothing,' he said. To the assistant he said, 'Sorry, miss.'

'Who's complained? About what?'

'Somebody has a grudge against you, mebbe.'

'I want to know who!' she cried, warming to her role. 'You can't just walk in here and—'

'I've said I'm sorry,' Tulloch replied. He led the way out without more ado.

They made their way to a nearby bench and sat down.

'The place had been cleared out in a bit of a hurry. There were gaps in the stock on the shelves. A nice tidy desk with the paperwork in pigeonholes, but one pigeonhole was completely empty.'

'So they had a quick clear-out.'

'Yes. This morning, I'd say.'

'*That's* what it was for!' Greg exclaimed.

'What was what?' Liz asked, bewildered.

'To delay us! That was what the shooting was about! He didn't want to do any harm; he just wanted to give enough time to Bygones to get rid of the stock.'

They sat thinking about that for a moment. 'He was taking a big risk,' Tulloch said. 'If you'd stuck to the motorway, he could never have got off a shot at you.'

'That's true. But if he had some idea of where we were going . . .'

'But Livingston is on the motorway—'

'Yes,' Liz broke in, 'but remember he was going by the notes from my handbag. There's a lot in there about houses that Chopin visited, and we actually did turn off to look at Calder House.' She paused a moment to look in contrition at Greg, who shrugged.

'Fairbairn had some information from the notes, so he was

probably expecting us to take a turn-off somewhere. Let's say he followed us all the way from the hotel, was ready for any route we took.'

'How d'you mean, ready?

'If we'd stayed on the M8 and he only wanted to delay us,' Greg put in, 'he could have arranged a problem for us as we drove into Livingston – somebody ready to stage a rear collision, or compete for a parking space – something like that.'

'He finds you very important, doesn't he?' Tulloch mused. 'Fairbairn, I mean.'

'Ye-es,' Liz agreed. 'Do you think anybody'd go to all that trouble, just to avoid a fine for tax evasion?'

Tulloch waited to hear her answer to her own question.

'For him, perhaps it's very serious – perhaps *deadly* serious. Perhaps he's trying to avoid a sentence for murder.'

'Ah,' Tulloch said. 'That's it.'

'So you think Fairbairn is Hampton?' Greg asked, surprised.

'Well, he could be, sir.' Tulloch laid it out for him. 'He's trying to make sure you can't get on his track. He asks his pals to get rid of any evidence of the Chopin connection and they do, because they think it's about their little swindle. But that's not what it's about really; it's about Hampton covering his tracks.'

'If you're right, he's done it very effectively,' Greg sighed. 'Unless . . . Could any of the stuff from the shop be around still? Where would they dispose of stuff quickly?'

'Ach, it's probably in the big rubbish bins in the service area. And don't think we're ever gonna find anything, sir, because those bins are enormous and there's a lot of 'em.'

'Could you . . . is there some pressure you could bring to bear on the shopkeepers? Get them to give information?'

The sergeant looked dubious. 'The chief superintendent would have to think that over, sir. I don't know what the legal aspect might be and by the time we got a yes on it, Hampton could be off in South America or somewhere.'

Liz was beginning to shake her head. 'I met Fairbairn. I'm not convinced he knows enough about Chopin to set up the manuscript fraud. Besides . . .'

'What?'

She turned to Greg. 'In London we were asking the museum people about visitors showing a special interest in the place.

They never mentioned a big middle-aged Scot with a grey moustache.'

Tulloch frowned in disagreement.

'I *met* him, Sergeant! He's a thickie. He could do something fairly fast like locking up his shop and running away. He might even come after us with a shotgun to give us a scare – direct action, you see. But Fairbairn didn't entice an old lady in Paris into parting with fifty thousand pounds.'

They sat in gloomy consideration of her conclusions.

Tulloch offered to drive them back to Edinburgh, but Liz said she had shopping to do. Tulloch was immediately anxious. 'No wee shops selling Chopin trinkets,' he begged.

'No, handbags and lipsticks, Sergeant.' She was already looking about for a suitable emporium.

Sighing, he let it go. He took His Highness aside for a moment. 'See here, sir, you've had a warning. And as your young lady says, he – whoever he is – knows where you're staying. I'd think about a move, if I were you, eh?'

'That might be good sense.'

'Let me know where you go.'

'Of course.'

Later, after an excellent lunch and a rather lengthy expedition to the Designer Outlet Centre, they returned to the Hill House Hotel. Greg was considering the sergeant's advice and wondering whether there was any point in staying longer in Edinburgh.

Hector McVay, as always, was hovering around in the entrance hall, ready to greet his guests as they emerged from the taxi. 'Well, then, I see you've had a successful outing,' he cried. He eyed the names on Liz's shopping bags. 'Dearie me, I'm longing to see what you look like in all that finery.'

Liz blushed a little. She'd spent more than she'd intended, but then it was therapy, wasn't it, after the experience of the morning?

'And did you buy what you wanted in the memento shop?' Hector went on.

Greg shook his head. 'The place you recommended has given up on that side of their business, Hector.'

'Oh, what a shame. We could look at the Edinburgh shopping guide. There are other places you could try, perhaps?'

'No, we did that when we first arrived. And we can't seem to get the address of the firm that supplies the items.'

'The address?'

'Yes, you see, Mr McVay,' Liz sighed, 'I had a price list that I think had their address and so forth, but it was in the handbag that was stolen.'

'Och, well, Ms Blair, that's no problem!' he said in triumph. 'One of my guests left a price list of those musical curios in her room last year and I just kept the wee thing, you know, for information for clients should they want it.' He bustled off to his office, and returned a moment later with a leaflet folded over a thin paperback. 'There you are then.'

They'd been waiting in the greatest suspense. Greg said, 'Thank you, Hector,' in a voice that was surprisingly steady.

He unfolded the leaflet and read it while Liz leaned over to see.

And there it was: an artwork heading, 'Keepsake Curios'; a description of necklaces, pendants, bracelets, miniatures, re-productions of paintings with silver or Britannia-metal frames, the items neatly divided into groups – 'Frederic Chopin alone', 'Jane Stirling alone', or 'Both characters represented'. The thin paperback was a copy of the romance *Fredric and Jane*.

The address of Keepsake Curios was at the foot of the leaflet: a business park near Dover, Kent.

Twelve

They had a conference. It was best, they decided, to go back to London. They needed to have a discussion with Chief Inspector Glaston, but face to face rather than by telephone – they had a lot to tell him. There was a train round about seven o'clock that evening, getting them into London by midnight. Before leaving, they'd telephone Glaston to ask for a chance to speak to him in the morning.

Then there was the matter of reporting progress to Mme Wiaroz. They could hardly ring a very elderly lady after midnight, so best to do that now; and, of course, Greg had to ring his home in Bredoux. But that could most definitely wait until tomorrow.

Liz couldn't help being pleased at the distance that had become established between Greg and the domineering ex-queen mother. And yet . . . She gathered he didn't go to Bredoux very frequently. It seemed that the old lady acted very coolly when he appeared. So he avoided visiting when he knew she was home. But that meant he didn't see his father very often, and ex-King Anton of Hirtenstein was blameless in the matter of offending Liz. She sighed to herself, thankful for the lack of interfering relatives on her side of the relationship.

By the time Greg called, Glaston had gone home, but the sergeant doing night duty took a message and a note of the London phone number.

Mme Wiaroz was delighted to hear from them. 'In Edinburgh! Ah then, you are pursuing the link with deplorable Jane Stirling. Excellent!'

'But I must tell you, madame, that I begin to think there is no newly discovered Chopin score.'

'But yes! I gave you the photocopy. That is the writing of my dear Chopin.'

'I'm afraid that's more than likely a forgery,' he said, as gently as he could. 'We've come across quite a little industry here, of fakes of all kinds – not only of Chopin, but of Jane Stirling.'

'Of *her*?'

'Indeed. Ms Blair bought a copy of a book – it's on sale in several shops – and it depicts a romance between Jane Stirling and Chopin.'

'Absurd! Utterly absurd! You must know that when such a rumour reached Paris, one of his Polish friends wrote in alarm to ask him if it was true. His reply . . . his reply . . .' She faltered. 'It's such a tragic reply! Chopin wrote that he was closer to death than to marriage.'

'Yes, I've been reading his collected letters.'

'And then, you know, he had to absolutely flee the country to get away from her!'

'Yes, so he did.' He was sorry now that he'd mentioned Jane Stirling. To get her away from her outrage he went back to the point he was trying to make. 'Madame, I was speaking of the supposed piano score. Everything I have come across here implies that the man Hampton goes in for fakery.'

'But the music! It was a mazurka – an unknown mazurka! I *know* it has never been seen before!'

He didn't have the heart to say that Hampton had probably got a friendly musician to write a few bars that would pass as a mazurka. It wasn't a difficult style to copy – a very recognizable rhythm, a line of notes that sounded Chopinesque – he could do it himself, he thought.

Céleste Plagiet came on the line. 'Monsieur Couronne? Excuse me, please, but Madame was getting upset, and anyway her evening meal is ready.'

'I'm sorry. I didn't mean to upset her.'

'Of course, I know that. But she is grieving very much for Marzelina, and also we are in the midst of finding a replacement for the unkind Doranne. This is a difficult period for us.'

'I'm very glad you're taking so much care of her, Céleste.'

'Oh, how could one not! But please, monsieur, try to have good news for her; she needs something to lift the spirits.'

'I understand. Tell her that we are now following a trail that leads us south from Scotland. I hope we'll learn something useful in a day or two.'

'Thank you, I'll tell her.'

They said farewells. Liz had been listening to one side of this conversation in French and came to sit beside him on the bed. Although her knowledge of the language was mostly about the fashion business, she'd understood a word or two. '*Inquiéter* means to upset. Why was she upset, love?'

'Oh, it was over Jane Stirling. She's actually jealous of Jane Stirling.'

'What, a woman who's been dead for well over a hundred years?'

He made no reply to this.

She waited then asked, 'What is it?'

'Céleste told me that Madame is grieving very much over Marzelina.'

'Oh!'

He nodded. 'Yes, we've hardly given her a thought these last few days.'

She put an arm around him. After a moment he murmured something to himself.

'What was that?'

'Something Jean Renoir said: "A little flame that stays alive" – she ought to be there in our minds all the time.'

'Yes.'

'I have her photograph in my document case. Yet I haven't looked at it once since we left London.'

'But we know she's the reason we're doing this, Greg.'

'But . . . all this petty thievery . . . little shops selling knick-knacks – what's that got to do with Marzelina?'

She had no answer to that at first, but at length she said, 'We drank a toast to her when we started all this. I agree that our man seems to be nothing more than a petty criminal who made a big mistake . . . but that mistake cost Marzelina her life.'

'And we promised Madame Wiaroz that we'd find him. And that's where he is, isn't he? – among all that gift-shop junk.'

'And tomorrow we'll start finding out where he gets it, perhaps even who he is.'

They were quiet on the train journey, sitting very close, deep in thought. Towards the end they almost fell asleep, and had to rouse themselves for the taxi trip to Archway.

Most unusually, Mr Crowne was the first to be up and about next morning. His father was always up early in Bredoux, attending to the horses and pottering about in the little cubby-hole next to the stables. His grandmother never rose early and avoided the stables.

When Liz got up, she decided not to go for an early-morning run. Her back was still rather sore, and besides, she had unpacking to do. She paused to admire the items she'd bought on her shopping spree yesterday. Lovely things. All the same, she felt guilty about what she'd paid for the new handbag, and even more guilty about the perfume, a new one from Paco Rabanne.

When Greg put down the receiver, he was grinning to himself. 'Guess what?' he said. 'My father's just about to travel to England.'

'Really?'

'Absolutely! I caught him just as he was leaving for the airport.'

'How come?'

'A former pupil has a daughter, now about the right age to start on the early stages of *manège* – that's if she shows any talent.'

'Wait a minute. *Ménage*?'

'No, *manège*: advanced horsemanship. So Papa's coming to see her do something or other at the South of England Spring Show.'

'Which is held where?'

'No idea. But Papa will be in London after he's looked at this child and says he'd like to meet.'

'Meet you.'

'Meet *us*.'

It made her draw in her breath. Then she said rather carefully, 'Does your grandmother agree to this?'

'Er . . . He hasn't told her.'

'Ah.'

'Look, *cara mia*, my poor father has lived with her since he was born. I know that in the old days, before they had to hurry out of Hirtenstein, he was able to keep his distance because they lived in different parts of the palace – oh, yes, there's a palace,' he added, as she smiled. 'Europe's full of palaces, most of them turned into civic offices or museums. The one we used to have is the Hirtenstein Principal Bank.'

'But now your papa has to share a chalet-farmhouse with her?'

'Yes, has been doing so for nearly thirty years, and he's learned survival skills. One of them is not to tell her what she doesn't need to know.'

'So . . . what actually is . . . you know . . .why does he want this meeting?'

He considered for a moment. 'I can only guess. It's to see you. To see if you're anything like the wicked type that Grossmutti is so afraid of.'

'She's not afraid of me!'

'She certainly is. She's scared you'll marry me and use my name on a line of fashion accessories.'

She gave a peal of laughter. 'A great name for a selling product! "Fashions by Gregorius von Hirtenstein".'

He joined in her laughter but ended by saying, 'But she really thinks you have something like that in mind.'

'And your father wants to know if it's true?'

'Well . . . I'm sure he doesn't really believe any of that. He just . . . I don't know . . . Maybe it's simple curiosity.' Then he added hastily, 'I'm sorry. That sounds as if you're a scientific specimen or something.'

'It's OK. If I were old enough to have a grown-up son, I'd

want to know who he was running around with.' She was
thinking that perhaps it was a hopeful sign. Perhaps Greg's
father had some fellow feeling for them. She said musingly,
'Your father's never thought of marrying again?'

'No-o . . . But from time to time there have been signs of –
what shall I say? – romantic entanglements.'

'Lovely ladies with thrones and palaces in their background?'

'I think they're more likely to come from his horse-riding
circles. I never met any of them.' He added with a slight pursing
of the lips, 'And neither did Grossmutti, though I'm sure she
knew about them.'

'She would have disapproved?'

'Papa preferred never to put it to the test, if you see what I
mean.'

'Greg, your family is really strange.'

'Yes, but it's small – not likely to cause much harm.'

Once again she found it comic. When she'd recovered she
said, 'I'd better get breakfast going. Glaston will be here soon.'

The air was still redolent of toast and coffee when the
Inspector rang the bell. He looked rather worn and gladly
accepted the offer of a cup of what was left in the cafetière.

'I had a bit of a confab with our Edinburgh friend Sergeant
Tulloch first thing,' he remarked. 'He told me about the address
in Kentonlea Business Park, so I contacted Kent Constabulary
and they had a car do an early-morning recce—'

'Oh, no!' Liz wailed. 'No police! He'll shut up shop and
scarper, like Walter Fairbairn!'

'No, no,' he reassured her. 'It's not unusual to have a police
car take a look – they've had problems with kids setting fires
in the area, so they drive around from time to time, just to look
for evidence.'

They gave him a résumé of their activities. He was greatly
concerned when he heard about the shotgun episode.

'We can't have that! I'll get the Kent lads to handle—'

'No, please, Inspector, listen to what Liz was saying. There's
some sort of little fraud going on, and because of that the young
woman in the Livingston shop got very scared when Tulloch
produced his warrant card. This firm – Keepsake Curios – they're
probably involved in the fraud; but what we want is to make
contact with the man who killed Countess Zalfeda. Don't let's
have any police involvement for the moment.'

'We want to go to the firm while they're still unconcerned, you see.'

'But I can't let His High— I mean Mr Crowne – be in a spot where there might be violence.'

'There won't be any violence,' Liz declared. 'And Mr Crowne won't be there. I think it would be best if I went on my own.'

'No!' said both men with equal emphasis.

'Yes; don't be silly,' she insisted. 'If Greg's not going, it's got to be me.'

'But not on your own!'

'Of course not, sir. I'll send a man with her.'

'Good Lord, aren't you listening, Inspector? If there's a big official-looking guy looming over us, that's not going to encourage confidences, now is it?'

'Then the whole thing is off,' Greg announced.

'No it isn't.'

'Come on, Liz, you've been mugged and shot at already; I can't let you do this.'

She let a moment go by then said, 'And weren't we saying last night that we had to remember Marzelina in all this?'

'Liz!'

'Well, sir,' intervened Glaston, 'I'd get several degrees of scorching from my superiors if I let you go to this firm; and what Ms Blair says is true: a plain-clothes man from the locals would probably be a bit noticeable. However . . . they could supply a woman police officer, I'm sure.'

That was the agreement in the end. Glaston telephoned Kent CID and was promised a suitable plain-clothes officer. Liz telephoned Keepsake Curios to ask if she could visit the firm with a view to having some items made. An appointment was agreed for next morning. Glaston, satisfied, took his leave.

They both had business of their own to deal with – Liz was still supposed to be designing a spencer and wanted to spend some time on the internet. Greg contacted Amabelle for business news, then visited Smithfield about next year's festival programme.

They travelled by train to Dover in the evening, having reserved a room at the Greenthorpe, a hotel not far from the town hall and with a good reputation. Greg was still arguing against the plan for Liz to visit Keepsake Curios, but kept losing.

'How can I be in any danger?' Liz objected. 'I'll have a big burly policewoman with me.'

WPC Tyrrell proved to be slender and of only average height, and wearing a very feminine dark-red skirt and jacket; but as she walked from the reception desk to meet them in the hotel lounge, she had a noticeably springy, athletic stride. A fitness fanatic, perhaps.

'What's the plan?' she asked, taking a seat after introductions. 'We're going in to do what – buy something from them?'

'Well, we're "thinking about it",' said Liz. 'What we want is to get him talking about Hampton, so I'm going to chat about these attractive trinkets I've seen elsewhere.'

'Yes, but why do you want to buy them?' Ms Tyrrell insisted. 'We're talking bulk order, are we? What are we going to do with them?'

Liz was both pleased and rather offended at her manner. There was scepticism there. It proved her escort had her wits about her, but she didn't much like being treated like a complete amateur. 'You and I are going to set up a little business selling memorabilia—'

'About what?'

'Just wait a minute and I'll tell you. I did some work on the computer last night so I'm clued up about it. We're going in for stars of stage and screen of bygone days – people like Gracie Fields, Jessie Matthews, Leslie Howard, George Sanders.' She waited for the reaction.

'I . . . er . . . I think I've heard of Gracie Fields.'

'Well, take my word for it, they were big in British films pre-World War Two.'

'And people would want to buy that kind of thing?' That scepticism again.

'We give the impression that we think they would. We're ever so keen.'

'M-mm,' said the constable.

'We want miniatures put into frames; we want their photographs on pendants.'

'Sounds weird.'

Liz produced the bracelet bought in Music Hath Charms of Manchester. Ms Tyrrell took it, studied it and raised her eyebrows.

'Which of them is that? Leslie Howard?'

'That's Frederic Chopin.'

'Ah.' This time there was some irritation in the tone. Constable Tyrrell was aware she'd made a silly mistake.

His Highness had been sitting by, listening to all this and trying not to grin. He felt it was time to act as peacemaker. 'Liz thought you could be a couple of fellow enthusiasts for the forties and fifties – keen on black-and-white films and knowing that there are enthusiasts out there waiting to buy this stuff.'

'The fact that there's a fashion aspect to this makes it quite believable,' Liz said, taking the cue. After all, they were going to have to pull together to make this work, so she must get her acceptance of the plan. 'I work in fashion. Fifties revival has come and gone; forties is just waiting to emerge. I thought we might be . . . let's say, cousins, who've decided to put some money together and start a business.'

'Oh yes.'

'I'm your cousin Meg Peters. You're my cousin . . .?'

'Angela. Not Tyrrell, just in case he's got friends in the local force – I'll be Cousin Angela Waddon: that's my boyfriend's last name.'

'Right.'

'But I didn't do research on the internet; I don't know any of these so-called stars.'

'That's all right. I'll trot them out as necessary. All you have to do is enthuse.' She was about to add, 'You can enthuse?' but decided not to.

'We-ell,' said Angela unexpectedly, 'I do a bit of amateur dramatics in my spare time – musicals, Christmas shows, that sort of stuff. I can put on a bit of a gush if you want that.'

'Excellent!' Greg cried. 'That's just the kind of thing that will make it convincing.'

The constable turned her cool gaze upon him. It became clear that she knew of his ex-royal status, disapproved of him, and therefore of his lady-love. She said, 'Glad you're pleased.'

They went over it again, with additions. Angela Tyrrell glanced at her watch. 'Better get going, our appointment's for eleven, isn't it?'

They rose. Outside there was a not-very-new Ford, clearly the constable's own car. Before they got in Greg caught Liz by the arm and turned her to give her a kiss on the cheek. He murmured, 'Cold, but no fool.'

She nodded and got into the car. He was left to carry out his own plan for the morning: he was going to survey the shopping area to find out whether any of Keepsake Curios' articles were in stock in the gift shops. What level of commerce were they dealing with? Was the firm well known, well regarded locally, producing something that sold in quantity? A fairly useful thing to do, but really it was just to fill in the anxious couple of hours until Liz came back.

Liz was driven by her unenthusiastic partner in the direction of Canterbury; but they turned off by and by on to a grid of roads with largely prefabricated buildings on each side. Rather to their surprise, there was quite a lot of activity.

'I'm surprised so many are working Saturdays,' remarked Constable Tyrrell.

'Serving local interests, probably – catering, that kind of thing. As to Keepsake Curios, they're probably getting stocks ready for the tourist season, souvenirs and that kind of thing, perhaps.'

Keepsake Curios was housed in a structure of bright-blue plastic panels, but the interior was more subdued. There was an entrance lobby with a board registering the occupants. Keepsake Curios owned or rented the left side of the block, the offices on the first floor. Mr Jerrold, sales manager, was the third door from the staircase.

The reception area acted as a showroom, with glass cases housing items from the production lines. Little pictures of the White Cliffs featured in frames made of metal, pottery, plastic or seashells. There were also mugs and beakers with the White Cliffs, Dover Castle, sailing ships, modern cross-Channel ferries, and seabirds.

A young male receptionist looked up in greeting.

'Ms Peters and Ms Waddon. We have an appointment with Mr Jerrold.'

'Oh, yes, of course. He's expecting you.' He went to the inner door, tapped, put his head round to say, 'Ms Peters, sir, and a lady.'

Mr Jerrold came to shake hands and offer them chairs. Liz murmured, 'My cousin Angela Waddon.' He smiled, pausing before going behind his desk.

'Can I offer you anything? – tea? coffee?'

'I'd love a cup of coffee,' said Angela Tyrrell, simpering.

Jerrold went to the door and opened it. 'Coffee, Sam.' He then went to his rather worn office chair and sat down heavily.

'Now, as I understood you, Ms Peters, you're starting up in the keepsake business?'

'Yes, my cousin and I – we think we've identified a niche market so we're going to have a go.'

'And how did you come to hear of us, if I may ask?'

This was the delicate moment. He had to be told she'd seen some of the Chopin Collection, and if he was involved in the little scam, he might get cagey.

'Well, a friend of mine was wearing this really nice locket – sort of ivory,' Liz explained, 'and I asked her where she got it and she said near where she's studying – in Manchester, a college there, you know – and she happened to have the box and there it was, your list folded inside still, with your name and address and everything.'

'Ever so handy,' Angela put in, gushing. ''Cos I live quite near here – Dover, you know, near Connaught Park.'

'I know it,' said Jerrold.

'So I invited Meg to stay with me a couple of days so we could come and see you in person. That's always best, don't you think? – the *personal* touch?'

He smiled at her. To Liz, the simper in Angela's voice was overdone, but Jerrold seemed to be falling for it.

'I'm with you. And glad to hear our price lists are proving useful,' he said. 'I wondered if you'd learned of us through our ad in Keen Collecting.' He sighed a little. 'Never know where to spend your money when it comes to publicity.'

Sam entered with coffee in mugs from the firm's production line. They contained black coffee, and were accompanied by little packets of sugar and containers of cream. Liz feared the coffee would be freeze-dried and was proved correct. It was clear to her that Keepsake Curios was not doing very well.

The office had windows along one side. On a long, narrow, felt-covered table in front of it were samples of the product. Mr Jerrold rose to select a few and hand them to his guests. 'Is this the kind of thing your friend was wearing?'

It was a replica of the pendant with the Chopin silhouette, but showing a small painting of a kitten.

'Oh, that's pretty!' cried Angela. 'Oh, Meg, that would look just lovely with Gracie Fields on it!'

'Is that going to be your speciality?' he asked. 'Actual living people?'

'Gracie, yes, but she's been dead a while, Mr Jerrold,' Liz explained. 'Do you know of her? A wonderful voice, and big in comedy films. And there are others of those days who were just as big – James Mason, Basil Rathbone, Diana Wynyard – old favourites like that.'

'Mm-m,' said the sales manager, who had clearly never heard of this collection. 'Got the reproduction rights for all that?'

'Our solicitor is looking into that right now.'

'Colour, or black and white?'

'Oh, black and white – their films were all black and white, I believe.'

'Such a shame,' cried Angela. 'If only we could make them as attractive as your dear little kitten, Mr Jerrold!'

'But we can do a nice job of black-and-white print on the ivory casing,' he put in quickly.

'What really appealed to me,' Liz said, 'was the cameo on the pendant Nancy was wearing.'

'Oh yes, cameo – that's always a good seller: a Georgian miniature type of thing.'

'This was a composer – Chopin – in silhouette.'

'Oh, Show-pang – yes.' He was nodding with some satisfaction. 'We do that as a special line too.'

'Ever so *attractive*,' twittered Angela. 'And what a lovely idea, too. Romantic, I always think when I hear Chopin.'

'So they tell me. I'm not into music, myself.'

'So you do special lines, then,' said Liz. 'You'd be prepared to take on our Stars of Screen idea?'

'Certainly, certainly. We'd have to ask our artwork department, but I see no problem. We don't make the articles, you understand; we buy in the components and then insert or apply the artwork. So long as you can get the photographic material, we can do the work.'

'That's great. Don't you think so, Angela?'

'Absolutely. But we've got to think of the cost, Meg.' She set her coffee mug down on Mr Jerrold's desk and looked solemn.

Liz sipped coffee and was equally grave. 'Yes, you know, we're just starting up. May I ask what sort of prices you're offering to the customer who's specializing in Chopin?'

Smiling, he shook his head. 'I could give you an estimate. Wouldn't be fair to bring him into it.'

'But there's a lot of similarity, don't you think?' Liz urged. 'We've had this special idea, and he did too – very artistic, his product. He's an artist?'

'What, Firstead? No, he's more on the musical side, I think.'

'Oh, of course, Chopin!' cried Angela, clasping her hands in appreciation. 'He's a musician, I bet!'

'Well, he talked quite a lot about music when he came to discuss the project, I do remember. Had some idea of printing an actual bar or two of music on some of the items, but that didn't show up too well, so we didn't go on with that. That's a while ago, all that.'

'How long?' And then, thinking that too direct, Liz added, 'How long has he been making a go of it? Because it would be a help to know.'

'Let me see. About two years? Yes, that's about right. Let me just look.' He turned to his desk computer, tapped a few keys, and nodded with satisfaction. 'Right you are. In the autumn – a bit of a dead time for musicians in this area, I'd imagine.'

'This area?' cried Angela. 'He's from my part of the world too? Isn't that a coincidence, Meg! It's a *sign!*'

'A sign of success, you mean, my dear? It certainly seems so. It's done quite well for Firstead, and a good thing too – summer, you know, there's a lot going on: passengers for the ferries like a bit of something to go to if they stay overnight in Dover or Folkestone. But with winter coming on . . . musicians probably don't get many engagements.'

'Oh, I can imagine!' Angela went on, still beaming at Jerrold in sympathy. 'The Channel crossing in winter – dear me! – although with all the stabilizers and things, it's a lot better than it used to be.'

'Firstead did you say the name was? A local man, I gather from what you say – do you think he might talk to us about our idea? – give us a hint or two?'

Mr Jerrold laughed. 'You'll be lucky! Never get more than a word or two on the telephone from him, and not all that often, as a matter of fact.'

'Could you let us have his telephone number? Just a word or two on the phone would be such a help.'

'Sorry, no can do. *He* rings *me*; *I* don't ring *him.*' He seemed to listen to himself saying this and wonder if it sounded good business practice. 'He's on the move a lot, you see – takes his goods personally to his customers, so I only hear from him a couple of times a year – when he places his order, like before Christmas and before the tourist season in Edinburgh.'

'Edinburgh?' Angela was expressing surprise. 'Oh, he travels quite a bit!'

'I'd say so. For instance, he rang me about a month ago to put in his order and I think he was in London then. On the move – quite a live wire.'

'But in an emergency – surely you know how to contact him?'

Jerrold chuckled. 'Not likely to have any emergencies with a line like the Chopin Collection, am I? It's very specialized. Just a matter of knowing how many of which design, that's all.'

'But where on earth do you send the *bills*?' wondered Angela in a tone of bewilderment.

'Oh, various places – stops on his route, but they change a lot.'

'Ooh, I shouldn't like to trade like that,' said Liz, shaking her head. 'Don't you worry that he might not pay up?'

'Never failed yet. Cheque almost by return, if you want to know. But if you're worried about the money side, I can give you advice from my own experience. For instance, you shouldn't think of making much in the first year or so; be prepared to stick it out. And you'd have to keep good accounts, keep the paperwork under control.'

'Yes, we intend to. If Firstead can do it, so can we! I do seem to gather that he's from this area – perhaps he's in the phone book.'

'Might be.'

'I can just imagine him,' Angela said, with a sentimental sigh. 'A Chopin-lover, a nice romantic sort of man – tall and dark and with expressive brown eyes.'

'Oh, shut up,' thought Liz.

But Jerrold was delighted. 'Dear me, you ladies,' he cried.

'But he is like that, isn't he?'

'Can't remember, it's so long ago! Can't seem to think he was tall, but he might have been dark. Sorry, my dear.' He gave his desk a slight smack with his hand. 'But back to business. What about your Stars of Screen? Which components would you like to use?'

He began to quote prices for quantities. Angela Tyrrell retired from the conversation but listened with attention to Liz as she bargained and scribbled notes. About half an hour later they took their departure. Liz gave him a with-compliments slip she'd produced last night on her laptop with the logo 'Stars of Screen'

and promised to send him copies of the first four photographs
intended for the collection.

'You won't send him any photographs,' Angela remarked as
they drove away.

'Not unless we decide to go on with this, if it's useful – and
I can't see how it would be. No, I'm afraid Mr Jerrold isn't
likely to do any further business with us, poor old thing.'

Angela shrugged.

At the hotel she dropped Liz off. 'I've got to get back and
put in my report,' she said coolly. 'Hope something comes of
the morning's performance.'

'Me too. Thanks for your help.'

'No problem.'

Greg was hovering in the lobby, and through one of its
windows saw the constable drive off. 'I thought we might invite
her for lunch,' he said as he met Liz.

'She doesn't like us.'

'So she was no great help, then?'

'Quite the contrary: she proved quite the star of the morning.
Mr Jerrold of Keepsake Curios quite fell for her.'

'So you learned a lot?'

'Not much,' she sighed. 'Come on, I'm dying for a drink
and you can see what you make of it.'

Thirteen

The bar was quite busy. Clearly this was a popular venue
for the business crowd. They acquired drinks and took themselves off to a nook shielded by an oak partition.

'So . . . What did you think of Keepsake Curios?'

'Not doing too well,' Liz replied. 'I feel a bit of a rat. I more
or less promised poor Mr Jerrold an order, and I've no intention of a follow-up.'

'That happens,' Greg soothed. He himself had had to make
promises he knew he probably wouldn't keep. 'So let's put aside

your kindly feelings and have a review of his involvement in the Chopin Collection.'

'I think he isn't involved at all. He supplies the articles to a guy called Firstead, but the odd thing is, he's only ever seen the man once – and that was a couple of years ago.'

'Really? So how does . . .'

'How does he conduct business with him? Good question. See if this reminds you of anyone, my love. Firstead places his orders by telephone, and the calls might come from anywhere, according to Mr Jerrold. Firstead tells him to send the bill to an address which varies, according to where our friend may be at the time.'

'Accommodation addresses?'

'That's what it sounds like to me.'

'And does Mr Jerrold get paid?'

'By cheque, without fail. In other words, you'd think Firstead wants to keep Jerrold from making any sort of enquiry about him.'

Greg took a mouthful of *bière blonde*. 'The method sounds very like John Hampton making contact with poor Madame Wiaroz.'

'That's what I thought.'

They pondered over this. Then Liz went on: 'Constable Tyrrell was really very good. She managed to get our Mr Jerrold to talk about Firstead – the idea was to get a description, but all he could come up with was that he thought he was dark.'

'That's not very helpful.'

'*But* . . . she elicited the fact that he'd talked about music. We had quite a little discussion about how difficult it was to make a living as a musician, and it seemed that Jerrold viewed Mr Firstead as a local man.'

'Oh, *fantastique*! I suppose it's too much to hope that you got an address?'

She sighed. 'He doesn't have an address to give. He was shy about that, because of course it reflects on his business methods – but the poor guy can't be choosy about who he deals with. He needs the money.'

'You said Firstead communicates by telephone—'

'No, we didn't get his number, but what we've got to do is look him up in the phone book. If he's a local man there might just be an entry.'

'Let's do it.'

They finished their drinks, then went to the hotel reception desk to ask for the local phone book. They went quickly through to the pages where they hoped to find the shy Mr Firstead; but he wasn't there.

'Well, I didn't really expect anything,' Liz said. 'You can bet poor Mr Jerrold's already tried this and would have the number if it was there.'

They went into the restaurant. The lunch-time rush was coming to an end, so they were given a table almost at once. Since they were in Dover, they ordered Dover sole to follow the hors d'oeuvre.

'We have decided, have we, that Mr Firstead and Mr Hampton are one and the same?' Greg enquired.

'That seems very likely. Don't you think so?'

He sighed and nodded. 'The man at Keepsake Curios – Mr Jerrold – seemed convinced he's a musician?'

'Yes, lots of sympathy about how employment probably dies off once the tourist season is over, which explains how Firstead started up the Chopin trinket business. To earn a crust or two during the off season.'

'So he starts up a little business, and he chooses to base it on Chopin.'

'Yes.'

'Why Chopin? Is he, like Madame Wiaroz, a fanatic?'

'Hardly, Greg. He doesn't show much respect. But he knows quite a lot about him – probably listens to discs?'

'Plays the piano.'

'Yes, plays Chopin, of course – that seems to follow.'

'So according to this trail we're on, we're looking for a local-pianist-who-plays-Chopin.'

'And we know this man telephones his orders so . . . Don't you think . . . the police might get a look at Keepsake Curios' phone calls? From the phone company? They must list where the calls come from.'

'So we ought to ask Constable Tyrrell if they can do that.'

'I'll do it. She doesn't approve of you.' She pushed aside her avocado salad, got out her mobile and called the number given them in London by Chief Inspector Glaston. She asked to be put through to Constable Tyrrell. When she heard a curt 'Tyrrell', she began cheerily: 'Angela? Liz Blair here. We've just had a thought about Firstead –'

'Good for you.' This seemed to be said after swallowing a mouthful of food. Ms Tyrrell was having a sandwich lunch.

'Oh, I'm sorry, am I interrupting –'

'What *is* it, Ms Blair?'

'We thought perhaps it would be a good idea if you were to contact the phone company that Mr Jerrold uses, to see if you can get a list of who called him.'

'Fancy you thinking of that.'

'Well, you see, Mr Jerrold mentioned that Firstead generally put in his orders—'

'By phone before Christmas and in time for the tourist season. And so it might be possible to sift out which calls were made by Firstead. Well, oddly enough, I thought of that myself, Ms Blair, and the super has the matter in hand.'

Liz was taken aback by the open animosity in her tone. 'I'm sorry,' she murmured. 'I suppose it *is* pretty obvious.'

'And not easy to arrange, so you'd better forget it for the time being.'

'Oh.'

'Thank you for your input.'

'Er . . . How long might it be?'

'A day or two – this is the beginning of the weekend, after all. And now, if you don't mind, Ms Blair, I'd like to get on.'

'Yes, of course. Thank you.'

She disconnected. Greg had been listening to her side of the conversation. 'Unhelpful?' he queried.

'Crotchety is the word that springs to mind.'

'But they're already requesting the phone records.'

'Yes.'

Their second course was brought. They ate a couple of mouthfuls while thinking things over.

'The time has come', Liz said, nodding at him in encouragement, 'for you to send up smoke signals for help from the Musical Mafia.'

'I think you've got your metaphors mixed. The Mafia use the heads of dead horses.'

'Please, not while I'm eating sole *à la jardinière*! What should you use for musicians? A flourish of trumpets?'

He seemed to be concentrating on his food.

'You're not going to say you don't know any musicians in Dover?'

'We-ell . . . Not in Dover. I do know a man in Folkestone who conducts and trains the East Kent Choral Society.'

She stifled a grin. 'A former opera star?'

'No, an orchestral player.'

'What did he play?'

He coloured a little. 'I know you're going to laugh.'

'No, no.'

'He played the harp.'

She laughed.

Greg sighed. 'I don't know what it is about the harp that makes people laugh. It's a very important instrument.'

'But it's usually women in flowing dresses who play it.'

'Well, Rodrigue doesn't wear flowing dresses. And he's had quite a difficult life, so no funny jokes, please.'

'Dearest, I wouldn't dream of it. Especially if we're going to ask him to help. Are we?'

'Well, I'll see what I can do. But I'm going to finish my sole first.'

It deserved their attention. Later, over coffee, he made the call on his mobile. 'Rodrigue? *Ah, comment ça va? Ici Grego*' – and so on for some minutes of catch-up. In the end, after disconnecting, he reported: 'He'd be delighted to see us and have a little chat. Let's go out and get a taxi.'

The resort town was only a few miles along the coast. It was rather empty but had the dignity of its chalk hills and broad promenade to make it worthwhile even in a cool English spring. The building in which Rodrigue Selbige lived was part of a row of Edwardian dwellings that had escaped the bombings of World War Two.

He welcomed them into a high-ceilinged little hall, gesturing with his stick to a room on his right. Liz understood now why Greg had said he'd had a difficult life. He'd clearly been injured at some time, so that now he was very lame.

When Liz walked into the room, she saw the harp at once. And her designer's heart was immediately captured by its elegance, its glistening frame like a fairy-tale bridge to some land of sunshine.

Their host saw her reaction. '*Beauté san pareil, non?*'

'*Absolument,*' agreed Liz in her schoolgirl French.

Which caused M. Selbige to turn to English at once. 'Well, my dear boy, sit down; what can I do for you? I hope you aren't going to invite me to London to listen to one of your voice discoveries – I'm too old to gad about like that.'

'You'll never be old, Rodrigue. And no, it's about local talent that I need your help.'

'Indeed? I shan't let you borrow any of my singers – we're deep in rehearsal of a difficult piece by Debussy.'

'No, I'm trying to find a pianist.'

Rodrigue raised thick white eyebrows. 'Here? Don't you see thousands of pianists as you whizz through London or New York?'

'This is a local man. At least, I think so.'

'And he is called what?'

'Firstead. Do you know him?'

'Firstead?' The old man murmured the name over to himself. 'No, I think not, *mon ami*. But of course, my acquaintance is mostly with singers and with students of the harp. Why do you wish to find this man? He is a new young genius, perhaps?'

'Ah . . . No, nothing like that. In fact, Rodrigue, he may not be a very good pianist.'

That was a puzzle. 'Then why look for him?'

'Because he's done something rather . . . unkind – to an old lady who lives in Paris.'

The old gentleman lowered himself into a Queen Anne-style armchair. 'I am confused. This man you seek is local to Folkestone but now it's Paris?'

'It's to do with a fraud initiated on the internet.'

'*Ah, invention maudite!* So he, the man Firstead, worked this unkindness at long distance, and your premise is that he lives here?'

'Or hereabouts – there's a connection with a business firm near Dover.'

'I see. Well, Grego, I know several pianists; they come for little pay to play for my rehearsals. But to tell the truth, out of . . . let me see . . . seven, five are ladies.'

'And the two who are not ladies?'

'One is a pianist and organist who plays for our St Erman's Church, and so I think is not likely to carry out any frauds on old ladies. And the other is Robert Nicholson, who has never seemed likely to do such a thing in the twenty years I've known him.'

'Do you know of any others?' Liz put in. 'Do any of your choir members play?'

'Oh, of course, some do . . . He is an amateur, you think?'

'Well, we don't really know. We have reason to think he travels.'

'Travels – abroad? Or locally?'

'Why? Does someone come to mind?'

'Not immediately, but you know, my friend, during the summer season, there are what you call gigs, for bands to play in clubs and so on – or no, generally they have the electronic keyboard, don't they?' He mused for a moment. 'But those bands, they do travel. Some even come across on the ferry from France and Belgium just for the season.'

'Do you know much about them?'

'No, but I could ask some of my younger colleagues – if you think it would help.' He nodded to himself but then looked put out. 'But no – he does not come from abroad. You said this should be a local man.'

'Well, we think that's the more likely idea.'

'I will ask my young acquaintances to see if there are any pianists in the little semi-professional bands that play at weddings and so on,' he suggested, pursing his lips and looking thoughtful. Then he brightened. He had found this not very entertaining. 'Now, let me offer you some refreshment. A little *Abricotine* with a *macaron*, no?'

They sat with him for some time, nibbling the little brown biscuits and sipping the strange sweet liqueur. He summoned up several names from his memory, thought about them, then shook his head. This one had moved to Spain; another had taken up competition bridge.

Greg prompted, 'This Firstead might have come into quite a lot of money recently.'

'Ah, the profit from his wickedness, you mean?' But he could make no useful suggestion. 'I will think about it, nevertheless,' he assured them as they took their leave. 'You said the Hotel Greenthorpe, no?'

By now darkness was coming on. They went for a walk, Liz particularly feeling the need for exercise after a day spent mostly indoors or in some kind of vehicle. The lights along the seafront gleamed in the deepening twilight. It would have been very romantic except for the biting wind coming off the English Channel.

Greg felt Liz snuggle against him for warmth. He put an arm around her.

'Do you think your lovely harpist friend will get us anything useful?' she asked, looking up at him.

He felt the chances were very small. 'He's in a little side street as far as the musical highway is concerned. I'm not belittling the importance of regional musical societies, though. It's just possible that Hampton–Firstead is some frustrated virtuoso—'

'Yes, who's grown tired of not being appreciated—'

'And who's decided to wreak vengeance on people like Madame Wiaroz because she loves Chopin and the great interpreters of his music.'

'But that would mean he's a bit crazy, Greg. And this man seems very astute.'

'Well, he's good at covering his tracks. He seems to want to hide himself – uses false names – it seems likely that Firstead is just another alias. Perhaps he's a split personality. '

'You're doing the psychological profiling bit, aren't you? We just don't know enough about him for that to work.'

'Well, we know he likes to stay in the background. He used a long-distance approach to Madame Wiaroz.'

'But he was face to face with Marzelina.'

'We don't know that.'

'What – he was wearing a mask? Kind of noticeable as he goes into the museum entrance hall.'

'No, I mean . . . He was Charles Hampton, but perhaps Charles Hampton looks quite different from Mr Firstead.'

'False beards? Groucho nose and glasses?'

'I beg your pardon? Groucho?'

'One of the Marx brothers – I was only asking if you thought he'd used an actual disguise.'

'Oh, I see . . .'

'And in any case, he was out there in public when he snatched my handbag in Edinburgh.'

'Was he?' Greg asked, trying to picture the scene again. 'He attacked you *from behind*.'

'Ye-es. So he did. And then he shot at us while he sheltered behind the open door of his van—'

'And went racing past us before we could get a look at him.'

It occurred to Greg as he said this that Hampton–Firstead knew what they looked like; but they had no image of him – none at all.

He decided not to say that out loud. It wasn't a comforting thought.

The theorizing went on for the length of a walk along the Leas and back. 'Let's get a cup of coffee,' Liz said. 'I need something to warm me up. And to get the taste of those sticky macaroons out of my mouth!'

They went into a Starbucks. As they sat down with their drinks, Greg's mobile chirped. He got it out, flipped it open, then gave a big grin at Liz. 'Papa,' he mouthed at her.

'Good evening, my boy,' his father said. 'Are you doing something very enjoyable, eh?'

'I'm in a coffee bar in Folkestone, Papa.'

'Folkestone! Good heavens, I thought you were in London?'

'We had some business that brought us here.'

'Ah! And where will you be tomorrow at lunch-time?'

'In Dover.'

'What is this strange preoccupation with the coast of La Manche?'

'Oh, just some things we're looking into. Why were you asking about lunch-time?'

'I was proposing to come to see you. But Dover . . . One moment, Grego.' There was a conversation, aside. His father was addressing someone he called Jasmine.

Greg heard a ringing feminine voice say, 'Not at all, Anton. No, no problem.' Jasmine? Perhaps the mother of the young rider who might be going on to study advanced equestrianism.

His father came back on line. 'My kind hostess was going to drive me to London to see you. But now we learn you will be in Dover, so she says even more kindly that she will drive me there.'

'Well, that's great! Liz and I look forward to it. And, Papa – shall we meet Jasmine also?'

'Ah . . . No, my boy, she prefers not.'

'Very well, we expect you around lunch-time at the Greenthorpe Hotel. In central Dover.'

'Splendid.'

Liz had gleaned enough to know they had a lunch date next day with the ex-King of Hirtenstein. She was staring at Greg in consternation.

'What's the matter?'

'Tomorrow! I need to get my hair done!'

This was a non sequitur that caused him a moment's confusion. Then he remembered that she liked to look her best always. He said: 'Your hair is beautiful.'

'What, after a day by the sea coast? It looks like dried prairie grass. And I haven't got a dress, only jeans.'

'You look beautiful in jeans.'

'Tomorrow the shops won't open until eleven. I can't buy anything suitable in the time between eleven and lunch-time!'

'You look beautiful in whatever you're wearing.'

'Stop saying I'm beautiful! Oh, dear heaven, why didn't I pack a dress?'

'Liz,' he said in a serious tone, 'calm down. Papa is a nice simple fellow whose dearest love is horses.'

She suddenly began to laugh. 'So if I look like a horse, I'll be OK?'

'Not with me. You're faced with a difficult choice. Whom would you rather please – me or my papa?'

'Oh, the "whom" I'd rather please is you, you grammarian. But I really must do something with my hair.'

'Brush it a hundred strokes.'

'Shampoo – so let's get back to the hotel and I'll do that.'

They took the bus back to Dover. It set them down not far from the hotel. Once there, Liz dashed to the bathroom to set about the beautifying process. Greg ordered sandwiches and more coffee from room service. They ate with her hair done up in a towel, after which she set to work with dryer and brush.

The result was very pleasing. She sat looking at the view afforded by the dressing-table mirror. 'What d'you think?'

'I won't say it's beautiful because it gets me a scolding. I think we should go down and have a drink in the bar to celebrate.'

'By all means.'

There was a choice of venues. The bar to the left of the lobby was crowded, because it was Saturday night. The other possibility was downstairs, calling itself the Cellar Club. Since they were hotel residents, they had honorary membership. They decided to try the Cellar Club.

Since it was Saturday night, the management were offering 'AN EVENING WITH OLD FRIENDS!' A small jazz combo was playing when they went in. His Highness had learned a little about jazz the previous year, so he was quite pleased to sit listening with half an ear while they drank Manhattans.

'Er . . . How does one address your father?' Liz asked.

'How . . .?' This was a problem. Greg's male friends and companions from his schooldays called his father 'sir'. His father's friends called him Anton. Others in Geneva who knew him less well called him M. von Hirtenstein.

None of these seemed appropriate. 'I don't know,' he confessed.

'Well, think about it. Otherwise I'm not going to take any part in the conversation.'

The jazz group finished their stint to a ripple of applause. A compère came on to announce the next item on the entertainment programme. The name was greeted with enthusiasm. On came a comedian, who addressed the microphone in intimate tones. 'Have you heard the latest from the council on parking meters?' he began. The audience made sounds of appreciation. It appeared his speciality was inventing local gossip.

'Is there anything we have to avoid talking about tomorrow, Greg?'

He leaned forward to hear her through the laughter from the audience. 'Avoid? No, why should there be?' He thought about it. 'He's not keen on politics.'

'Neither am I, so that's OK. I can't talk about horses, Greg, I don't know anything about them.'

He took her hand. '*Queridita*, he's not coming to see us to talk about horses.'

'But what, then?'

'I've no idea.' He thought it over. 'My father's a kind man,' he said, smiling to himself. 'I imagine he may be going to apologize for Grossmutti.'

'Oh.'

'So you just have to smile nicely and say, "That's OK."'

She made pretence of resisting the idea. 'I can't say she's an unkind old despot?'

'Preferably not. After all, that's his mama you'd be talking about.'

'Dear me, so it would. All right, I promise to be good.'

He laughed, told her she was always good, and they found their way to other, more engaging topics. After a while they became aware that the comedian had been replaced by a musical act. A singer in a long Edwardian dress was entering on the introductory bars of the 'Jewel Song' from Faust.

Liz covered her ears in protest. 'Is this what passes for entertainment in the Cellar Club of a Saturday night?'

But she needn't have bothered. The whole point was that the singer kept making a mess of it. The audience was laughing. Liz returned to her problems of next day. 'What about this lady that's giving him a lift into Dover? Shall we be talking about her, or her little girl, or anything like that?'

'Well, I'll be asking Papa what she looks like – the little girl, I mean. She might become a pupil.'

'When you lived there, did you do any teaching?'

'Me? No, no; stable boy and helping to exercise the horses – that was my role. You've never seen Bredoux, of course. It's not big. We only had room for two of our own, and the other boxes were for the pupils' horses.'

'And since you've left, who does all the donkey work?'

'Oh, a devoted teenager from the village.' He chuckled. 'There are always devoted little girls where there are horses. I think there's quite a lot of psychological theory about that.'

The singer gave a sudden soprano shriek. '*Ah, je ris de me voir en ce miroir –*' Even to the untrained ear of Liz, she was singing flat. She broke off, berated her accompanist. The audience were laughing and cheering.

'Noisy in here,' Liz said plaintively.

'Not a bad voice, if it was used properly.'

'Surely we could find something more entertaining to do, lover?'

'Ah! But what about the bruises?'

She leaned forward to speak in a husky, seductive whisper. 'We'll manage,' she said.

They made their way between the tables and out to the foyer. In the lift they kissed and stayed close to each other.

As he put the key card into the door she said, 'I won't have to curtsey at our lunch date, will I?'

He laughed and swept her up to carry her in.

They slept late next morning. They had a continental breakfast sent up, but Liz was in too much of a fuss over choosing clothes to think of eating.

'How about this?' she asked, holding an olive-green shirt against her bosom.

'Too like army fatigues.'

'Well, this?' A black sweater.

'Too funereal.'

'Well, that's it, sugar. No, wait: how about the sweater with this?' A cyclamen-coloured scarf.

'Perfect.'

She was doubtful, but the limits of her travelling wardrobe forced her to agree. She sat at the dressing table taking immense care with her make-up. 'What time should we expect him?' she asked in a voice that was slightly shaky.

'Early. Riding people get up early at home to look after the horses, so they generally eat breakfast about six, and feel hungry again about midday.'

'Oh Lord!' A glance at her watch showed only twenty minutes to go until noon. 'Come on, let's get downstairs.'

They settled themselves in the hotel lobby, near a window so they could watch for His Majesty. The weather wasn't at its best, a sea mist dulling the sky, so that passers-by had their coats buttoned up. Hotel guests came out of the lift clearly looking forward to a lazy Sunday indoors, drifting to the newspaper kiosk to buy magazines or a paperback.

A new-looking grey Freelander pulled up at the kerb outside. A man in his fifties and wearing a beige body-warmer got out, kissed the driver on her cheek and waved as she drove off. Then he turned to the hotel entrance.

His Majesty ex-King Anton of Hirtenstein proved to be a head shorter than his son. He was slight in build but wiry, his skin weathered, his brown hair beginning to go grey. He cried a greeting, hugged his son, slapped him on the shoulder, then turned at once to Liz.

'Ms Blair. I'm so glad to meet you. I have looked forward to this.'

He offered his hand and Liz took it. He clasped it warmly.

'Thank you . . . I'm . . . glad to meet you too . . . monsieur.' Monsieur – that's what she should call him.

There was nothing the least bit intimidating about him. He didn't even look regal. He was wearing a thick navy sweater under his sleeveless down jacket, and brown trousers. He could have been any man home from a morning ride.

But all the same, he was Greg's father. She was 'meeting his parents'. The thought held her tongue-tied.

Anton turned to his son. 'Here you see a man who has forked hay, exercised a skittish mare, schooled a young Percheron, and been driven some seventy miles to see you. Shouldn't you offer this man a drink?'

'This way,' said Greg, and led them into the bar. It was fairly busy, but Sunday trade grew brisk at a later hour than a weekday, so they found a table.

'What would you like to drink, Papa?'

'Aha! That dark English beer with the foam on top?'

'I believe it's Irish, but I know what you mean. Liz?'

'Emm-m – mineral water with ice and lemon, please.' Keep a clear head, she was thinking. She cast a glance of appeal at him: Don't leave me!

But he walked off.

His father studied her. 'You must forgive me if I seem to stare at you. I've often tried to imagine what you look like.'

'Oh! I . . . er . . . Well, what do you think?'

'He is a lucky man,' Anton said. Then, with a serious little frown, 'But he has been so unhappy this past year, my dear. And of course it was no secret in our household that madame my mother was to blame for the break-up. I am so sorry, Liz. You must forget everything she said to you.'

'Yes.'

'Grego had hardly ever been able to speak of you because of the air of disapproval; and it would have been improper for us to whisper together behind her back. But this past year, since he moved out to his own place, we have met now and again in Geneva, and I have heard a few things from him. I know that you have been close to him through many difficult times. And I thank you. I thank you from my heart.'

'Yes. I understand. Thank you.'

'Tell me something about yourself. You are a fashion expert, yes?'

'Well, sort of.' She knew better than to go into a long discourse – men as a rule weren't interested in colour trends and fabric weights; but she mentioned a few of the things that brought her her daily bread, and Anton was smiling and nodding when his son returned with a tray of drinks.

'Here you are, Papa. Let me see what you make of it.'

Anton accepted the glass and put his nose close to sniff at the surface of the brew. His son guessed that never in his life had Anton of Hirtenstein drunk this rich bitter stout. He was watching with amusement.

To tell the truth, Anton made little headway. He was only on his third mouthful when a clerk from the reception desk came to speak in a low voice to Greg.

'Excuse me, Mr Crowne, an officer from Dover CID is in the lobby and would like a word.'

Greg flashed a glance at Liz. She made as if to get up, but then sat down again. They couldn't both hurry out and leave Anton on his own. Greg nodded, rose, and followed the clerk.

Constable Tyrrell was standing in the lobby with a tall, alert-looking man, both studying the clientele in a seemingly casual way.

'Mr Crowne? I'm Chief Inspector Valmouth. I thought I ought to come and give you a bit of a warning. Can we talk?'

'Of course.'

'Over here, please.' An alcove with no one else nearby. 'We were lucky, sir, with our inquiries about telephone records – started yesterday and got immediate co-operation from the duty supervisor. We've been checking through the list since yesterday evening and then again early this morning – using a reverse directory, you know; and we've come across something rather worrying.'

'In what way?'

'We've been able to distinguish calls to Keepsake Curios from known addresses, businesses that we could verify as genuine from other sources. However, seven calls over the past eleven months have either been from mobiles we've verified as no longer in use, or from public callboxes. And one of the public callboxes is that one there.'

He nodded to the telephone on the wall facing him. It had a plastic hood over it, but was by itself – an arrangement by a thoughtful management for anyone who wanted to have a very private conversation.

Greg knew what was coming next. He would be asked to move. Low though he came on the pecking order of VIPs, officialdom wanted no trouble over him. He said, 'We were just going to have lunch.'

'That's you and Ms Blair?'

'And my father.'

Chief Inspector Valmouth's thick eyebrows went up in astonishment. 'Your father? Here?'

'Yes.'

'Well, sir . . . In *that* case . . . We'd like you all to leave this hotel.'

'But the man's not here now,' Greg objected. 'Hampton–Firstead or whoever he is. How often has he used this phone?'

'Twice. But for all we know he might use this place as his local.'

Greg had to think what the word 'local' meant in this context. He had to admit it was possible. 'Have you questioned the staff?'

'We did what we could, sir, but we haven't really got much of a description, now have we?'

'You mean he could be the man behind the bar, or the hall porter . . . Yes, I see that.' He had to admit that, in Valmouth's place, he'd be making the same request. 'All right, Chief Inspector. I'll tell them we have to pull out. But let's not scurry like rats, eh? Can I ask for your help?'

'Certainly, sir; that's why we're here.'

'Ask the desk to book us a table for lunch at some decent restaurant. I'll go and explain – my father will understand, of course. Then we'll move out and have our meal. There remains the problem of our belongings – Ms Blair's and mine.'

'I'll arrange for a chambermaid to pack them up for you, sir, and we'll deliver them to you. We'll book you in at another hotel, OK?'

He sighed inwardly. It probably meant that there would be a plain-clothes man looking in on them from time to time, wherever they were housed. Was the purveyor of knick-knacks worth all this trouble?

Well, yes, he was, because if they were right in their reasoning, the purveyor of knick-knacks had killed Marzelina.

Fourteen

A taxi was waiting to carry them off to their new lunch venue.
They found themselves entering a cheerful Italian restaurant, filling up with family parties, since it was now getting on towards one o'clock.

They ordered Parma ham as antipasto with a simple salad for the vegetarian, and *pansoti al preboggion* to follow. Anton, asked if he would like a drink while they waited, ignored the suggestion of his son that he should try the dark beer again. 'I see they have Falconera,' he murmured, consulting the wine list. 'Much more suitable.'

'Doesn't it annoy you, monsieur, having to dash out of one place and into another, just because the police say so?' Liz enquired.

'Oh, it happens. Some people like to shout at us, or spit at us, or throw things at us. It's best just to avoid them if we can.'

'Papa,' said his son, 'you ought to telephone the Greenthorpe so they can let your *chauffeuse* know where to find you.'

'Ah, no need: she lent me this.' He produced a mobile from a pocket. 'I give a little call when I'm ready to leave and tell her where I am.'

'And she drives seventy miles again to pick you up?' Liz asked, looking dubious.

'No, no, she's here, in Dover.'

'She hangs around waiting for your phone call? Papa, that's devotion!'

Ex-King Anton held out his hand and twiddled his fingers. '*Soin des ongles*. She is amusing herself well, or so she told me.'

'And you'll go straight back to Sussex?'

'Oh no, we're going on to London. Jasmine has a little pied-à-terre there. I leave for Geneva in the morning.'

Greg nodded in complete acceptance, and Liz hid a smile.

They had a long, easygoing time together. As they were attacking layered almond cake for dessert, Valmouth telephoned Greg to let him know they were now booked in at the Collinet Hotel and that their clothes had been delivered there.

Soon after, Anton called up his transport. He hugged his son fiercely then turned to Liz. 'Not goodbye – *au revoir*, Liz.' He took her hand and kissed it.

'*Au revoir*,' she replied, wondering if in fact she was likely to see him again.

They went with him out to the forecourt. Jasmine put out a hand for him to see the result of her manicure – rosy-pink paint on her nails looking quite at variance with the rough green tweed of her coat. He went around to the passenger door, gave them a little salute over the roof of the vehicle, got in and was whirled away.

Greg and Liz went back into the restaurant for a second cup of coffee. 'Will he talk about this to your grandmother?'

'Maybe. When the moment seems good.'

They asked for directions to the Collinet, then set out on foot, in need of exercise after the pasta with its rich walnut sauce and the wine. When they presented themselves at the desk, there was a flurry of welcome. The hall porter produced their luggage, which was taken up while they were registering.

The place was smaller than the Greenthorpe and was inclined to be 'cosy'; but it was pleasant enough, so they settled in.

Liz, unpacking her travel-bag, came across the plastic carrier in which she'd wrapped all her purchases from the curio shops in Manchester and Edinburgh. Among them was the paperback about the romance of Chopin and Jane Stirling.

She'd paid very little attention to it. It was a pack of lies – that she knew; but now she sat down to examine it.

It was thin – only ninety pages. The title page announced it as *Jane and Frederic: A Love Story*. Below that came the author's name. By Adam Lishinski.

'Who's Adam Lishinski, I wonder?' she said.

'What?'

'Adam Lishinski. He wrote the love story.' She held up the paperback.

Greg was staring at her.

'Another pseudonym for Hampton–Firstead, I suppose?'

'No,' he said. 'Adam Lishinski is a real person.'

'Yes, of course he's *real* – it's another version of our dear friend HF, don't you think?'

'Yes, but . . . wait.' He leaned across the bed to take the book from her. He opened it, standing in thought with the title page open. Then he put it down and zipped open the document case in which he was carrying books and papers. From it he took a hardback volume, much thicker than *Jane and Frederic.* He turned to the index at the back, then flipped pages.

'Ah!'

'Ah, what?'

'Adam Lishinski is the anglicized version of a real name, and it belonged to the doctor in Edinburgh.'

'What doctor – oh, the one Chopin stayed with?'

'Yes, and so . . . and so it seems to mean Hampton–Firstead has read a biography or a collection of Chopin's letters.'

He sat down on the opposite side of the bed. They were silent for a moment.

Liz said, 'But we knew he must have done research.'

'Yes, but if he wrote this himself, doesn't that mean that we could trace him through the publisher?'

'The publisher's name ought to be on the reverse of that page,' she suggested, and scrambled over the bed to sit alongside him.

He turned the page over: 'Published by Fantasie Publications, Hythe, Kent. Printed by Keyprint, Sandgate, Kent.'

Liz threw herself at the bedside table to pick up the phone and call Enquiries. 'Hythe, Kent. Fantasie Publications – that's spelt with an "ie" on the end.' She listened. She shook her head. 'Then will you give me the number for Keyprint – that's in Sandgate, Kent.' A longer wait. 'No? No, I've got no postcode.'

She looked across at Greg. 'No luck.'

'Try another service.'

She obeyed, but the result was the same. Nothing. No telephone number for the firm that she was enquiring after.

Greg was examining the paperback. 'There's no price printed on the cover,' he reported.

'Turn it over; it should be on the back.'

But there was no price, nor were there any of the other symbols. No logo, no bar code, no figures giving the registration of the title for trade records.

'Well . . .'

'This is the work of an amateur,' Greg sighed.

'Desk-top publishing, perhaps.'

'That's on a computer, yes?'

She gave a little gesture of exasperation. 'So much for getting his real name from the publisher.'

'It's just like a *Gemeindezeitschrift.*' When she frowned in enquiry he said, 'Parish . . . community . . . periodical?'

'Oh, a parish magazine? It's a bit above that level – the cover's quite well done, don't you think? But you can buy software for all that, I think.'

'And it seems to tell us nothing except that he consulted books to get the information.'

'No . . . It *suggests* something more. It bears out what my friend Mr Jerrold at Keepsake Curios said. He lives in the area.'

'What makes you say so?'

'All these place names? They're spread out along the coast nearby – Sandgate's more or less part of Folkestone; Hythe is about five miles further on. And he chose a firm near Dover to make his trinkets.'

'So the Greenthorpe Hotel might really be his "local", as Chief Inspector Valmouth said to me.'

She said, 'Oh my!' at that. Then, after a pause, 'If we ever get really close to him, so that the police can get a warrant or something . . . we might be able to find evidence of what he's been up to in his computer.'

'That's possible. He made his first contact with Madame Wiaroz by computer.'

'But you can do that in a computer café.'

'Yes, but the book? You could hardly produce that by hiring time in a computer café.' He turned over the pages and exclaimed in surprise. 'Look! He's reproduced the opening bars of the Mazurka in G major.'

'You sound as if you've seen an old friend,' she said, smiling.

'I had to learn it in my schooldays for one of my music exams.' Then he turned the book so that she could see. 'Liz . . . could that be how he produced the piece of music he sent to Madame Wiaroz?'

'You mean on his computer? – with faded ink and all that? I don't know,' she confessed. 'But if we ever find out where he lives, and his computer's still there . . .'

'We ought to give this – and the other things we bought – to the police.'

'Ye-es . . . But which police? The Dover force? Or Scotland Yard?'

They remained undecided for some minutes. Then Liz said, 'The local boys would be glad to get rid of us, I imagine. They're afraid we're going to get damaged and cause them trouble. What do you say we tell them we're going back to London, and we take all this stuff with us and give it to Mr Glaston?'

'I suppose so.' Yet he sounded unconvinced. 'But, Liz – I don't want us to go back to London.'

'But the cops are scared that Mr HF is practically breathing down our necks –

'He's not a problem if you think about it. He doesn't know we're here – how could he? And *we* don't know *he's* here, now do we? He may live locally, but we were told by the shop-keepers in Manchester and Edinburgh that he'd been there, deliv-ering goods. That was only a couple of days ago.'

'We-ell . . .'

'So although you're saying he lives around here, he might still be in Scotland – or anywhere, if comes to that.'

She frowned at him. 'You just don't want to go.'

He had the grace to look embarrassed. 'No matter what my father said about just obeying police orders, I don't like being chased out.' He shrugged and waited for her protest.

But she thought about it for a long moment. 'All right,' she said at last. 'We'll stay. So we're going to give the book and so on to Chief Inspector Valmouth.'

'That doesn't follow. We could send it to London. If there are fingerprints on any of the items, they have better facilities for processing them, I would think.'

'But Greg . . . It seems rather bad manners, leaving the local people out of the loop – don't you think?'

He was uncertain. He genuinely didn't know what was best to do. 'Let's leave it for now,' he said, putting the book back into the plastic carrier bag.

She took it from him, put it into her travel bag, put that in the wardrobe and closed the door on it. There – that was disposed of for the time being. But she wasn't sure it was the best solu-tion.

Once they finished unpacking, Greg telephoned Rodrigue Selbige. He expected little help from him and was proved correct. 'I asked some of my choir,' he said in a chatty tone, 'after church

this morning, you know. There are about four who play the
piano and . . . well . . . I know them, Greg; they are not criminal
types.' He was a little indignant at the idea.

'Do you know any people who are keen on music – I mean,
as part of the audience? Any constant concert-goers?'

'Oh, of course. My choir depends on them. Be sensible, my
boy; you can't really suspect innocent music-lovers, surely?'

But the man they were after was some kind of music-lover,
he said to himself as he thanked the old man and disconnected.

On the dressing table Greg found the folder with leaflets that
gave information about local entertainment in Dover. The offerings were few. As people here kept telling him, nothing much
was happening in 'the off-season'.

Now it was evening-time. They had eaten too well at lunch
to feel the need for dinner. On the contrary, they needed fresh
air and exercise. They set out to make themselves better
acquainted with the town, heading, of course, at the instigation
of Liz for the High Street and its big shopping centre.

The place had been busy earlier, but now the shoppers had
all gone home. Greg was patient as Liz examined window
displays, but his mind was elsewhere. Sensing boredom, she let
him lead her south through the market square so that by and by
they could hear activity at the docks, the ferries sending out
warning whoops as they set sail for Calais, the occasional growl
of some big cargo-moving machine.

After a while they had to admit that it was cold and not very
entertaining. They found themselves a cosy bar off Townwall
Street, where a guitarist was providing entertainment. As they
went in he was playing 'Zorba's Dance' to the accompaniment
of erratic hand-clapping from the customers. Greg felt Liz hesi-
tate – her glance at him said: At the end of this wearying day,
can I subject you to this? But he nodded and urged her forward.
He had nothing against Zorba.

Still in a self-denying mood, they ordered non-alcoholic
drinks. Now the customers were singing along with 'You Are
My Sunshine'. Once again Greg had to smile reassurance at Liz.
There were worse things in life than a discordant rendering of
an old song.

The truth was, he hardly heard it. His mind was busy elsewhere, involved in an argument about the disposal of the articles
that made up their 'Chopin Collection'. If he handed them over

to the Kent force, he was sure Chief Inspector Glaston would be furious. If he by-passed the locals, it would be seen as an insult.

But did that matter? The main inquiry, originating from the murder of Marzelina, was being directed from London. And yet . . . If they actually found out the whereabouts of Hampton–Firstead, it would be the local force that would take him into custody.

Now Liz was making notes on an old envelope about the window displays she'd noticed. Part of her occupation was to advise fashion shops about what to put in their windows. Her thoughts were busy with one thing; he was busy with another. What good was it to be together again and yet be so separate?

On the whole it wasn't a very enjoyable evening. They were home and preparing for bed just after ten. As Liz was brushing her teeth, Greg came into the bathroom.

'All right, then,' he said. 'First thing tomorrow, we'll hand the Chopin Collection things over to Chief Inspector Valmouth.'

But it didn't quite happen.

Over breakfast in the little dining room they were reviewing where they could make further enquiries today about local musicians. Greg suddenly put down his butter knife and said, 'Where did we hear a pianist recently?'

She was at a loss. 'Ah . . . I don't know.'

'Saturday night? In the Cellar Club?'

'Oh . . . The jazz group?'

'No, that was sax, string bass and electronic guitar. No, it was the singer – remember the accompanist?'

'Of course!' But though she'd heard a piano, she could hardly recall the player. She hadn't paid any attention.

'Come on, eat up; we want to go and ask his name.'

'Ask who?'

'His employers, at the Greenthorpe.'

'But aren't we supposed to avoid—'

'Liz, our piano-playing villain isn't likely to be there on the spot at eight-thirty in the morning.'

'No, you're right. OK, just let me swallow my toast and we'll go.'

It was only a short walk to the Greenthorpe. Greg asked the desk clerk if he could speak to the manager.

'Of course, sir,' said the clerk, aware since yesterday that Mr Crowne was someone of importance.

A moment's telephone call, and out came Mr Lethwaite. 'Mr Crowne! What can I do for you?'

'The pianist that accompanied the comedy singer on Saturday night – I'd like his name and address, please.'

'The pianist?' Lethwaite echoed in amazement.

'Yes, I'd like to know where he lives.'

'But . . . but . . .'

'It's important.'

'I see. Yes, of course.' There had been something rather princely about Mr Crown's tone of voice. 'Just a moment. Perhaps you'd like to step into my office while I look it up.'

They trooped in after him. It was a small section behind the reception desk, quite tidy but rather Spartan compared with the luxury of the public rooms. Lethwaite stooped over his computer keyboard. Greg and Liz waited impatiently the other side of his desk.

'Entertainments,' he muttered, tapping keys. 'Er . . . April . . . Saturday . . . Flip Quartet, Rhythm and Blues . . . Chérie Chanteuse, Ups and Downs in Music . . .' He straightened. 'His accompanist isn't mentioned.'

'But surely you must know who to make the cheque out to?'

'Ah, well, you see, my assistant looks after the performers, and, you know, they like cash.' The manager was embarrassed.

'Another little tax-avoidance scheme,' murmured Liz.

'But you know who his accompanist was, surely?'

'Well, no; that's my assistant's area.'

'May we speak to your assistant, please?'

'Of course.' He picked up a phone on his desk and made a connection.

Liz said in a tone of protest, 'You keep on saying "his": are you telling me that was a *man*?'

'Yes, of course. A man *en travesti*,' said Greg.

'A drag act?'

'Is that what you call it in English? What is "drag"?'

'I don't know – long skirts, probably, because a man couldn't wear short skirts: his legs would give him away.' She was shaking her head in disbelief. 'But the voice, Greg? He sounded like a soprano.'

'Not a bad voice. He'd make a good counter-tenor with proper training.'

The assistant manager came in, looking slightly worried. A summons to the office usually meant trouble.

'Ronald, Mr Crowne would like to have the name and address of the accompanist to Chérie Chanteuse.'

Ronald didn't respond with the query that immediately struck him: 'What on earth for?' Instead he said politely, 'I'm sorry, sir, I'm afraid I don't have that.'

'Don't have it?' cried Mr Lethwaite, either truly astonished or pretending. 'That's not very businesslike!'

'Perhaps not, sir, but it works. I pay Harry, Harry pays his accompanist. It's always the same with double acts or groups like, say, Flip's – it's easier if one of them deals with the money side.' His expression was reproachful, as if he was telling him something already well known – and perhaps it was.

'Well, then, Harry. His name and address will be in here, will it?'

'Yes, sir, under "Entertainers, Details".'

Lethwaite pressed keys. His screen reformed. He ran down a list. 'Here we are, sir,' he informed Greg. 'Harry Crayshaw, Martel Cottage, Hillside Lane, Dover.'

'Thank you,' said Greg, writing.

'May I ask what this is in reference to?' the hotel manager asked, with some anxiety. 'I hope there's no complaint about our entertainment?'

'Not at all,' Greg assured him, and urged Liz out of the office.

They stopped in the hotel lobby. 'What now? Are we going to Martel Cottage?'

Greg shook his head at her. 'Remember I said we'd turn over all that Chopin Collection stuff? We'll call Valmouth and hand it all over to him, including the singer's name and address.'

'Oh. Well, I suppose you're right.'

Greg made the call. There was a short conversation, which on Greg's side included some defensive chat and an apology for being at the Greenthorpe Hotel for whatever reason.

'We're in disgrace,' he said. 'We're to wait, but outside.'

They went out into the street, the matter of collecting the plastic carrier with its plastic trinkets momentarily in abeyance. Today was fine, with a hint of sunshine though the wind was chill. They had been waiting less than five minutes when an unmarked car came surging to the kerb. Out got Valmouth, followed a moment later by WPC Tyrrell.

'Now what's all this?' demanded the chief inspector, clearly very put out. 'I thought it was understood you'd stay away from the Greenthorpe!'

'Never mind that,' Greg said, with something like as much force as Valmouth. 'Liz and I have been trying to track down this man for ages. And now I think we may have found him!'

'You're talking about Hampton? Or Firstead?'

'No, it could be a different name. We've been supposing that he's a musician, a pianist, and that he lives somewhere around Dover because he chose a local firm as maker of his trade goods.'

'Yes, yes, but that's no reason to—'

'You know Liz and I have been trying to track down a pianist that might fit the bill. We've just got the name and address, here at the hotel, of someone who could be right.'

Angela Tyrrell was looking peevish. 'So who is he, then,' she demanded, 'this guy we're supposed to arrest?'

Greg paid no attention to her irritability. 'We think he might be the pianist who accompanies Harry Crayshaw, a – *un personnificateur.*'

'A drag act,' Liz supplied.

'What?' She gave a snort of derision. 'You're not talking about poor old Chérie Chanteuse? That's absolutely loony!'

Everyone was taken aback. Valmouth drew his brows together and said coldly, 'If you have information about the man, Tyrrell, please let's share it.'

Ms Tyrrell sobered at once. 'Sorry, sir, but I know Harry Crayshaw, and he'd never be involved in anything dangerous or scary. He's a pussycat.'

'And you know this, how?'

'We-ell . . . he's a member of my amateur dramatic group. Plays the Dame in our Christmas pantomime, for instance.'

Her superior received this with a mixture of embarrassment and exasperation. 'Apart from his dramatic abilities – *who is he?*'

'Er . . . he's lived here all his life, like me, and so has his family. Connected with the ferry service from way back – him and his father and his father before him, I think. He's lived in the same house from way back. He gave up work . . . let me see . . . might be three or four years ago – wanted to see if he could make a go of the Hinge and Brackett idea.'

'Hinge and Brackett,' Liz murmured in Greg's ear. 'Two men in drag, singer and piano – quite famous, I believe.'

'*And what about his pianist?*' Greg asked the constable. 'Can you vouch for him too?'

'Of course not,' she said, beginning to realize she'd put her foot in it. 'Don't know anything about that.' Then, building defences, 'But I know Harry – he'd never engage anybody dodgy.'

The chief inspector was vexed. He'd rushed here, anxious about this royal encumbrance, only to have the situation dissolve into something like farce. He didn't want to waste any more time over it.

'Right, then, let's just wipe all that off the scoreboard,' he said. 'And if you don't mind, sir, I'd like *you* to stay away from this hotel in future.'

'But look here,' Greg insisted, 'the reason you wanted us out of this building was because our quarry – the man we're trying to find, Mr Firstead or Mr Hampton or whatever name he's using – he had used the public phone here a couple of times. And now we have the possibility that it's a man who *performs* here – isn't it quite likely he'd use the lobby phone?'

'But Tyrrell is vouching for this bloke Crayshaw—'

'But not for his accompanist.'

'Listen, Harry's not the sort to get involved with low-life types.'

'There you are,' urged Valmouth.

Greg sighed and gave a little bow. 'Very well, Chief Inspector.'

Valmouth frowned at him. 'You're not thinking of going to that address on your own, are you?'

Greg gave a nonchalant shrug.

The detective sighed. Was it possible to stop him? He felt like clapping handcuffs on the man; but then he gave in. 'All right, but Tyrrell goes with you.'

Angela Tyrrell made a movement that might have been protest; but a glare from her boss quelled it. 'How will you get back to the office, sir, if I'm ferrying him around?' she enquired, hoping he'd change his mind.

He simply glowered, so she led the way out to her car.

She drove them north and west out of Dover, through dwindling rush-hour traffic, into an area of plentiful trees and green lawns. Then came fields, and a considerable hill, after which they turned off to the right.

Martel Cottage had clearly been built for a farmworker but had been extended and improved over past years. A brass knocker on the heavy front door was in the shape of a hammer, influenced by the name Martel, Greg supposed. A toolmaker's home at one time, perhaps.

The constable knocked. They had a glimpse of someone looking out from the bay window to the right of the door. She knocked again, and after a moment the door was opened by a rather handsome man in jeans and shirt.

'Angela! How nice to see you!' He let an enquiring glance roam over her companions. 'What can I do for you?'

'Got a minute, Harry?'

'For you, always,' he said, standing back to let them enter.

They came into a narrow passage with small rooms opening to the left and the right. To Liz, it was recognizable as a two-up, two-down of days long gone by. Some time ago an extension had been added to the back of the house, and it was to this that they were led by Crayshaw.

A comfortable and neat living room welcomed them, with an agreeable warmth to counteract the chill of the morning. Several framed theatre posters decorated one wall; a signed photograph of a famous actor stood on the bookcase.

Crayshaw himself had something of a theatrical air. His shirt was of very rough black linen, worn open at the neck with a knotted grey cravat. He ushered them towards chairs with a wave of the hand, then stood looking expectantly at the constable for an introduction.

'Oh, sorry,' she said. 'Ms Blair, Mr Crowne; they're helping me.'

'Hot drink?' he offered. 'Tea, coffee, hot chocolate?'

'No, thanks, Harry; we're not staying long. I just wanted to get some info from you.'

'Good lord. This isn't *official*, is it, Angie?'

Her embarrassed glance flickered towards Greg, who kept an expression of polite interest..

'In a way it is, Harry. You were on at the Greenthorpe on Saturday night, weren't you?'

'Oh, yes. Clientele pretty thin. You know what it's like this time of year, dear: only the townies, no holiday types.'

'Who was your straight man?'

'At the piano? Marty Quinn. Why do you ask? – Oh, don't tell me you suspect *him* of anything! Not dear old Marty.'

'Got his address handy?'

'Well . . . as it happens . . . no. Why d'you want it?'

'I'd just like a word with him, that's all.'

'Don't tell me that awful wife of his has been after him again about the child support. Child support! He pays when he can, poor old boy.'

'How do I get in touch with him, Harry?' There was a touch of asperity in her voice now.

Crayshaw shrugged affectedly. 'As a matter of fact, you can't, dear. He lives for the most part in France – to avoid the tax man, you know – and he was telling me he'd got a gig in Hamburg as from next Thursday, so he was going straight there when he left on Saturday.'

'Harry!' said Angela with irritation. 'When you hired him for Saturday, how did you contact him?'

'I didn't, darling: *he* contacted *me*. Couple of weeks ago. Asking, you know, if I had anything going because he needed a quid or two, and I said I had this gig coming up at the Greenthorpe, so he nipped over on the hovercraft Saturday morning.'

'That seems rather a casual way of doing business,' Greg remarked, smiling so that the words seemed inoffensive.

'Oh, Mr Crowne, in the theatre, you see, *friendship* means a lot. I can always rely on someone to help me out at the piano.'

'Someone who had experience of public performance, I suppose?' Greg enquired. 'Someone who'd been properly trained?'

'Trained?'

'Well, I think I heard that quite a few' – he searched for the phrase – 'pop stars? – they can't read music.'

'That's true.' Crayshaw smiled and shook his head. 'But all my straight man has to do is to keep starting the first few bars of the 'Jewel Song' from Faust. Then I interrupt him and he breaks off. A child could do it.' He flourished a hand in the air to demonstrate how easy it was.

'So it's always Gounod? You never need him to play anything taxing – no Rachmaninov or Chopin?'

'Good Lord, no.' The other man stared at him, then blew out a breath. 'No, so long as he can master the bit that accompanies Marguerite's gazing at herself in the mirror –' He broke off. 'You know the opera, I gather.'

'Not one of my favourites.'

'But good for a laugh, eh?'

Angela Tyrrell was annoyed by this excursion into the classics. 'So you don't have a regular accompanist – is that it, Harry?

'Now, Angie, you know what it's like in the entertainment business. If I could rely on getting an engagement every month, or even every six weeks . . .' He pondered the matter. 'But you see, even if I was able to get on the regular circuit, that wouldn't really help, because I'd have to have someone travelling with me, and expenses for two would be – goodness me – a bit of a problem. So unless I hit the big time, which of course we know will happen any moment, dear, I just hire someone who's available.'

'And you pay him cash on the nail?' she queried, now in control of the situation.

'You got it, baby,' Crayshaw replied in the tones of Kojak.

'So how many different chaps do you work with?'

'Oh, let me see . . . I had four pub engagements in Bristol in December, so Steve helped me out then. New Year's Eve and New Year's Day I had gigs in Sheffield, so that was Arnie; and then there was the one for that club in Southampton, so that was David. So that's three, and with Marty that makes four so far this year. And as I've got quite a few dates later on, there'll be others here and there.'

Angela hesitated then asked, 'Any of them up to anything shady?'

Crayshaw was offended. 'What – drugs, you mean? Angie, you know me better than that!'

'I'm not accusing you of anything, Harry. But has anybody seemed to be a bit flush with money recently?'

'Ha! That'll be the day.' This time it was the John Wayne drawl.

Liz had been glancing around the room. 'I see you have quite a few collectibles from the world of theatre.'

'Just a few.'

'There's money in that, I hear. I'm thinking of getting into that – memorabilia about stars of the black-and-white screen. Any hints?'

''Fraid not. I was just lucky once or twice with the posters; I got them quite cheap. And the photograph comes from when I was on the boats – he was a passenger.'

Liz got up to examine the handsome face from a decade ago.

'It's always nice to have a little something coming in on the side,' she murmured, in a speculative tone. She turned back with a smile. 'Your friend that had to rush off to Hamburg, for instance – from the sound of it, he needs a way to keep the Child Support Agency off his back.'

'Oh, *Marty* – he's a bit slow – he wouldn't know how to make a profit from anything except music.'

'Well, he could concentrate on musical items, then,' Liz suggested. 'Posters and programmes about the Beatles – or about Liberace – or even Chopin.'

Crayshaw frowned at her and shook his head. 'Can't imagine anybody making their fortune at *that*.'

Constable Tyrrell was getting to her feet. She said, 'Well, thanks, then, Harry. Won't take up any more of your time.'

'No problem, dear. See you at the auditions next week?'

'Of course.' As he led them to the door she added, 'You hoping to get the Robert Cummings role?'

'I should be so lucky,' he sighed. At the door he gave her a hug and a kiss. ''Bye for now, darling.'

Outside, Ms Tyrrell stalked to her car. Greg paused for a moment to draw in a breath of fresh air. The warmth of the cottage had become somewhat cloying after a while, owing in part to the aftershave of their elegant host.

In the car, as the constable was switching on the engine, Liz leaned forward from the back seat to enquire, 'What was that about the audition?'

'Our drama group is putting on a musical adapted from an old film – something light for our summer show, you see.'

'And I'm sure you are going to win a part,' Greg said.

'Might do,' she said, shrugging off the flattery. 'I'm after one of the character roles. Poor old Harry. He's too lightweight for the lead.'

She started the car and drove off, giving her attention to her driving while she negotiated a difficult crossroads, then said, 'So we had no luck finding your problematic pianist, eh?' She sounded quite pleased about it. She still disapproved of Greg.

'Sad to say. Perhaps it's a herring.'

'A *red* herring,' Liz supplied.

'Yes, thank you.' If they'd been alone he'd have asked her where you could catch a red herring, but with Constable Tyrrell listening, it would raise no smiles.

'And none of them seem to be venturing into the collectible business.' She was scoffing at the memory of Liz's remarks. 'Dunno what you thought you were doing, with all that about programmes and stuff.'

Liz said nothing. She had wanted to bring in the name Chopin, as Greg himself had done earlier. On neither occasion had Harry Crayshaw been interested, so it seemed none of his accompanists had classical ambitions.

The constable delivered them to the Collinet then sped away. 'We should have got her to wait while I brought down my carrier bag,' Liz remarked as they entered the hotel. 'That would have proved there was a bit of money to be made from collectibles.'

'What, and have her sneer at us again? No, we'll ring Valmouth to tell him to expect it. The police station's just along the road.'

They went up to their room to carry out this intention. Liz wrote a note explaining where she'd bought each item. Greg then rang Chief Inspector Valmouth.

'Ah yes, Tyrrell's just been reporting to me about that,' was the response, in a rather urgent tone of voice. 'She was a bit dismissive but I'm quite interested in it – because a thought has just struck me. You saw her pal Harry in his drag act on Saturday night, yes?'

'Yes.'

'It occurs to me that his pianist, Marty, really might be our man. Because, you know, he might have seen you.'

'Oh?' said Greg, trying to catch his train of thought.

'My information is that he – this crook – got your hotel address in Edinburgh, followed you, and had a go at you on the road to wherever it was . . . that shopping centre. So he knows what you look like.'

'He does.' That was a realization that he'd been living with.

'So what if he saw you in the Cellar Club on Saturday night and got the fright of his life? You know, he was off to Hamburg before you could say Jack Robinson.'

'You could be right,' groaned Greg.

'And Harry Crayshaw didn't have an address for him. So he's kind of elusive, wouldn't you say?'

'That makes him sound like the man who contacted Madame Wiaroz and offered her the manuscript.'

'I thought so. And like the man Tyrrell says ordered the goods from Keepsake Curios.'

'Same man, same method?'

'And you know, we hear that this Marty Quinn told Crayshaw he was going to Hamburg. But do we know if that's true?'

Greg was going over the conversation in his mind. 'Crayshaw said Quinn came over on Saturday on the hovercraft.'

'Uh-huh. We'll check on that. Marty Quinn . . .' Valmouth didn't sound hopeful. 'There's such a lot of cross-Channel movement at the weekends, though . . .'

'I suppose so. But you know, Chief Inspector, none of that may be reliable. If it's the same man we're looking for – the man who killed Marzelina Zalfeda – he covers his tracks. We don't know whether he really lives in France, or came over on the hovercraft, or was really going to Hamburg.'

Valmouth muttered a string of profanities. When he'd recovered his temper he went on: 'Isn't there *anything* concrete to go on?'

'Well . . . We acted on the idea that he was interested in music – interested enough to know that a Chopin manuscript would earn money. We went on from that to think he might have started with something less spectacular, so that put us on the trail of the Chopin Collection. And whoever was marketing that line of business is desperate not to let us get close. That much is definite.'

'But that might just be because he's up to a small-time swindle over VAT.'

'That's true, but what else have we got to go on?'

'I wish I knew. My problem is, Mr Crowne, I don't know how much of my resources to put into this.'

'I understand.'

'Um-m . . . It's not going to hurt if we check the ferry services, I suppose. And I'll send Tyrrell back to get a description of Quinn from her friend Harry Crayshaw.'

'He implied that Quinn was in trouble over . . .' He turned to Liz for help. 'Why had Marty Quinn gone to live in France? To avoid something about his child?'

'Paying maintenance.'

He passed on this information to the detective, who groaned. 'Oh, Lord! It's useless to ask for information in that area; they've been in a mess for years.'

'I'm sorry, Mr Valmouth.'

'Not your fault. We've got to work with what we've got. Leave it with me, then; but if you think of anything . . .'

'You might get something out of the trinkets we collected in Manchester and Edinburgh – fingerprints, perhaps. I'll bring them along to the police station.'

'Yes, and we might try Keepsake Curios again, more officially this time.'

'Worth a try.' They exchanged farewells.

Greg gave a summary of the conversation to Liz.

She shook her head. 'I think the trouble is that Mr Valmouth isn't altogether convinced our man is here. I expect there are a lot of people who come and go over the Channel on a regular basis.'

'He asks us to let him know if we get any bright ideas.'

'Oh, Greg . . . I don't feel in the least "bright"!'

They delivered the carrier to the police station, then spent the rest of the day in the public library looking at reference books and regional directories. They still had an inner conviction that they'd find their man among the lists of musical people – a performer, a teacher, perhaps a reviewer of concerts and recitals. They made a note of those that they might contact next day.

At length, dispirited, they tried to cheer themselves up with dinner and a cinema visit.

Liz rose early. She felt her bruises from the Edinburgh assault had cleared up enough to allow her to take a morning run. She pulled on tracksuit and trainers and set out. She returned home feeling that her muscles had been restored to their usual efficiency, and was looking forward to a long, hot shower.

To her surprise she found Greg up and dressed. 'Breakfast will be here in a minute,' he told her. 'Valmouth is going to collect us in about half an hour.'

'Why? What's happened?' She could tell it was serious.

He grimaced and shook his head. 'Keepsake Curios burned down last night.'

Fifteen

Chief Inspector Valmouth arrived in a car driven by a male constable in plain clothes. Liz and Greg got in the back. Valmouth turned in the front passenger seat to give them the news.

'Reported early this morning by a normal patrol. It was well alight by that time, and because those outer panels are plastic it was difficult to deal with – noxious fumes, they call it.'

'How did it start?' asked Greg.

'Well, somebody broke a window on the right-hand side of the ground floor then squirted in a lot of something flammable. The chief fire officer says probably barbecue-lighter fuel. The ground floor on that side is where your pal Mr Jerrold has his workshop, where his staff put together the various gimmicks he sells. Seems to be pretty much gutted – or melted, seems to be what it is.'

'So it's only on the ground floor on one side?'

'We'll see when we get there but I gather the whole building suffered a lot of heat and smoke damage. It's a small block, that building. The floor on the right, above the workshop . . .'

'The office,' Liz supplied.

'Yeah, the office – it's a wreck, I hear. The floor fell into the workshop, taking a lot of burning stuff with it.'

'So who set it alight?' she asked.

'Well, there are three theories,' said Valmouth rather grimly. 'The favourite is the kids that have been messing about there since January. Practice makes perfect – they did fires in dustbins and tried to set a parked car ablaze one time, but now they've worked out how to do it properly.'

'That's the one I'm backing,' the constable put in unexpectedly.

'The second theory is that Jerrold hired someone to set the fire . . .'

'What?' Liz cried.

'Of course, for the insurance,' said the constable, nodding to himself.

'No, no! I've met him. He's a nice old chap.'

'He's a nice old chap who's not doing too well,' Valmouth said. 'Mapley's right. Arson for insurance is a very likely explanation.'

'No, it's them ruddy kids,' insisted Mapley.

'The third possibility is that the fire was started by our missing Marty Quinn. Which is why you're here.' The sat-nav system interrupted with an instruction for the driver, so for a moment Valmouth fell silent. Then he went on: 'I'm not saying it's a likely idea. 'Cos it would have to mean that Quinn's been in the area for days, keeping an eye on you, and knew you'd been to see Keepsake Curios, Ms Blair.'

'But if that's correct, that means that the place was burnt down to get rid of information about Quinn – or, as Mr Jerrold calls him, Firstead.'

'That's the idea.'

'But I really believed him when he said that he didn't have any,' Liz insisted.

'Perhaps he has information that he doesn't know he has? And as he's on the scene now at the business park, I'd like you to chat him up, miss, if you wouldn't mind.'

'Oh.' She wasn't attracted to the notion. The poor man would be in shock. Was it right to badger him at a time like this? She turned to Greg for an opinion. Greg met her gaze, shook his head faintly in commiseration, but seemed to be telling her that she must co-operate.

Yes, she must, she told herself. An innocent young woman had been killed in London. If the man they were seeking had anything to do with the fire, she must help to establish that fact.

They approached the business park. The reek of burnt chemicals hung in the air, acrid and offensive. The fire trucks had gone, but groups of people were gathered around the perimeter of the scene, presumably staff from other buildings anxious to know what was happening.

The damaged structure presented a lopsided appearance. The blue plastic panels were buckled and distorted but not consumed. Window frames, twisted out of their mountings, hung loose or had fallen in contorted shapes to the ground. The hall doorway was askew, like the entrance to some cartoon witch's cottage. The door itself lay, misshapen, on the forecourt. Fragments of burnt paper were drifting in the upward air current.

A small official vehicle with the logo of the Kent Fire Service stood closest to the building. Mr Jerrold, the owner of Keepsake Curios, was talking to a man in a navy-blue uniform. Constable Mapley parked the police vehicle neatly nearby.

The two by the official car turned to see who would emerge. Mr Jerrold gave a little cry of surprise at seeing Liz. 'Ms Peters! News travels fast! How did you come to hear of this terrible business?'

The fire officer was shaking hands with the chief inspector. 'Mr Valmouth? My name's Ibbot. Mr Jerrold here's just been telling me that he's seen those fire-raising louts hanging around the place in the last few days.'

'There you are,' muttered Constable Mapley to no one in particular.

But that's what he *would* say if he'd had the fire set himself, Liz thought. 'I saw those vandals up to mischief' – ready-made culprits.

Remembering the request of the chief inspector, she moved closer to Jerrold, to say, in tones of sympathy, 'What a dreadful shame! All your lovely things!'

'Dreadful, dreadful,' he sighed. She glimpsed tears in the corners of his eyes. He was in mourning for the wares that he had invented and produced for hundreds of tourists who would now never know of them.

He didn't have this place burned, she said to herself. He loves it too much. She said, as if trying to be businesslike, 'I suppose that means the end of my little venture – unless you think of starting up somewhere else?'

'Your venture . . . Oh, yes . . . your acting people . . .' He seemed a little confused, a little dysfunctional. 'I'm not . . . I'm not looking ahead yet, you know. This has been such a . . . such a calamity. It's all gone, you see. I don't know if I could really start again.'

'But you have records of all your customers,' she urged. 'I'm sure they'd rally round.'

'Ha!' There was just a touch of irony in the sound. 'My customers will want supplies for the tourist season. They'll soon find someone else.'

'But for next year. If you made a new start, you could contact them for next year's gifts.'

'I only wish I could. But everything's gone, the office is . . . just a . . . a complete shambles. They wouldn't let me go upstairs even for a minute or two because of the . . . the fumes, you know, but they tell me our computers are . . . well . . . hopelessly damaged and our filing cabinets fell . . . into the ground floor . . . so anything on paper is just ashes.'

Liz was beginning to feel bad about misleading the poor soul. Yet she had to do what she could to get information. 'But perhaps you might have duplicates of some of your files at home, mightn't you?'

He bent his head in gloomy regret. 'Madge . . . my wife . . . she doesn't let me bring work home. No, there's almost nothing there.'

Greg was meanwhile listening to the conversation between the chief inspector and the fire officer. Mr Ibbot was congratulating himself on the fact that the plastic of the building was a recent invention and hardily fire-retardant. 'Could have had a much more serious affair,' he said. 'Those lads had no idea they were wasting their time, to a large extent.'

'You're pretty confident it was the boys?' Valmouth asked, stifling a sigh. The local force had been trying to find them since the New Year, without success. Several known tearaways were on the suspect list, but there was never anything useful by way of evidence.

'It's likely, don't you think? Although . . .' Ibbot paused in thought. 'Although it *is* a new venture, actually getting the accelerant inside the building. Up till now they've just laid rubbish against the outside and set it alight. But there!' he added. 'You can just imagine them saying to themselves, "We never get a really big blaze; let's try something more dramatic".'

'Well, let's consider other possibilities . . .'

'You mean arson for insurance?' Ibbot glanced aside at Jerrold, who was deep in conversation with Liz. 'Possible – I don't dismiss it. But you know, there's usually more finesse about a professional arsonist. He tries to make it look like an electrical fault, or something of that sort. This is . . . Well, I favour the kids, myself.'

'Righto, we'll work on that assumption, Mr Ibbot.'

'I'll let you have a copy of my report.' The fire officer moved away to carry on his investigation.

Valmouth turned to Greg. 'So that's the view, sir. Perhaps I brought you out here for nothing.'

Greg nodded towards Liz, who was still listening with bent head to Mr Jerrold. 'Liz is finding out what she can. Let's wait until we hear what she has to say.'

'*He's* not known to us in any way,' Valmouth confided. 'Not even a traffic violation.'

'So it sounds as if it really might be the work of the children. Only . . .' He paused. 'I don't believe in coincidences.'

Valmouth nodded. 'Yeah. Just seems too convenient that when we get on the track of this Marty Quinn, Keepsake Curios goes up in smoke.'

'That's assuming that Marty Quinn, Charles Hampton and Mr Firstead of the Chopin Collection are all one and the same man.'

The detective made weighing movements with his hands. 'I'm still trying to make my mind up. We've found no evidence that anyone called Quinn came over on the hovercraft on Saturday, nor that anyone made the return trip at the weekend.'

'But if we was going to Hamburg? He might have gone by air.'

'Not so far as we can tell. But then, you see, it might turn out that Marty Quinn is a stage name, or just another alias.'

'The entertainer – Mr Crayshaw – he could probably tell—'

'That's where Tyrrell is now.' Valmouth tugged hard at his ear. 'I let her off too lightly over that. She should have got a better description from Crayshaw, and why not pictures? Crayshaw must have publicity shots of himself on stage, probably even video – I bet he's got his accompanists on film, too.'

They headed back to the car. After warmly shaking hands with Jerrold, Liz joined them. They stood in a group before getting in. 'I tried to get the conversation round to Firstead,' she reported, 'but really he's in such a state he just can't concentrate.'

'So you think he's not responsible for the fire?'

'I'm sure not.'

'It's the kids,' Constable Mapley said, opening the back door for them.

'Maybe,' his boss said, unconvinced.

On the way back to town they exchanged suggestions about the fire. Valmouth was deciding to keep an open mind. 'We're going to go on trying to find Quinn. I'll never be happy until I know he's either in or out of the picture. We'll see if the fire service can produce anything by way of evidence from how the fire was started – I'm not hoping for fingerprints, but who knows? – there may be something about the method. And we'll look into Jerrold's finances—'

'No, no,' protested Liz.

'Got to, Ms Blair.'

Greg asked if they could be set down at the offices of a hire-car firm. 'I'm sick of not having our own transport,' he confessed.

'Ah . . . of course, sir,' murmured Valmouth. 'And you will let us know the car registration and so on, won't you?'

Greg nodded agreement. Naturally the chief inspector wanted to keep tabs on him.

The hire firm offered Peugeots. They chose a one-year-old and headed off towards the waterfront, in need of a place to talk. It was hours since they'd left the hotel after only a snatched cup of coffee. They parked in big area not far from the famous White Cliffs, then walked until they found a quiet café.

Liz left Greg to order coffee and rolls. She'd changed out of her tracksuit in such a hurry that she was sure she looked a mess. A few minute spent brushing her hair into shape and applying lipstick made her feel a little better.

Yet all that was unimportant. She was unhappy. Looking into Mr Jerrold's finances! She felt the poor man was being undeservedly suspected. She came stomping back into the main room ready for a quarrel about him.

'It's just totally unfair! That poor soul's lost everything and he's being talked about as if he's a criminal!' She threw herself into the chair alongside Greg, banging her handbag on the ground beside her.

'The chief inspector has to—'

'I think Chief Inspector Valmouth ought to show a little common decency to him in view of his loss!'

'Mr Valmouth isn't by any means convinced Jerrold is to blame,' he said soothingly. 'In fact, he finds the fire too much of a coincidence.'

That put a stop to the flood of protest she'd been about to unleash. 'Oh. Well . . .'

He was glad to see that she had stopped to think things over, and pushed a cup of steaming coffee towards her.

She took it and swallowed a huge mouthful. 'It *is* weird, isn't it? Every time we go anywhere and ask questions, somehow that avenue seems to get closed off.'

There were fresh croissants and little pots of black-cherry jam. It all served to improve her mood. Munching, she said, 'Let's agree that Mr Jerrold isn't to blame for the fire.'

'Liz, I've never even met the man! Much though I admire your wisdom and your brains, I don't know if I can just go by your opinion.'

'My wisdom and my brains tell me to agree that it's too much of a coincidence. I have a strong suspicion that our elusive friend Slinky the Shadow is the arsonist.'

'And I'd agree with that, I suppose,' he said in tones of great doubt, 'only that I can't see how Slinky the Shadow knew Keepsake Curios was some sort of danger to him.'

'But that's obviously because I went there and asked questions.'

'But how could he know that?'

That gave her pause. 'We-ell, I'm supposing Slinky is Marty Quinn, and Marty Quinn saw us when we were in the Cellar Club on Saturday night . . .'

'But you weren't wearing a placard saying "I've been to Keepsake Curios", now were you?'

'What?'

'You went to Keepsake Curios with Constable Tyrrell on Saturday *morning*. Marty Quinn saw you – if he did see you – on Saturday evening. How could he possibly know?'

Her brows drew together. She frowned at him. 'Wait,' she said. He waited. After a long moment of thought she said, 'Who did know I'd been to Keepsake Curios?' Before he could reply she began to talk it through. 'The police knew, because Constable Tyrrell went with me. Mr Jerrold knew. The young guy at the reception desk knew – but he didn't take part in the discussion, so he's got no idea we were fishing about the Chopin Collection.'

'So we discount him?'

'I think so. Your harpist friend, Mr Selbige – did we mention Keepsake Curios to him?'

'No, we asked him about pianists who might have come into money.'

'Then . . . I don't know how Quinn knew I'd been to Keepsake Curios.' She was trying to conjure up all they had done since Saturday morning. 'Have we been talking about it where someone could have overheard us?'

'In the hotel, you mean?'

'Well, yes, I suppose so.' A possibility struck her. 'Chief Inspector Valmouth came and rooted us out of the Greenthorpe on Sunday in a bit of a panic. He'd learned that someone had telephoned Keepsake Curios from the phone in the lobby. When he asked to talk to you, did it get loud? Could anybody have heard you saying the name Keepsake Curios?'

He tried to summon up the scene. It seemed to him they had conversed in normal tones in a secluded alcove.

'I don't think so. And yet . . .'

'What?'

'That was the morning after we'd been to the Cellar Bar. Perhaps Valmouth was right. Perhaps Marty Quinn was still in the hotel and witnessed all that.'

'Oh, don't say that!' She was shocked at the thought that their enemy could have been so near.

'And so he decided to tidy up another loose end by destroying Keepsake Curios.' But he couldn't quite accept it. He tried to marshal the train of events in his head. 'Let's accept the idea that he was there on Sunday, and overheard . . . or got some hint somehow from the presence of the police . . . and felt that Keepsake Curios was a chink in his armour . . .'

'Go on.'

'Why wait thirty-six hours to do something about it?'

She began counting on her fingers. 'Lunch-time Sunday to lunch-time Monday, that's twenty-four, and on until the middle of the night on Monday – yes, that's right: that's thirty-six hours or more.'

'You'd think that right away, on Sunday night – that would be a better opportunity . . .'

Alarm was making her quick to respond. 'So did we do something on Monday that made Marty Quinn think it was urgent?'

'We went to see Harry Crayshaw.'

'Yes, that's all we did.'

'Well, that's not a small thing. He gave us the name of the pianist: Marty Quinn. That seems to be an important moment, if our version of events is right.'

'But Greg – the same objection remains. Just because we got the name, how does it follow that Marty Quinn *knows* that? Are

you saying that Crayshaw is in cahoots with him – that he
warned him?'

He was beginning to wonder if it could be so – but Crayshaw
had been so open and co-operative.

Liz strengthened his doubts by her next words. 'Constable
Tyrrell is a pal of Crayshaw's. I mean to say, she vouched for
him – knows his family history and all that.'

'Yes.' He tried to see it from different angles. 'But if you're
friends with someone, and you hear the police are looking for
him . . . do you perhaps give him a hint?'

'But Greg, he said he didn't know where Quinn had gone –
I mean, Hamburg, yes, but not an address or anything.'

'Yet he might have been lying out of sympathy for Quinn,
because of the trouble with his wife. And don't forget, Liz:
Crayshaw had no idea *why* Constable Tyrrell was making inquiries.
We know that Charles Hampton, who may be Marty Quinn, is
wanted for murder. But that word was never mentioned to him.'

'Of course.' She was nodding. 'If he thought Quinn was only
wanted because of money problems, he probably wouldn't think
it important.'

'Perhaps we should mention this idea to Mr Valmouth . . .'
The thought was unappealing. It would sound like a reproach
that Tyrrell had been too soft with her fellow thespian.
Nevertheless he got out his mobile and made the call.

It was the constable herself who picked up the phone. 'Oh,
hello,' she said in a brusque, preoccupied manner. 'Is this important? I'm just typing up my notes, I just got back from talking
to Harry again.'

'Ah. That's why I'm ringing. I was going to—'

'He's absolutely baffled at the idea his pal Marty could be
involved in anything like the fire at Keepsake Curios. I think
we can rule that out.'

'Did you make it clear to him that—'

'Oh, I gave him a really hard time – he was really taken
aback, came over all remorseful; but he's got no information
that's worth anything.' There were sounds of movement alongside the phone, as if she were turning notebook pages.

'There was some talk of getting photographs?'

'He had to go through his press-cuttings book looking for
pics of Quinn. I've brought back a couple.'

'Perhaps Ms Blair and I could have a look at them to—'

'Much good it'll do you! Harry's centre-stage and there's this guy in an evening jacket sitting at the piano, hardly visible.' Her patience was clearly at an end. 'Did you want the boss for something? He's out of the office at the moment.'

'No,' Greg sighed. 'It was just a thought, but it seems you've covered it.'

'Right, then, so long.' The phone was noisily put down.

Liz was waiting to hear what had been said. 'You didn't seem to get in more than ten words!'

'No, Constable Tyrrell has put a scare into Harry Crayshaw and now he's given them photographs of Marty Quinn. So I think we must agree he's not trying to shield him.'

'You think he genuinely doesn't know where he is.'

Greg put up a hand and dragged at his hair in frustration. 'The fact is that the fire was set Monday night.'

'Yes, of course.'

He let a moment go by then went on: 'So if Crayshaw is reliable, if he's telling the truth when he says Quinn went to Hamburg . . .'

'What?'

'Quinn *came back* from Hamburg to do it?'

They were both shaking their heads almost immediately.

'Well, no. That seems unlikely,' said Liz.

'I think the fire-setter was here in Dover.'

'But then . . . who is he?' She tapped the table with her fingers. 'Is it just those wicked kids? Don't say it's poor Mr Jerrold – I won't believe that. And if it's Marty Quinn, is he hanging around keeping an eye on us? *And how is he keeping up with all the action?*'

They had no answer to their questions. For a few minutes they sat in baffled silence.

Then Liz began again from a new angle. 'For the moment, let's put aside trying to establish who set the fire. Let's go back to Firstead, who ordered the goods for the Chopin Collection.'

'Very well.' Anything, rather than remain tangled in this catch-22 situation.

'When you start up contacts with a new firm,' she ventured, calling up memories of her own business dealings in the fashion world, 'there's usually quite a lot of cordiality, perhaps a drink to put everyone at ease; but it ends with signing a contract. Isn't that what happens when you're dealing with concert-hall managers – people like that?'

'Of course.' He was attentive.

'Our criminal pal Slinky the Shadow must have signed a contract with Mr Jerrold.'

'Which is why he'd want the paperwork to go up in flames.'

'Yes, though it would be signed in a false name and with a false address, wouldn't it?' She was recalling the wrecked buildings. 'He sent emails, and perhaps they gave some clue or other, something that could be traced.'

'Well, the police will be looking at the computers. But I think they're more or less wrecked.'

'Mm . . .' A pause. 'Business isn't very brisk for Mr Jerrold,' she suggested. 'Don't you think he might remember a meeting that gave him a regular customer?'

'But you and Tyrrell asked him about that.'

'Yes, but you see, we never asked any direct questions.' She frowned at herself when she thought about it. 'We'd assumed aliases, because we were afraid that if I gave my real name, Mr Jerrold would recognize it – that's because we thought he might be a chum of Slinky the Shadow. We couldn't come out and say, "Look here, we're after the man who set up the Chopin business."'

He was following her line of thought. 'You think the police should griddle him about Firstead?'

'Do what?'

'*Faire contre-examen.* Toast him?'

'Oh, you mean *grill* him.'

'Tyrrell has been to put a scare into Mr Crayshaw about Quinn, and it seems to have worked.'

'Oh Lord, no – poor soul, he's in shock and he knows the police suspect him of burning down the place himself. He's appalled at them and their outlook.'

'Well . . . It needn't be the police.' He gave her a questioning glance. 'We could go.'

Sixteen

A phone book provided them with the home address of Kenneth Jerrold. When Liz called, he sounded subdued, uncertain.

'But didn't we speak about this already?' he ventured. 'I thought I told you? I won't be back in business again for a long, long time.'

'Yes, we did have a chat,' she said. 'It's something else – quite important. May we come and see you?'

'Well, I've got people here . . . But after all, what does that matter? If it's important I suppose . . . Well . . . come if you want to.'

The house belonged to the era of the nineteen-thirties – a mock Tudor façade in a decent expanse of garden. There were two cars in the driveway, which meant that Jerrold's visitors were probably still there.

The door was opened by a little lady who must once have been a beauty – fragile, fair hair owing much to her hairdresser's talent, but still with a fine skin and forget-me-not-blue eyes. 'Ms Peters?' she greeted them, her attention on Liz.

'Yes, and this is my friend Mr Crowne.'

'How do you do? Please come in, but I must ask you to be careful about anything you say to my husband: he's really not himself.'

She ushered them into a big living room with old-fashioned sofas cushioned in floral prints and frilled shades on the lamps. A fire was crackling in the open hearth. Kenneth Jerrold and another man were sitting with teacups and plates of biscuits before them on a low table. It seemed, after all, there was only one visitor.

'Ah . . . Ms Peters . . . Good of you to come . . .' Their host was looking somewhat lost. It was clear he'd forgotten why he'd agreed to their visit. 'Tea? Madge, would you see to that for us?'

His wife gave him a comforting smile then bustled off on tiny high-heeled feet. He made welcoming waves towards chairs. They sat down. He nodded towards the other man. 'This is Teddy Fielding, who manages the art department –' He broke off. He was remembering that there was no longer an art department. 'I've been seeing my staff, you know . . . telling them . . .'

'How d'you do,' said Fielding, smiling at Liz with appreciation. He was younger than his employer – in his forties, perhaps, with a fashionable bristly shadow round his mouth and chin, and straggling dark hair worn long enough to cover his ears. 'Bad business, the fire, eh?'

'Dreadful,' said Liz. 'And that's what we came to discuss with you, Mr Jerrold.'

'Yes. Too bad about . . . What was it we were going to make for you? Teddy, what was that project for Ms Peters?'

'The actors, wasn't it, Ken?'

'Oh yes. I remember. Teddy was quite interested in that, weren't you, Teddy?'

'Better than kittens and ruddy dolphins,' said Teddy with a shrug.

'That was inspired by your Chopin Collection,' Liz replied. 'Greg and I thought that was very attractive.'

'Yes, indeed,' Greg agreed, 'particularly for me because I'm in the music business.'

'Money in that,' Teddy rejoined, his eyes lighting up. 'What area – on disc, or offering for download?'

'Oh, Greg's an old fogey,' Liz cried. 'He collects vinyl!'

Teddy laughed, and so did Mr Jerrold, although he looked as if he wasn't quite following. He wasn't the kindly, affable man whom Liz had first encountered. His face had sagged, his skin was greyish.

'Yes, of course, vinyl,' Greg said, unoffended by the amusement. 'When it comes to someone like Chopin, pianists always make a richer sound on the old recordings.'

'I think you told me that a Mr Firstead had set the Chopin idea going,' Liz put in swiftly, intent on keeping the conversation on track.

'Er . . . Firstead . . . yes . . .' Jerrold was frowning. 'I won't be able to let him know that we're out of business, now will I? I haven't got a current address for him.'

His art department manager shook his head. 'Too bad if he

cancels out,' he remarked. 'I kind of enjoyed doing his stuff. But of course all my designs and dimensions went up in the fire.'

'Do you talk to him a lot about the collection?' Liz asked. 'I'd still like to go on with my project, but I wonder how much research I'll have to do, how much consultation you have to have with the designer.'

'Well, we *did* spend quite a bit of time together, I suppose, but only on his first visit. Let me see . . . It would be – what, Ken? – four years ago now?'

'What?' Ken asked, at a loss.

'Mr Firstead and the Chopin stuff. Four years ago?'

'Yes. Oh, yes – Mr Firstead. Liked the oval pendant a lot.'

'Right. But he had some wacky ideas too: he wanted to put music – I mean musical notes, on lines, like what a pianist would need –'

'A score,' Greg supplied.

'That's it, a score – not all of it, just a few lines. He wanted that photographed on a sort of beige background, to look old, you know, and then put in a frame like a photograph. I told him it would never sell and we had a bit of an argument. Said if he put a signature on it, it would sell.'

'Chopin's signature?'

'I suppose so. But I made him see sense, so he gave that up. But some of the other things were pretty. I think he did quite well out of it.'

'The pendant with the portrait – that was a good idea,' Liz prompted. 'That was Mr Firstead's idea.'

'Oh, yeah, that was really funny. He went on quite a bit about which portrait to use, and of course me – I'd never seen a portrait of Chopin in my life. I sketched what I thought was him but it turned out it was somebody else I'd seen – Wagner, I think.'

Greg laughed.

'There you are: you can see how clueless I was,' cried Teddy, enjoying his role of raconteur. 'So in the end, to get the right sort of look, what I did was, I sketched an oval frame like the pendant, and then sketched Firstead himself in the frame. He saw how good it would look and placed quite a decent order.'

'You sketched Mr Firstead himself?'

'Yeah, yeah; quite a nice-looking guy – can't recall the details but elegant, you know: good cologne and stuff. Only a quick

black-and-white sketch, but I thought it went well.' He sighed.
'That's gone up in smoke like everything else.'

Greg and Liz exchanged a glance. It seemed to them that
they'd just heard the reason for the fire at Keepsake Curios.

Madge Jerrold came trotting in bearing a tray with fresh tea,
cups, saucers and little cakes from a commercial packet. 'Here
we are,' she said with cheerful briskness. 'Sorry it took so long.
Running out of goodies, we've had so many visitors.' She sat
down to busy herself with pouring tea.

'Did you get the feeling that Mr Firstead was a musician
himself?' Greg asked. 'A pianist, for instance?'

Teddy was acting as waiter, handing round the plate of cakes.
'Um-m, I don't recall . . . I know he was very keen to buy my
sketch from me, which I suppose might have been useful to him
for publicity, you know, if he was out there performing on the
black-and-whites.'

'But you didn't sell it to him?'

'No way. It was a nice piece of work. I might have exhib-
ited it one day if I ever really began to do any serious work.'

'But if you were thinking of it as a good piece of work, surely
you took it home with you?' Greg urged.

'Nah,' said Teddy, sitting down and biting into his iced cake;
'I had a load of stuff like that there in the desk – all gone.'

'Could you do it again?' Greg suggested.

'What?'

'The sketch. Could you do it again, from memory?'

'Why on earth should I?'

'So that I could get an idea what my actors will look like,'
Liz put in hastily. 'For the oval pendant; I'm thinking of Robert
Donat, for instance.

'Never heard of him. But if you get me a photograph, I
can soon give you an idea what he'd look like in an oval
pendant.'

'It's a shame you don't still have Mr Firstead . . .'

'Oh, Mr Firstead,' said Madge Jerrold unexpectedly. 'I
remember you mentioning him, Ken. A nice, regular customer.
He'll come back once you've set up in a new place, dear.'

Her husband shook his head. 'No way to let him know where
I've gone. That's if I ever do start up again.'

'Oh, he'll get in touch, dear. I remember you said he was like
a faithful friend.'

'I wish I had the chance to meet him,' Liz sighed. 'He's made a success of the kind of thing I'm planning.'

'Don't know that he'd be all that willing to help,' said Teddy, musing over his memories. 'Kind of guarded about himself, I thought. He talked quite a bit about Chopin, seemed to be in the know about him – something about his family having some sort of connection with him.'

'With Chopin?' Greg exclaimed, astonished.

Teddy met his startled glance. 'Well, yeah. Seems to me that's what he said. Somebody – his grandfather or great-grandfather or somebody – met him. Could have, couldn't he? Chopin was what – nineteen hundreds?'

Greg was so astounded he was left speechless. Mrs Jerrold said, 'How interesting! Actually met him, did he?' To her husband she said coaxingly, 'You never told me that, dear.'

'What? Who're we talking about?'

'Chopin – Mr Firstead had a relative who met him, Teddy is saying.'

'Well, that's what he said,' warned Teddy. 'Folk say all kinds of things. Mind you, it seemed true enough at the time. I mean, he wasn't claiming this relative was up there with Chopin – not a player or a singer or anything. I think he said he was a servant or something. Looked after him.'

'Looked after Frederic Chopin?'

Teddy was puzzled by the intense interest he'd evoked. 'Good heavens, I don't remember it exactly. I just seem to think he said he was doing this Chopin line of trinkets because there was a family connection, and the guy had been very ill on a sea trip and this relative had held his hand or mopped his brow or something.'

'And the piece of music Firstead showed you . . .?' Greg said now.

'What about it?'

'Did he say that . . . Did he claim that it had been given to him?'

Teddy shook his head. 'Don't think so. No. He just showed it to me, and we discussed it, and I said it was a no-go.'

'Did it look old?'

'Old?'

'You said he wanted to put it in a frame, printed on dark paper. Was the original worn-looking – might it have been Victorian?'

'Don't recall. Well, maybe. Look here, this was years ago when he was telling me this. And the only reason I was interested was because I was going to have to do the artwork for his collection.'

'It's a fascinating story,' Liz put in as if thrilled. 'I do wish I could meet him!' She sipped tea so as to make a pause and cool down the situation, then went on: 'So we'll just hope he gets in touch in the near future, won't we, Mr Jerrold?'

'Oh, of course, of course.'

'So did you get the impression he's a local man, Teddy?' she asked, turning again to him.

He smiled at her. He was happy that she found him interesting. 'You're really keen to get his advice, aren't you? Wish I could help you, darling, but all I can say is he talked a bit about Chopin, and he wanted a better line of goods than most of our customers. He liked the sketch I made of him, which shows he had good taste, eh?' He thought it over. 'If it's any help, I got the impression he . . . well, he had a good opinion of himself. Dapper, if you know what I mean. Spent more on his appearance than I do!' He grinned, rubbing a hand on his bristly jaw.

'Oh yes, I remember you mentioning that!' cried Mrs Jerrold, touching her husband's hand. 'Quite fastidious, you said. Do you remember that, dear?'

'What?'

'About Mr Firstead. Ms Peters is interested. You and Teddy thought him a cut above some of the other clientele.'

'Mr Firstead?' Her husband shook his head. 'No way to get in touch with him, you know, dear.'

She tried to keep smiling despite his total lack of comprehension. Teddy said quickly, to cover up the non sequitur, 'He'll turn up, all handsome and elegant and smelling of roses. And we'll ask him where he gets his hair cut.'

'Oh yes,' agreed Kenneth Jerrold, at a loss. He fidgeted with his teacup then remarked, 'Excellent references. You can be sure I'll give you an excellent reference when you apply for a new job, Teddy.'

Mrs Jerrold stifled a sob and turned away her head. Teddy said in a comforting tone, 'I'm not worried, Ken. And don't you fret: everybody else will find a niche somewhere with the summer season coming on.'

Liz rose. 'Thank you very much for all your help, Mr Jerrold. You've been very kind.'

Greg got up too as their hostess prepared to usher them out. At the front door she said, 'The doctor says it's just post-traumatic shock. He'll be more himself in a day or two.'

'Of course. I hope we haven't made things worse for him.'

'Not at all, not at all; anything that gets him to talk is good. Hope to see you again when the outlook's a bit brighter.'

In the car, Liz covered her face with her hands and shook her head. 'I feel awful. Poor man!'

'Firstead did that to him,' Greg replied. There was a bleakness in his voice.

She leaned against his shoulder for comfort. 'We're fairly sure of that now, aren't we? – that Firstead burned down Keepsake Curios?'

'The sketch – that was the thing that made him do it.'

'I feel that must be true.' She straightened, patted at her hair, wriggled her shoulders to pull herself together. 'But are we any closer to him? He's like one of those insects that disguise themselves on a twig: we just can't get a look at him.'

'Dapper. What does that mean, Liz? It's a new word for me.'

'Ah.' She tried to find a few synonyms. 'Well turned out –'

'Turned out of what?'

'Neat, rather finicky – Beau Brummell – have you heard of him? I think he was "dapper". He was famous for his clothes and his good manners.'

'Ah well, if he was a *beau*, I understand. So we think Mr Firstead is a beau, and therefore we're looking for a handsome man.'

'And somehow . . . not burly, not a galumphing sort of man.'

He looked at her with enjoyment. 'What a wonderful language! Three extraordinary words in two sentences – "dapper", "finicky", "galumphing" – and it all helps to build up an idea of this elusive man.'

'Slinky the Shadow,' she sighed.

He started the car and made his way carefully out of the drive on to the busy road. The rush hour was under way. There was a pause while he slid into the traffic stream. Then he said, 'Hampton is Firstead – I think we can take that as almost certain. Now we have to ask ourselves the question: is Hampton also Marty Quinn? Is the man we're looking for a piano-playing fan of Frederic Chopin who makes an uncertain living playing in nightclubs?'

'If only Mr Fielding had kept that sketch!'

'Well, there's still another chance to find out what he looks like. Constable Tyrrell got photographs of Marty Quinn from Crayshaw.'

They agreed they ought to report to Chief Inspector Valmouth. Liz made the call. They were invited to come straight to the divisional office in Dover.

Mr Valmouth listened with attention to their story. He nodded several times as they were bringing it to a close. 'I agree with you: I think it's a pretty safe guess that it's Firstead who is responsible for the fire.' He smiled a little. 'Scared, wasn't he? Saw you in the Cellar Club, cottoned on to the fact that you were getting close and decided to destroy the best piece of evidence we might have got.'

'But he doesn't know you *have* got something: the pictures from Mr Crayshaw.'

'Here they are,' he responded, opening the file on his desk. He produced a couple of glossy prints.

Greg took them, Liz leaning close to examine them. He sighed. As Angela Tyrrell had predicted: they weren't much use. Chérie Chanteuse was shown in all her glory, long, sequined gown clinging to her body all the way down to the frills at her ankles. Her head was slightly turned, one hand outstretched towards her accompanist. He was shown off to the side, hunched over the keyboard, hands clearly playing a very heavy and sustained chord. This had been their good-night to their audience, the artiste acknowledging the good work of her pianist.

'I've sent these on to Glaston in London,' said Valmouth. 'There might be something they can do – enhancement, that sort of thing; but Glaston wasn't optimistic.'

'Perhaps Mr Fielding could use these as a prompt to his memory? And redraw his sketch?'

'We'll give it a try.'

'I suppose he wouldn't be in danger?' Liz put in with a little shiver of nervousness. 'Because Mr Fielding once had a good look at Firstead?'

'Oh, that's pushing it a bit far,' said Valmouth. 'After all, Chummie burnt Keepsake Curios down when it was empty. And though he took a shot at you on the road in Scotland, it was an amateur attempt with a scatter-gun. He hasn't killed anyone.'

'Except Countess Zalfeda,' Greg said, with a sudden glint of anger.

'Yes. Of course. I didn't mean I was forgetting that.' Valmouth was vexed at himself. 'That's if it's the same man.'

'It seems very probable that Charles Hampton of the original fraud and Firstead of the little tax-evasion scheme are one and the same – don't you think?'

'Well . . .'

'And that Firstead is also Quinn.'

'No, that doesn't follow.'

'Quinn and Firstead are either one and the same man, or Quinn is an accomplice,' Liz insisted. 'Because it's after we were noticed by Quinn that the fire happened in the business park. Either they're the same man or they're connected.'

'An accomplice – why not? Somebody had to forge the fake mazurka and probably produce that paperback you bought, about the romance between Chopin and the Scottish lady. And since Quinn's a pianist, he's the likely man to know how to write the music.'

Greg was looking unconvinced. 'I can believe Hampton had other people involved. There were quite a few selling his trinkets and making a little bit of money. But forging a piece of Victorian manuscript is different. And in any case, the *one* accomplice we're pretty sure of who's taken part in the big fraud is the person that collected the money for him – and that was a woman he's left far behind him in London. I think he's inclined to be *immer einsam* – on his own – you have a word for that.'

'A loner.'

'Yes. And therefore I think he acts alone, playing the part of these three men, one after the other. Hampton in London, Firstead when he gives his orders at Keepsake Curios, Marty Quinn when he goes back to his everyday life.'

'But he's got fifty thousand pounds stashed away somewhere now, Mr Crowne. Why is he hanging about here?'

When Greg replied, it was slowly and with caution, thinking it out as he spoke. 'This was at first a money-making scheme. When he had to kill Marzelina in the museum, he became very scared. He felt he had to lie close – no, I mean, lie low. He was going to acquire this big sum of money, and –' He broke off.

'What?' Valmouth prompted.

'Fifty thousand is not a very big sum of money, really,' Greg reflected. 'He could have asked for much more. So don't you think he is not a very expert criminal?'

'Well, Glaston tells me he could have asked for millions, if that manuscript had been genuine,' Valmouth agreed. 'But if he's the kind of guy that thinks he asked for a fortune, why isn't he off somewhere safe, doing something with it? – living the high life on the Costa del Cash?'

'I think . . . Perhaps because he wanted to do something with it *here*. Or perhaps he wanted to use the same trick again and earn more money, and he has this scheme which he knows how to work from *here*.'

'There's a reason,' Liz put in, frowning at their bemusement. 'If we ever catch up with him, we'll find out what it is.'

'One thing we could do,' he suggested. 'We could show the photographs of the pianist to a friend of mine, if you permit, Mr Valmouth.'

'Oh? Who's that? Someone reliable?'

Greg explained about Rodrigue Selbige, the choirmaster. Liz had recovered her spirits enough to smile at the fact that Greg didn't mention the harp-playing. Valmouth shrugged agreement and produced an envelope for the photographs.

It was now after six. M. Selbige, when contacted, said he'd be delighted to look at the photographs and, as it happened, was coming to Dover. 'I conduct my choir in a rehearsal at the Connaught Hall,' he announced with some pride. 'You know, that is part of the Maison Dieu, in the town centre. So therefore it would be more convenient to you, if we meet there, no?'

'That would be excellent. What time, Rodrigue?'

'Let us say eight? My singers and I, we will start work at seven, and after an hour it is good to have a break and discuss the improvements needed. There's a coffee bar where we could sit for a few moments.'

That allowed time for them to eat. They were both ravenous by now, so they rushed back to the Collinet to shower and change. A wine bar with a good menu provided a quick meal; they were able to walk to the Maison Dieu at a leisurely stroll. The entrance to the concert hall was under the clock, but they were guided by the sound of soft harmonies, rising and falling like gentle waves on a seashore.

'What's that?' Liz, asked in a whisper, catching Greg's sleeve.

'That's one of the choruses from *The Blessed Damozel*, if I'm not mistaken.'

'It's kind of weird!' She shivered a little although her padded jacket was good protection against the chill of the building.

'Debussy is kind of weird,' he agreed. 'They're still rehearsing, so let's just wait here.'

They sat on a bench in the passage. They heard the choir halt and start again, then again, then at last bring the music to a long, fading close.

'Gee,' said Liz. She didn't say she was glad it was over, but he grinned and squeezed her hand. Their taste in music was never going to coincide: she liked Nerina Pallet; he liked Jessye Norman.

There were sounds of chairs scraping, some discussion, then footsteps as the singers drifted out of the hall in search of refreshments. They paid no heed to the two on the bench, thinking they'd probably come for the political meeting in the council chamber on the other side of the building.

M. Selbige appeared, flexing his arms. 'Alas, I always grow tense at the subtleties of Debussy,' he said, smiling at them. 'What did you think, my friend? A good sound?'

'Not bad, although you need a few more tenors.'

'Tenors – ah, they are hard to come by!' He led the way to the coffee bar, where one of his choristers was acting as server. Seeing him arrive, one of the singers quickly found a tray, put three plastic beakers on it and brought it to the table they'd chosen. 'Thank you, Stanley. My friend Greg says you are being drowned out by the sopranos.'

Stanley smiled and nodded in agreement, then left.

Liz sat by, sipping her coffee, while Greg and Rodrigue Selbige exchanged incomprehensible remarks about the cantata that was being studied. Sensing at last that she was being ignored, Selbige directed a glance of apology at her. 'You did not come here, mademoiselle, to hear this chit-chat. Something about photographs, was it not?'

She produced them from her big shoulder bag. 'You know we were asking about pianists, Mr Selbige. Do you happen to know the name of the man at the piano in these pictures?'

He took them, put them side by side on the table. He pulled at his bony chin. 'These were taken some time ago?' he suggested.

'Er . . . We don't know that, I'm afraid. They came from the publicity album of the performer on the dais.'

'A very elegant lady,' said Selbige. 'She's a singer? Strange that I don't know her.'

'She's a nightclub performer,' said Greg, feeling disinclined to explain that the lady was no lady.

'Oh, I understand. Yes, of course; poor Daniel – he had to take what he could get.'

'Daniel?'

'Daniel Dushke, I think it is. Not a very good photograph, but his posture at the piano was always bad.'

'Daniel Dushke? 'Liz repeated, on a sigh of confusion. 'We understood the pianist was a man called Marty Quinn.'

Selbige picked up the better of the two pictures and held it about twelve inches from his nose. He peered at it. 'He and I were not close in any way, but I'm confident it is he. He played for me at rehearsal three or four times, but he was always very careless over tempo, and of course you can tell by this ' – he slapped the photograph down on the table – 'he used to hunch over the keyboard in a way that showed he had not been well taught. I'm not surprised that he took engagements in night-clubs, not at all.'

'You said "used to", monsieur,' Liz urged. 'He isn't in the neighbourhood any more?'

'My dear lady, he is in heaven, I hope. He died – let me see – I think it was two years ago.'

'Died!'

'Oh yes. Life was not kind to him: he nearly starved getting out of – where was it now? – Romania? Bosnia?'

'He was a refugee?'

'At some point in his life, yes, he had to make his escape from his homeland, and the hardships of that . . . His health was very poor and he made such a small income from his playing. I think in the end he was perhaps taken by some form of pneumonia.'

'Are you sure this is Daniel Dushke?' Liz insisted.

'Oh, yes. No one else ever crouched at the keyboard in that fashion, my dear.'

And since he'd been dead two years, he certainly hadn't been playing for Chérie Chanteuse on Saturday night at the Cellar Club.

Seventeen

M r. Selbige bustled off to start work again with his choir. They heard the piano give the chord, then the unaccompanied voices striking up with some uncertainty. Liz said, 'Let's get out of here.'

Under a lamp outside in the street they paused to look again at the photographs.

'We should have known,' Greg muttered. 'Dapper, finicky – all those words to describe him, and we accept this photograph of a man in a wrinkled old evening jacket?'

She could only nod and sigh in agreement. They started back towards their hotel, disheartened and tired after a day of shocks.

En route Greg paused. 'We should show these photographs to the entertainment arranger at the Greenthorpe.'

'Oh yes, let's!' Anything to counteract the disappointment of failing.

At the desk in the Greenthorpe Hotel they asked for the entertainments manager. This was greeted with some incomprehension. 'Ronald someone,' Liz prompted. 'We spoke to him yesterday.'

'Oh, Mr Gillimore. He's the undermanager. Just a moment, sir; I think he's gone off duty.' He pressed buttons on his desk phone, looking surprised when the call was answered. 'Ronald, there's a lady here asking to speak to you.' After a pause he turned to Liz. 'What's it in connection with, madam?'

'It's not a complaint,' she reassured him. 'I just want to ask about Chérie Chanteuse again.'

When this had been passed on, the clerk offered her the phone. 'Can I help you?' Mr Gillimore asked stiffly, clearly very vexed.

'Mr Gillimore – Ronald, isn't it? – you remember I was asking about Chérie Chanteuse and his pianist. Could you spare just a minute to look at a couple of photographs?'

'I'm on my way out. I'm in rather a hurry.'

'Where are you – in your office?'

'I'm in the garage just about to drive out!' It was a snort of irritation.

'Righto, then, we'll meet you there – just hang on ten seconds, will you?'

She handed back the phone with a bright smile then turned swiftly to Greg. 'Garage. He's on his way to a heavy date, I think, so come on!'

They followed the signs to the garage, where they found Ronald Gillimore sitting in a silver Ford with the door ajar. Liz swung her handbag round to fetch out the photographs. 'Can you tell us the name of this pianist?' she asked, offering them.

He leaned out to look. He shrugged. 'Don't know.'

'We got these from Harry Crayshaw, who told us this was the man who was playing on Saturday evening. But that's incorrect –'

'I told you, I hardly ever meet the guys who back up the acts.' He peered at the photographs. 'That's the Cellar Bar, right enough – I can tell by the background though it's not a good shot. But I think it's from a while ago – those look like the old screens and we've changed to a more orangey shade now.'

'Thank you,' Liz said, retrieving the photos. 'Have a nice evening.'

He nodded, smiled in relief at getting away and closed the car door.

Liz and Greg went up in the lift to the main floor. Once there, they sat down in the lobby to look again at the photographs.

Greg said, 'Crayshaw handed over these pictures to Tyrrell when he must have known they don't show Marty Quinn.'

'They're not good pictures. Perhaps his eyesight is bad?'

He gave a grunt of derision.

'Well, then, the next thought is that he doesn't want us to find Marty Quinn.'

'That's the one I favour. Though I'm not sure why.' He tapped the photographs. 'If Marty Quinn and Firstead are one and the same, then he's nothing like this untidy character. He's "dapper" and "good-looking".'

'And the reason Harry Crayshaw doesn't want to help us find him is because . . . because he doesn't know anything about his criminal side. He thinks he's got marriage and money problems.'

'I think we need to have a word with Mr Crayshaw.'

'You bet.'

They went back to their hotel, where Greg sent a message to the divisional office so as to keep Mr Valmouth informed. The night sergeant noted it down, grunting a little in disapproval at their actions.

Liz used the equipment in the hotel room to make tea for herself. Greg found a bottle of Evian in the fridge. It was now getting on towards ten o'clock. The Colinet was the kind of place that went very quiet around this hour of the night. They sat by the bureau, feeling isolated in a world of perplexities.

'Keepsake Curios was set alight to get rid of the sketch of Mr Firstead,' said Greg. 'You agree with that?'

'Yes, I do.'

'Firstead had a reason to do it that had come to his notice recently. He never tried to burn it down before.'

'No, he didn't.'

'So something happened recently that startled him.'

'"Marty Quinn" saw us on Saturday night and told him.'

'But "Firstead" didn't do anything on Saturday night –'

'But perhaps Quinn *is* a separate person – a pal – but couldn't get in touch with him on Saturday night, Greg. Nor on Sunday. It was only yesterday – Monday – that he was able to contact him.'

Greg considered the suggestion. 'Does that mean that Firstead is not, after all, a local man?'

'Don't say that!'

'Let's put aside the Greenthorpe for the moment. Let's say Firstead *is* a local man. He ordered his goods from a local firm; he chose names from around here for the fictitious firm that published and printed the book about the romance.'

'Well, yes, I still think that holds good. So perhaps he doesn't need help from the Marty Quinn guy – perhaps he got some hint somehow that we were getting interested in Keepsake Curios – perhaps he saw Tyrrell and me when we went there.'

'But that implies that Firstead's been close to us ever since he found out who we were from your stolen handbag in Edinburgh.'

She shivered. 'I hate that idea!'

They were interrupted in their discussion by the ringing of Liz's mobile. The client who was expecting a design for a spencer wanted a progress report. He was spending a late-night session at his office catching up with outstanding projects and was very annoyed. She made excuses, promised progress, then sat down with her laptop to do some work. Greg decided to make contact with the computer at his office in Geneva. They were busy for an hour or so and then, very weary, called it a day.

Liz went for a morning run. Greg got up by and by, made himself a life-saving cup of instant coffee, then sat down in his dressing gown to list things to do today.

They were somewhat delayed in making a start, led astray by the delightful idea of sharing the shower; but over breakfast they made the decision to go first to Harry Crayshaw, and then plan what should come next.

'We ought to let the chief inspector know,' Liz suggested.

'Ye-es . . . but he'll only send Constable Tyrrell with us, and she's such a *compadre* of his she's likely to . . .'

'Shy away from calling him a liar.'

'Yes, that's what I was thinking. Because, he *is* a liar, isn't he, Liz? He must have known perfectly well that those were not photographs of Marty Quinn.'

'So what's our attitude? Are we going to give him a call to say we're coming? Or turn up and give him a surprise?'

'I vote for the surprise method.'

'Me too. I've met a lot of chaps like Harry in the fashion world – great at their own thing but a bit unwilling to play their part in the real world. He needs a jolt to get him to pay proper attention.'

'So we'll go and explain to him that he's not allowed to muddle things up under the illusion he's helping an old friend. This situation is too serious for – you have a very good phrase in English – giving help and support to friends?'

'The Old Pals Act.'

'Marvellous,' Greg said, grinning in appreciation.

It was still not much after nine o'clock of a bright April morning when they drove into the lane. Greg parked the car in an area scooped out of the hedgerow a little beyond the row of cottages.

There was no reply when they knocked the hammer-shaped knocker at Martel Cottage. They knocked again, waited; but there was no sign of life.

Liz led the way to a side entrance at the end of the row. She knew something of the lifestyle from childhood holidays spent in the country. In days gone by, home owners would often hang a sign on their front doors telling callers where to find them – 'Out the back' or 'In my garden' in brown pokerwork on a strip of varnished pine. But nowadays that was too much like an invitation to walk-in thieves.

There was a narrow path along the back boundary of the rear gardens. Most of the cottages had built extensions to house an extra room and a modern kitchen, from which sounds of activity could be heard – radios playing, the clink of washing-up.

From Martel Cottage there was no sound. Next door a very elderly man was tying knots in the withering leaves of his daffodils.

'Good morning,' called Liz.

'Morning.' He straightened, a hand in the small of his back. 'Not a bad day.' He moved away from the flower bed with relief, coming to talk to them over his burgeoning beech hedge.

'You're out early,' said Liz.

'Oh, my, this isn't early for me! Up with the sun, I am.' He was smiling at her from a face that had seen many years of early-morning sun. White stubble clothed his cheeks and chin, but the hair on his head was sparse. 'Looking for someone?' he asked.

'Mr Crayshaw?' Liz said.

'Oh, him.' He took a pipe out of the pocket of his worn cardigan and without filling it put it in his mouth. 'He's not home yet. Off last night on one of his big showbiz occasions.'

'That's why we want to talk to him,' she said. 'There's a problem with one of his shows at the weekend.'

'Oh yes, at the Greenthorpe. Very *prestigious*.'

Greg laughed. 'You know all about it!'

'My Lord, do I not! Me and the wife, we have to listen to every detail. The Greenthorpe was a triumph – wild applause: he's sure to get a return engagement during the summer.'

'And his accompanist was perfect,' Greg added.

'Eh? No-o, can't say Sherry Shantoose is very free with compliments to anybody else.' He took the pipe out of his mouth and studied it a moment with a critical gaze.

'We wanted to talk to him about his accompanist,' Liz took it up. 'Marty Quinn? Do you know him at all?'

'Not me. He keeps showing us new batches of publicity stuff, but I don't recall him ever talking about any of the pianists.'

'But he told you everything went well at the Greenthorpe?' Greg enquired. 'The pianist didn't lose his place or seem startled?'

The gardener looked at Greg with interest, as if he rather wished something like that had happened. He pulled on the empty pipe.

'Um-m. He didn't talk as much as usual about that show, now I come to think about it. There was a bit of a problem, but it was with the fastening of his "evening gown" – took it off in too much of a hurry.' There was undisguised scorn in his tone. 'And what do you think – he's probably going to ask my wife to mend it for him.'

Liz couldn't help being intrigued. Clothes were always of interest to her, and especially anything in women's wear made for a man. 'Does he have a dresser? That thing he was wearing on Saturday night – it practically needed a shoe-horn to get into it.'

He shook his head. 'It'll be a while before he can afford a dresser, although he's been at it three or four years now. He's always calling on Alison to mend a zip, or put a stitch in where he's pulled off a glittery bit. Poor Ally, she hates it – those clothes all smell of make-up and vanishing cream . . .'

'It's very good of her to do it,' Liz sympathized. She knew what clothes were like after a fashion show. 'I suppose he has a stage dressmaker?'

'Somebody in London. We always get a fashion show when he brings a new one back – costs the earth, I should think. But there, Harry's always been one to spend money on himself. Good clothes even offstage – when he was on the ferries, he always used to stock up on good brandy and aftershave and silk ties.' He gave a rueful smile. 'We used to be glad of the duty-free brandy and cigarettes, so we can't complain now that he's got stage-struck.'

'What time is he likely to be home?' she asked, getting back to the nitty-gritty.

'Who knows? Guildford, it was, last night. He's got a bit of a fan club there, though why anyone . . .' He let the sentence die away. 'Shall I tell him you were asking for him?'

'No, we'll give him a ring later,' Liz said rather hastily. 'Thank you very much; we'll let you get back to your daffodils.'

'Yeah,' he said without enthusiasm, and moved away from his beech hedge.

When they got back to the car, they had a debate.

'Should we hang about in case he comes home soon?' Greg suggested.

'Oh, duckie, if he was on at a club in Guildford he probably didn't get to bed until the wee small hours. And then he's got to get himself up and have breakfast and pack away his props . . .'

'Props?'

'His evening gown and wigs and fan and the piano score for his accompanist. And then he has to drive back.' She paused. 'Guildford isn't really all that far, Greg. What if the accompanist there is the famous Marty Quinn?'

He leaned on the roof of the car and groaned. 'Please don't say things like that. Marty Quinn is beginning to haunt my dreams. We hear about him, but we never catch up to him, like *Reinike Fuchs*.'

'Who's he?'

'The sly old fox. In the fables.'

'This guy is more than a fable, as you well know, chum.' She got into the car.

'Where are we going?' he enquired. 'Back to Dover?'

'Oh, Lord!' She considered, fair head on one side. 'No offence to that delightful town, but I've had enough of it for the time being.'

'Well, we could drive on to Canterbury.'

'Cathedral-visiting?' Her tone told him that was not her idea of fun.

'I could go to the cathedral. You could go to the shopping precinct.'

'Ah. That sounds like a plan.'

'But first we have to inform Chief Inspector Valmouth that we're going there.'

'Oh, bother Chief Inspector Valmouth!' But she sat quietly while he tapped buttons on his mobile.

The call was answered by Mapley, the sergeant who had driven the chief inspector to the fire scene the previous morning. 'The guv'nor's in a meeting with the top brass at the moment, sir. Can I take a message?'

'I just wanted to say that Ms Blair and I are at Martel Cottage. We were hoping to speak to Mr Crayshaw . . .'

'Mr Crayshaw – really? Why was that, sir?'

'Because the photographs he gave to Constable Tyrrell were *not* of Marty Quinn. A friend of mine told us last night that the man in those photographs is called Daniel Dushke and he's been dead for some time.'

'What name was that, again?' the sergeant asked.

'I think you already have that. I left a message last night.'

There followed ten minutes of spelling out names and explaining why they mattered. 'I'll pass this on to Mr Valmouth,' said the sergeant. 'Not urgent, is it?'

'I suppose it is not.'

'Because you see, we're having a visit to the town hall from a big noise on Friday and we've got to lay on security, so there's a lot of hoo-ha going on. He might be tied up for quite a while.'

'I understand.' Of course he understood. He often had to be a minor guest at such occasions – a marriage, christening or funeral of some distantly related royal, usually. 'It's just that Mr Valmouth asked me to keep in touch.'

'I'll pass it on, sir.'

Duty done, they set off for Canterbury. Mr Crowne had suggested it because it gave him the chance to look at the cathedral's western crypt. He had a group of instrumentalists due to perform there during the Canterbury Festival in October.

The city was a place where the fashion business had never so far taken Liz. She launched herself upon this unknown shopping area like Columbus setting out for the New World.

When they met at last at the rendezvous for lunch, she was carrying shopping bags with the logo of at least four famous firms. She'd found a shop selling fabrics that might be suitable for the making of the as-yet-mythical spencer and, of course, had invested in a few goodies for herself.

'I've been thinking,' she remarked as they ate lunch in a handy vegetarian restaurant. 'It was looking at the clothes in the department store that put it into my mind. You know Crayshaw's neighbour talked about his stage outfits being made in London . . .'

'The spangled dresses. Yes?'

'And said, quite rightly, that they probably cost a fortune.'

'I accept your judgement on that.'

'Well, I'm sure he couldn't buy that kind of thing from an ordinary dressmaker. There must be specialists who make them – part of a sort of in-group that know a lot about each other.

There are probably agents who arrange the bookings, and perhaps put them together with a band if they need one.'

'Or with an accompanist.'

'Yes, that's what I was thinking.'

'You think that Mr Glaston should be making enquiries among that group in London to see if he can find Marty Quinn among the available pianists.'

'Worth a try,' she suggested.

'Perhaps. I don't know. It's what you would call a long shot, isn't it?'

'But why not? Harry Crashaw keeps on being unwilling to help where Marty Quinn is concerned. I get the impression they're great pals.'

They ate for some time in silence. Then Greg said, 'We'll go back to the cottage after lunch, to try Mr Crayshaw once more. If he continues to be unco-operative, I'll ring Mr Glaston and suggest the London circle of *travestimenti*, if you really think it exists.'

'Of course it exists,' she scolded. 'Do you think I don't know the rag trade? There are makers of kinky shoes, and super-sexy undies – there's sure to be a band of dressmakers for drag artists.'

The sun was sending out its full afternoon warmth when they drew up again in the parking area beyond Martel Cottage. They knocked once more at the cottage door, and again without success. An elderly lady was next door, putting pots of geraniums on her window sill.

She turned to them, smiling. 'Are you the young people who were here this morning asking for Harry?'

'Yes; this is Greg, I'm Liz,' said Liz, at once making friends.

'How do you do; I'm Jim's wife, Allison.'

'I take it Harry's not come home yet.'

'As a matter of fact, he arrived a little while ago, full of himself, sharing out a box of chocs given to him by an admirer, would you believe! But later he all of a sudden said he had something important to look after and went rushing off again.'

She saw their look of weary defeat and went on sympathetically: 'I'm sorry. I did mention you were asking for him, but to tell the truth, he didn't seem pleased.'

Greg intervened at once. 'How did it come about? He told you he had to leave again and then you said, "There were people here asking for you", or the reverse?'

'Sorry?'

'Did he leave *after* you told him we'd been here?' Liz interpreted in her easy-going tones.

'Yes. Yes, as a matter of fact he did.'

'Ah!' said Greg. 'When did he leave?'

She looked perplexed, then pushed her front door open to call, 'Jim! Jim – could you come here a minute, pet?'

Jim appeared, drying his hands on a towel. 'Oh, hello; you've just missed him,' he said on seeing them.

'So your wife has just been telling us.'

'Yes, Jimmy, what time was it when Harry drove off?' asked his wife.

'Lemme see. We had to accept one of the chocolates from his box, but we said we didn't want to eat it because we were going to have lunch. So that would have been about one o'clock. Then when we were clearing the table he called across the back fence—'

'Yes, he had one of his dresses over his arm; he was going to ask me to mend something. He's *always* catching those high heels in the hem.'

'So that would have been about two,' Jim pondered. 'I'd say he took off about a quarter of an hour or so after that.'

Greg glanced at his watch. Nearly three.

'Have you any idea when he'll be back?' Liz asked.

Jim grimaced and shrugged. 'Not any time soon,' he said. 'He was dragging his big wheeled suitcase with him when he went out to his car, and when I asked him if he was off to a gig he said something about France.'

'France!'

'That's a nice step up for him,' said Alison. 'I don't think he's ever had any foreign engagements before.'

'Yeah, nice if it keeps up; it'll be like the old days, eh? Brandy for me, perfume for you, posh aftershave for him – duty free's less stingy than it used to be, old love.'

'Thank you,' said Greg, and steered Liz away. She was startled at his urgency.

They hurried to the car, got in, then he said, 'Everybody keeps mentioning his aftershave.'

'Do they?'

There was a long pause while Liz , puzzled, sat staring at Greg. Then he said, with emphatic recognition, 'It's him.'

'Who?'

'Charles Hampton.'

'Yes, Charles Hampton, we're trying to—'

'"He smell of nice soap."'

'Who?'

'*Charles Hampton!* It's what the woman in the letter shop said about him. "He smell of nice soap." That's right, isn't it?'

'Yes, it is, and so what?'

'Don't you remember? When we first came here to talk to Crayshaw, his living room was stuffy and very – what's the word I want? – odorous, I think.' He pinched at his nose. 'It was his aftershave. I remember I was glad to get out into the fresh air.'

'It *was* a bit whiffy but—'

'It's him: he's Charles Hampton *and* Mr Firstead *and* Marty Quinn – at least, wait!' He held up a hand to warn her to keep quiet. After a moment of startled thought he said, 'There isn't a Marty Quinn. Of course there isn't. He invented him to put us off the track.'

'Crayshaw invented him? But Greg, somebody had to play the piano for him at the Greenthorpe—'

He broke in impatiently. 'That was a Mr Anybody – he talked about a whole group of people that he could call up when he needed an accompanist: it was one of them. The man who played for him at the Greenthorpe was *not* a man called Marty Quinn.'

'But why – oh, just so we would go off on a wild goose chase?'

'That's why he supplied photographs of some man who is dead, to keep us wasting our time. *He's* the sly fox –' He broke off.

'You're going too fast for me, lovie.'

He hurried on, disregarding her. A new and devastating thought had come to him. 'It was *him* who went to the bank and posed as Marzelina to cash the letter of credit.'

'*What?*'

'In a wig and a dress – yes, he didn't need a woman accomplice; it's *him*, on his own – it's him all the time!'

Eighteen

Chief Inspector Valmouth needed to hear it twice. 'You're saying that Chummie has been using three different identities?'

'Two identities. Marty Quinn is a . . . a *testo di Turco* . . . a person you throw things at . . .'

'What?'

'At a fair.'

'Oh, an Aunt Sally. Marty Quinn is an Aunt Sally.'

'Exactly. An imaginary figure you waste time on. We have wasted time on him. But it hasn't prevented us from understanding the truth, Chief Inspector.'

'Huh!' grunted Valmouth. 'I put out a warning to watch for Crayshaw at the ferry docks because you seemed so determined about it, but really . . .' He directed a gaze of serious enquiry at Mr Crowne. 'Where's your evidence, sir?'

'I just explained . . .'

'Look here: I gather you've been involved in a couple of cases other than this. Scotland Yard speaks well of you. But you know we can't do anything unless we have grounds for it. You say that this bloke living here in Dover is the man who killed your friend the countess but . . . but . . .' He was embarrassed.

'You feel that a man from your community could not kill someone in London?'

'Well, you see, he's part of the neighbourhood – takes part in charity runs, acts in the shows of the amateur dramatic society. His family's been here for generations.'

'Yes!' cried Mr Crown on a note of triumph. 'You remind me! The manager of the art department at Keepsake Curios said the man he knew as Firstead talked about a grandfather – or was it a great-grandfather – who had looked after Frederic Chopin.'

'So what? Where does that fit in?'

'Chopin – the fraud was based on claiming to have a manuscript by Chopin. The *Crayshaws* have lived in Dover, as you say, for ever . . .'

'Yes, but Tyrrell knows him quite well and I don't recall she ever said any of his family was a servant to a man like Chopin.'

'On the ferry!' was the impatient reply. 'It's well known that Chopin was already very ill when he came to England in 1848. He had to come on the ferry – how else could he come?'

'Well, all right, yes . . .'

'And isn't it a fact that the Crayshaws have served on the ferries for generations?'

Valmouth put a hand up to his brow and rubbed it. 'Yes. I do remember that being said. But even so—'

'Crayshaw grows up in a family that has this story about looking after Chopin. Isn't that what stewards do on the ferry boats?'

'Well—'

'And Chopin was notorious for being seasick – he writes about it to his friends.'

'So OK – Crayshaw might have a reason for being interested in him and setting up a business. So you're saying he invented this identity: Firstead.' Valmouth wagged a finger. 'Why does he need a different identity?'

'To avoid VAT on his goods,' Liz put in at once, speaking up after a long silence. 'He started it all as a little swindle; then he got the idea of selling the music score of a missing mazurka. That gets him into the big time.'

'Fifty thousand pounds,' snorted Valmouth. 'That's hardly big time.'

'It is to him, Mr Valmouth,' she insisted. 'If you think about all this, it must come across to you that he's an amateur – don't you agree? That's why he panicked when he realized he'd strangled Marzelina with her scarf.'

'And then he scuttled out of London,' Greg added, 'tidying up the deliveries of his goods in Manchester and London. And perhaps thinking he could stay hidden and keep it all going as a business.'

They sat waiting for his reaction. Valmouth sighed. 'It makes a kind of sense. But I repeat: where's the evidence?'

'If you search his house?' Greg suggested. 'Something on his computer? The paperback book about the romance between

Chopin and Jane Stirling – we've thought about that quite a lot and we've come to the conclusion it's a – what's the term, Liz?'

'A desktop publication.'

'It might be there, waiting to be reprinted if it should be selling well.' Greg paused. 'And the fake manuscript might be there too.'

'Ah. If we found the manuscript! That would be something.' There was a pause of consideration. Looking a little less anxious he went on, 'I'll arrange for a warrant. And while we're in the house, we'll look for photographs of him to distribute around the docks. We can just detain him if we catch up with him. No need to bring a charge at the outset.'

'You'd look for pictures in his publicity collection? They will show him in his stage costume, surely.'

'He must have other snaps – Christmas, holidays. We certainly don't want any of him in his girlie get-up.'

Greg looked startled. 'Wait!'

'What?'

'When he left his cottage he told his neighbour he was heading for an engagement in France – and according to the neighbour, he was pulling the big suitcase in which he carries his stage clothes.'

'So what?'

'Chief Inspector, he has make-up and wigs, all sorts of props' – with a glance of acknowledgement at Liz for the word. 'We may be looking for Chérie Chanteuse, not Harry Crayshaw.'

The chief inspector was aghast. 'You're saying he may be *in drag*?'

'Why not?'

'But . . . but . . . OK, he's got long glitzy dresses, but street clothes? He surely never appears on stage in anything that he could wear outside!'

'He could go into any chain store and buy what he needs,' said Liz.

'But . . . but . . . He could never get away with it. I mean to say, a man done up in a long dance dress and make-up is pass-able, but in short skirts? His legs and big feet would give him away.'

'He could be wearing jeans and trainers.'

'But Ms Blair, if he wears jeans, then he looks like a man.'

'What, if he buys girlie jeans with a sequin pattern down

the front? And wears high-heeled boots and a girlie wig? He can look like a woman if he shaves close and wears daytime make-up.'

The chief inspector looked as if he wished the floor would open up and swallow him. After a long moment of grim thought he picked up his desk phone and made a call. His office door opened to admit Constable Angela Tyrrell.

'Tyrrell, is your old pal Chérie Chanteuse capable of carrying out his drag act in the light of day and out in the street?'

Tyrrell was amazed. She stiffened and only just managed not to reject the idea with loud denials. Instead she said, 'I don't know, guv.'

'When he does these plays and things with your theatre group, he plays the female roles?'

'Of course not. Only in the Christmas show. He always plays the Dame.'

Greg was struck by a thought. 'Didn't you say he was auditioning this week for a part in the summer play?'

Her unfriendly glance was telling him that she wished he'd never come into her circle of acquaintance. 'He wants to audition for the male lead,' she remarked with veiled insolence, '*not* for the soubrette.'

'Isn't it strange, then, that he's off to an engagement in France?'

'Oh, I think that's just a wrong steer, Mr Crowne.'

'It's what he told his neighbour . . .'

'What, old Jim Kennerley? He got it wrong.'

'It was you who said Mr Crayshaw's family had been in the ferry service for generations, wasn't it?' he went on, casting his mind back.

'What if they were?'

'Did he talk about their connection with Frederic Chopin?'

She shook her head. 'Chopin? He had enough on his hands learning the songs in the musicals, just like the rest of us.'

'He can read music?'

'Well . . . yes . . . we all can. Not sight-reading, of course, but in the end we learn our parts pretty well.'

'So he could write down a line or two of melody?'

'What do you mean? Copy it?' She looked very doubtful. 'I wouldn't think so. There's never any need: we get the music photocopied.'

Greg was thinking of the piece of manuscript that had been sent as a sample to Mme Wiaroz. He'd hoped that the forgery would be on Crayshaw's computer. Perhaps not, after all.

'You'll be going to make a search of Crayshaw's home,' instructed the chief inspector. 'Look out some photographs of him in ordinary clothes and a couple of him in his drag outfit.'

She looked mutinous but nodded acceptance.

'I'll send Landforth with you to examine the computer. Crayshaw *has* a computer?' he added.

'Of course he has. We send out all our rehearsal dates and things by email.'

'Right, I want that looked at and if there's anything about Chopin on it, I want it brought to the lab for investigation.'

'Yes, sir.'

His tone made her understand that her promotion prospects had suffered a severe setback owing to her friendship with Harry Crayshaw. She was much less sure of herself as she went out.

The chief inspector was now quite anxious to get rid of Greg and Liz. There had been plenty on his desk before, and there was a lot more now. As they were leaving, Greg ventured to ask, 'You say you sent out an alert at the docks – any results so far?'

'Hardly,' was the terse reply.

'And the French police – they'll be keeping watch for him?'

'Of course.' The chief inspector let it be seen that he was not pleased. This pair had presented him with a culprit who fitted all the hints they had collected, but in his opinion they had scared him off by actually going to his home. All the same, he was going to keep watch for Crayshaw at all the exits leading to France – though, of course, Crayshaw might not have any real intention of going to France.

'We should have told him we were going to Crayshaw's house,' mourned Liz as they emerged into the uproar of the city centre at home-going time. 'He's peeved at us.'

'Yes, you're right. But then you would never have got Mr Kennerley to speak to you so willingly, because we would have had a policeman with us.'

'Tyrrell is furious.'

'Tyrrell knows she made a big mistake from the outset in refusing to think of Crayshaw as a criminal.'

They walked back to the Collinet. It would soon be time for

dinner. They decided to do some catching-up with their personal affairs then think about where to eat.

Greg rang Mme Wiaroz. The telephone was answered by Céleste Plagiet. 'Ah, Monsieur Couronne! Excellent to hear from you, but this time, I hope with good news for Madame?'

'I think she will be pleased, Céleste. May I speak to her?'

'One moment.'

The instrument was passed on. 'Monsieur Couronne?' quavered the old lady. 'Céleste is smiling so I hope this is not going to depress me!'

'This is a progress report, madame. I believe we are close on the heels of Charles Hampton.'

'Ah!' It was an exclamation full of emotion. 'He will be arrested?'

'We hope so, in the not-too-distant future. We are in Dover now, Mademoiselle Blair and I. The police are watching for the man at the entrances to the ferry service.'

'He is leaving the country?'

'We believe so. The Calais force has also been alerted to look out for him under the various names he has adopted. His real name, we believe, is Harry Crayshaw, an actor.' He refrained from telling her that the man who had killed Marzelina was a comic turn.

There was some slight commotion at the Paris end of the line. Céleste came back on. 'Madame is in tears,' she reported gently, 'but they are tears of joy, monsieur.'

He was alarmed that the old lady might have read too much into his remarks. After all, Crayshaw was still at large. He said to Céleste, 'Please tell her that there is still some way to go before the man is brought to justice, mademoiselle. But the police are now fully in action with data that should help to catch him.'

'Yes, yes, I will tell her. Thank you, Monsieur Couronne, but I must break off now, because Madame needs a little care and attention.' She hung up abruptly, leaving Greg wondering whether he should have made the call.

'How did it go?' Liz enquired. She had no idea, since the conversation had all been in French.

'Madame Wiaroz is a bit overcome,' he explained. 'But I think she's happier.'

They realized they were quite weary. It had been a long and

eventful day. They decided to stay in the hotel for dinner and were rewarded with a very good meal of traditional English fare, even for Liz, the struggling vegetarian.

They were in the bar having an after-dinner drink when Greg's mobile rang. It was Chief Inspector Glaston calling from London.

'Valmouth's put me in the picture, sir. You've landed him with a messy assignment, haven't you?'

Greg didn't know whether to agree or apologize. He asked, 'Do you think we're on the right track?'

There was a pause. 'My gut feeling', said Glaston at last, 'is that this girlie guy is our man. But you need more than a gut feeling to convince the Crown Prosecution Service.'

'Of course. Perhaps something will be found on his computer.'

'Well, you know, that might take a while.' He hesitated then went on: 'In the meantime, try to stay out of Valmouth's hair, will you? He's got a lot on his plate at the moment.'

'You mean the arrangements for the civic visit.'

'I don't know whether you're aware, but the man who's visiting isn't popular – he made quite severe cuts in his business and put a lot of people out of work. So Valmouth's had to lend some of his men to beef up security.'

'So the watch for Crayshaw might not be very widespread?'

'I didn't say that.' But that was what he meant. Greg sighed, but managed not to agree to his next remark, which was to the effect that Mr Crowne and Ms Blair might as well leave Dover and return to London.

When he'd passed on all this to Liz, she was downcast. 'So as far as Mr Valmouth is concerned, it's a case of "Don't call us, we'll call you."'

'I think that was the message. In fact, I think it means that if we try to contact Mr Valmouth, we'll be politely told to go away.'

'Or we might be fobbed off with Constable Tyrrell, whose abilities, of course, we greatly admire.'

Greg said a few words under his breath about their dilemma but luckily in a language Liz didn't understand.

'Shall we push off, then?' she asked, '– go back to London?'

'What do you think?'

She gave it some consideration. In truth, she felt that perhaps there was little chance of being useful now in Dover. The police had the matter in hand.

Yet she knew that Greg would hate to give up. He had known Marzelina, however briefly. To know the identity of her murderer and yet not see him in handcuffs was hard, unacceptable, almost intolerable.

'We could see how it looks tomorrow,' she suggested. 'It's true Mr Valmouth is mad at us today, but he might feel less irritated in the morning.'

This he doubted, but it was getting late. They were both tired; their ability to reason things out wasn't at its highest.

'Let's sleep on it, then,' he agreed.

Chief Inspector Valmouth relented enough to telephone next morning, as they were eating breakfast in their room.

'Just thought I'd let you know. We found his car. In the long-stay car park at the railway station. It's likely he got on the London train yesterday evening before we got a picture for identification.'

'The London train! But he said he was going to France.'

'Well, that might have been the first thing that came into his head. Or else he didn't want the neighbour to know where he was really going.'

'But the police at the docks are still on the lookout?' Greg asked.

'I haven't changed the instructions.'

'And the Calais force?'

'So far, but I can't keep that going for long. He's in the wind now, I'm afraid.'

Greg groaned inwardly. 'And the car? Was there anything useful in it?'

'Nah. The big suitcase that the neighbour mentioned was in the boot. A very classy gown swathed in anti-acid tissue paper and zipped up in a polythene dress-carrier. And evening shoes, some stage make-up – that sort of thing. If he had packed any ordinary clothes, he's taken those.'

Greg put the phone aside to say to Liz, 'He's left the case in the car – the one Jim, the neighbour, mentioned to us. His stage things are still in it.'

'All of them?'

'It appears so – his gown, his make-up –'

'Wigs?'

'What?'

'He must wear a wig for his performance.'

Greg spoke into the phone. 'The night we saw him, Crayshaw was wearing a wig. It was –' He broke off to appeal to Liz. 'What shade was the wig he was wearing at the Greenthorpe?'

'Dunno, duckie. I don't think I ever looked at him.'

'Well, I think it was blonde, and . . .' He made large motions around his head.

'Bouffant?'

'He had a blonde bouffant wig, Chief Inspector.'

'Well . . .' A pause while Valmouth looked at the report on his desk. 'I don't see a wig mentioned.' Greg could hear him grunting to himself in annoyance. 'So I should warn the railways police to ask if a blonde woman took the London train last night? Great.'

'I'm sorry,' sympathized Greg.

'Much good it'll do. I really rang just to say you might as well think of it as a lost cause now, Mr Crowne.'

'But I just telephoned Madame Wiaroz last night to say . . .' He let the protest die away. No use burdening the policeman with personal woes. Instead he asked, 'What about his computer? Have you learned anything from that?'

'The techie boys are still trying to work out the password.'

'He must keep accounts . . . records . . .'

'So far all they've got is on the surface: household bills, attempts at writing publicity for his act. No accounts for his earnings in the clubs, by the way.'

'No, we were told at the hotel that he was paid in cash.'

'Sneaky little git!' snarled Valmouth.

Greg thought it wise to say 'So long' and disconnect.

Liz had listened intently to what she could hear. 'I gather they think he's made it out of Dover.'

'It seems so. His car was at the station *parking*.'

She pouted. 'That means nothing. He could have put it there just to make us believe he's gone somewhere in the UK.'

'But instead has gone cross-Channel, as he said at first?'

She hesitated a long moment before saying, 'I think he's stayed around.'

'In Dover?' The idea startled him.

'Well, why not?'

'Why should he? He's in danger here.'

'Not if he's in a good disguise. We asked about his wig – if he's got himself into a daytime version of his drag act, he could pass unnoticed if he wanted to. I mean, Greg – he doesn't have to get himself into a glamorous get-up: he could make himself look like a washerwoman.'

'No, no, he likes to be an opera diva.'

'You're forgetting he wanted the chief male part in the summer show.'

'Ah! Yes, that had gone from my mind.'

'We don't know what he might have had in his make-up box. He might be wearing a curly moustache and thick eyebrows by now.'

He laughed, but asked, 'Tell me: why should he stay in Dover?'

'Because there's something here that's important to him, perhaps. Or because he knows the police are going to be busy with this VIP visitor, so he can hang around for a bit and then slip away.'

'Is this women's intuition at work?' he teased.

'No, it's my feeling about Crayshaw. The wily fox, remember.'

They went back to their croissants and coffee.

By and by Greg said, 'The neighbour – Jim?'

'Kennerley, I think is his name.'

'Mr Kennerley could perhaps tell us quite a lot about Crayshaw.'

'Well, that's true.'

'And perhaps he might know his future plans. Do you recall, you said once that he wanted the money from the manuscript for a special reason? Perhaps Mr Kennerley might know what that is.'

'And that might help to work out where he's got to now.'

'Perhaps we could ring Mr Kennerley and ask if we might go to see him.'

'Do you think Mr Valmouth would approve?'

'Let's not ask him.'

They got the number from enquiries and rang.

Mrs Kennerley answered. 'Oh, yes, of course – Greg, from yesterday. I recognized your voice at once.' When she heard his request, she replied, 'Well, as a matter of fact, we're just going out.'

'Oh.'

'Jimmy has an appointment at the health centre.'

'Oh, dear. Anything serious?'

'Just aches and pains in his back, you know – old age.'

'Then perhaps we could call on you later?'

'Well, as a matter of fact, the health centre's in Dover, and that's where you are, isn't it?'

'Well, yes.'

'We could meet and have a chat. We generally go to the Coral Café for a cup of coffee after he's been pulled and pummelled at the clinic.'

'Let's meet there, then.' They agreed a time. He reported the engagement to Liz, who smothered a grin. The Coral Café didn't sound quite their cup of tea.

Since it was in a town-centre location, they took their time in getting ready. Liz hadn't had a morning run, so she insisted they walked there. The city was busy but had no appearance of being full of holidaymakers yet.

The Kennerleys were there ahead of them, already tucking into large, luscious wedges of cream cake. The waitress hurried to attend to the newcomers at a wave from Jim. Clearly they were valued patrons.

'It's like the Tower of Babel at home,' Jim declared when they'd settled opposite. 'Yellow tape all around Harry's house, two cop cars taking up all the parking lay-by, and a couple of reporters hanging about trying to find out what's going on.'

'And what *is* going on?' Liz enquired.

'Hanged if I know! What's he done? Stolen the bar takings?'

'Now, Jim, you know they told us it was a serious matter,' scolded his wife. She turned a shrewd eye on Liz. 'You and your friend weren't enquiring after him yesterday for nothing, now were you? But I never thought you were police.'

'Nothing like that,' Greg said. 'We think Crayshaw did something very bad to a friend of mine.'

'Oh, never! Harry? He hasn't got the guts to do anything really bad.'

'Not intentionally, perhaps.' Mrs Kennerley's opinion tallied with Greg's: he thought of Crayshaw as a man who had got out of his depth. 'You know him well,' he said. 'Where would he go if he was trying to evade arrest?'

She thought about it. 'To tell the truth, I can't quite get my head around the idea that he's on the run. We've known him for years; he's a Dover man, his roots are here. His family has lived in that house from way back.'

'His family has always been connected with the ferry service, I believe,' Greg said.

'That's right,' Jim agreed. 'Followed his dad's example – ship's steward. His dad died in an accident on the docks, so they extended the cottage with his insurance money. His granddad, so Harry used to say, was on the boats when King Edward used to nip across to see his lady-love in Paris.'

'Now, Jimmy,' his wife chided.

'The one Harry's mum liked to talk about was – let me see, it would have been a great-granddad. Ernest, I think his name was. She used to say he'd attended to this famous French chap back in the old days – she was French, Harry's mum; nice little thing but a bit airy-fairy, never could really believe a word she said. But she liked this story because he was French, the famous chap.'

'He wasn't French, Jim; he was Polish.'

'No, no, Allie, I'll remember his name in a minute.' He slapped his forehead. 'My memory these days! But I'm sure he had a French name.'

'Chopin?' Liz suggested.

Jim stared. 'How did you know that?'

'We heard something about it a while ago – something about looking after this important passenger who was ill on the trip to Calais.'

'Fancy you knowing that! Yes, it was some yarn like that about him –' He broke off. 'That's that composer; I remember now – that's why it was important. Mrs Crayshaw used to go on about that: how marvellous it was to have even been in the same room with him; and then, of course, there was the fairy tale about having something that belonged to him.'

Greg and Liz were afraid to say a word in case they interrupted his flow of memory.

'Huh!' remarked Mrs Kennerley with some scorn. 'Nothing to be proud of, in my opinion, picking up other people's leavings!'

'Chopin left something?' Greg prompted in a quiet voice.

'Yes, so the story went; he was so ill he had to be practically carried ashore in Calais – or no, I think it was Boulogne. And of course his cabin was a mess, so the steward cleared it up and brought some of his stuff home.' Alison pursed her lips. 'I think that probably happened a lot, you know – sort of finders keepers.' She let it be seen that she didn't approve.

'What did the steward bring home?'

That made her stop and think. 'What was it Annette was always talking about? Gloves, was it, Jim? Or was this the passenger that left his ivory hairbrush?'

'Hanged if I know, dear.'

His wife smiled apologetically at Greg. 'It's six years since she passed away, poor little thing,' she explained. 'Always pale and anaemic, she was. I don't really remember all she said about Great-Granddad and the things he brought home. To tell the truth, I thought she made it up.'

'Did Harry never mention it? You see, we believe he had a little business based on things to do with Chopin.'

'Harry? What makes you think so?' Jim Kennerley asked, startled.

'It seems he went on business trips supplying trinkets to gift shops in Manchester and Edinburgh.'

'No, no,' he protested, 'when he goes away it's always to do his act in clubs and pubs. He wants to be a second Danny La Rue. On telly and all that.'

'Danny La Rue?' Greg turned to Liz for clarification, but she was as baffled as he.

'Oh, you're too young to remember him,' said Alison Kennerley. 'He was in the same business as Harry – dress-up artist, you know. Harry decided to have a go at that when he was made redundant, but he's never likely to equal Danny. Really spectacular *he* was. Magnificent costumes – you never saw anything like it. He played the London Palladium. Harry always said he'd get outfits like that one day.'

Liz drew in a breath and let it out. She put a hand over Greg's and squeezed it. 'That's what the money was for,' she murmured.

'For sensational costumes?'

'Yes, so as to get himself noticed, to have marvellous publicity pictures taken, to get into the West End and be a real star.'

'Fifty thousand pounds for costumes?'

'And for what they'd bring him: fame, admiration, the chance to have his scripts written by good writers – all that.'

He was silent. The Kennerleys sat watching in some disquiet. Their information seemed to have caused the young man a great deal of pain.

'And this is why Marzelina died?' he said in an undertone to Liz.

She could think of nothing to say to that.

The Kennerleys hadn't caught the words but thought it best to change the subject.

'Do you think his house will go up for sale?' Alison asked. 'My daughter's looking for a place.'

Liz smiled in sympathy. 'I wouldn't hold your breath. If he's off in France somewhere, trying to keep out of sight . . .'

'But he'll have to come back, surely? What's he going to do about money?'

'Perhaps he has funds he can access,' Greg said, thinking of the money from the letter of credit, transferred to an offshore bank.

Alison looked gloomy at the idea of the next-door cottage being empty and untended for a long time.

Her husband said musingly, 'I could see Harry settling down in France somewhere. He's always liked French things. That act he does – it's based on something like a French opera, you know; that's his mum's influence.'

'You say he used to be cabin crew?'

'Oh yes, and always popping back and forth since he packed it in.'

'He travels to France a lot?' Greg queried.

'Oh yes, we all do. Shopping's so much cheaper over there,' said Jim. 'When I did up our living room, I got all the new electrics at Cité Europe.'

'And Harry liked to go there for *his* kind of stuff – he bought fans and things for his act,' explained Mrs Kennerley who, like Liz, had an interest in fashion and its accessories. 'He goes for his favourite shaving cream and things – made in France; you can't get them here.'

'And so he went on the ferry taking his car? Or how did he travel?'

'Like most of us, cheap day shopping ticket,' said Jim, as if it was a thing everybody knew. 'Alison and I, we get a coach trip – takes you across on the boat and then on to one of the big shopping malls.'

'And did Harry do that?'

Jim pursed his lips. 'He could usually wangle a free ride – knew his way around, you know, from being on the job.'

So it seemed likely that Crayshaw had boarded a ship without having to pass through any of the usual passenger checkpoints.

They stayed only a few minutes longer with the Kennerleys then said goodbye, expressing gratitude for their help. Outside, Greg used his mobile to speak to Valmouth, who muttered imprecations at the news that Harry knew how to by-pass the checkpoints.

'It would be worth talking to Mr and Mrs Kennerley,' Greg suggested. 'They know a lot about Crayshaw without being aware of it.'

'Yeah, thanks,' said Valmouth with heavy irony.

The Coral Café had been chosen by the Kennerleys because it was near the health centre. They turned a corner or two into the main road.

'Are we really doing any good?' Greg wondered. 'Valmouth was really not pleased.'

'Don't think like that!' cried Liz. 'He didn't know all the stuff we just found out, now did he?'

'Well, no.'

She hesitated before going on. 'We owe it to Marzelina,' she said.

He looked down.

'We do,' she insisted. 'And to ourselves. *We* know more about everything than the police – at least, I mean, *you* do: you know about Chopin and the music and all that.'

'I was so hoping Mrs Kennerley would say documents had been saved from Chopin's cabin.'

'Me too.'

'Chopin was always ill when he made the crossing. He often used the Folkestone-to-Boulogne route because he thought it wasn't so rough.'

'Poor soul,' murmured Liz.

'He had a companion with him that last time – Leonard Something . . .' Greg was trying to picture it. 'Chopin is ill, his friend Leonard tries to look after him . . . Perhaps opens a valise to get out a clean shirt for him . . .'

'You're thinking he could have got out some of Chopin's papers as well.'

'It's possible, don't you think? – looking for something in someone else's case? Yes, and then in the difficulties of getting Chopin ashore, he forgets to pick up what he pulled out.'

'It *is* possible, Greg.'

'So . . .

'What are you thinking?'

'Perhaps Crayshaw actually owns a Chopin manuscript.'

'Well, we thought about that before, love. He may have a real mazurka or a phoney one.' She walked a pace or two then stopped. 'Whichever it is, he probably intended to use it more than once, I'd imagine.'

Greg stood facing her, trying to match her thought processes. 'You said he probably would need a disk or a DVD, if he made a counterfeit. So he has one or the other – the software or the real manuscript – and it's a precious thing. Where do you keep a precious thing?'

'What?'

'Where do you keep something extremely valuable?'

'In a bank? In a strongbox?'

'And banks close at about four in afternoon. And so he would be unable to get it yesterday when he went on the run. *And so . . .*'

'*And so* he has to stay in Dover.' She glanced at her watch. 'The banks opened about an hour and a half ago. Oh . . .' She groaned. 'He's probably gone by now, then.'

This was such a disastrous conclusion that they hardly knew how to face it. They stood staring at the traffic edging along the main road, where cars and holiday coaches were queuing to enter the car parks.

The coach park was just across the street. Two big vehicles emblazoned with 'Cross-Channel Shopping' were waiting their turn to enter.

'Day trips!' exclaimed Liz.

They exchanged glances then hurried across, to walk in after the slow-moving coaches. There was a gathering of passengers waiting to board on a traffic island signposted with the names of coach companies.

They made their way towards the island boarding point. Passengers were offering tickets to a courier as they clambered on.

'Is there a booking office where we could ask about Crayshaw?' Greg asked, glancing about.

'He could probably use any travel office in the town – but Greg, he wouldn't have to present himself in person. You can book on your mobile phone: you contact the firm and ask them to text the ticket, and then you show that to the bus conductor.'

Greg clutched his hair in exasperation. 'We'd better pass that on to Valmouth.'

'Good heavens, I'm sure he already knows, sweetie.' She could see he was almost going out of his mind with frustration. 'Let's hang about a bit,' she said. 'See if we can pick up anything.'

It was a bright mid-morning in April. Business was fairly brisk for the shopping trips, but coaches came in with plenty of seats available and often went out not completely full. So as not to be noticeable they found a watching point at a kiosk selling coffee and sandwiches. Anyone hanging about at a bus station with a cup of coffee is taken to be a traveller waiting for transport.

Time went by. A uniformed transport official told them the coaches now stopping and moving out would deliver passengers for the ferry departure at twelve twenty.

'But it's only eleven o'clock now,' Liz protested.

'Oh, yes, but you have to allow check-in time.'

'How long's that?'

'Three-quarters of an hour or so, this time of year. A lot longer in high season.'

'And when's the next sailing after the twelve twenty?'

'The afternoon sailings are about one o'clock and two o'clock.' He glanced at their plastic beakers of coffee. 'The coffee on board is a lot better,' he remarked.

'Er ... yes ... We're waiting to travel with friends who're coming from London.'

Satisfied they were bona fide travellers, the official turned away.

'Well, I don't think Crayshaw showed up for any of the twelve twenty buses,' Liz sighed.

'Should we ring Valmouth and tell him what we're doing?' Greg wondered.

'What, and get ticked off again? If and when we see Crayshaw, we can tell him to alert his men at the docks.'

Coaches came and went. The one o'clock passengers were carried on their way. No one who looked like Crayshaw appeared in either his male or female form.

'Do you think this day-trip idea was a mistake?' Greg murmured.

Liz had been thinking it over. 'Well, he's got this problem with his clothes – I mean, if he's using a disguise. We're supposing he has to get something from a bank or somewhere. He has to turn up there, looking like Harry Crayshaw, doesn't he?'

'Well, that's true.'

'Then, if he's using some sort of costume, he has to go somewhere to put on his make-up and change his clothes. Where would he go to do that?'

'I don't know. The same place that he spent last night?'

'That's what I think, duckie. Some little bed-and-breakfast place. There must be hundreds of them in and around Dover. And you can bet Valmouth hasn't sent out an alert to places like that, so Harry could come and go as he likes.'

'Nine thirty he's at the bank when it opens. Ten o'clock he's back at his hotel if he's changing into his disguise.'

'Then he comes to the coach station to board the bus. He probably couldn't make it in time for any of those going to the noon-time sailing; he seems not to have come for the lot going for one o'clock. Let's wait and see if he's with the two o'clock crowd. It's worth giving it that much of a try.'

'And then what?' he asked, expecting her to say they should get Valmouth to send someone to take over.

She said, 'Then we go to lunch. I'm getting hungry!'

He laughed. She was a source of continual delight to him.

As the coaches for the two o'clock ferry began to roll in, passengers began to gather on the boarding island. One or two minicoaches arrived, depositing others who were to join the queue.

Liz took Greg's empty coffee beaker and went with it and her own to a big waste bin at the far side of the terminal. She crossed the path of a party from one of the minibuses, being shepherded by a stewardess towards the coach now at the stop. She wove her way through them, threw the beakers into the bin.

Next moment Greg saw her flying back towards him at top speed between the lumbering vehicles. The group from one of the minibuses was boarding a coach, their shepherd bringing up the rear.

Liz was waving at him and calling out, but it was impossible to make out what she was saying because of the noise of the motor engines.

She reached him, collided with him, and gasped for breath as he held her up.

'That's' – gasp – 'him!'

'What?'

'The stewardess with that group! That's him.'

'What?

'His aftershave! I didn't' – gasp – 'realize until I was a yard or two – past him. That was Crayshaw!'

Nineteen

Greg looked wildly past her head. The passengers for the coach were all aboard, the stewardess stepping up after them, the door closing.

He glimpsed a slim woman in a trim uniform of striped trousers, roll-necked black sweater, striped jerkin and jaunty peaked cap. Presumably the uniform guaranteed access to the ferry service. The cap had a hatband with lettering, unreadable as its wearer turned away. The name on the side of the coach was Foremost.

The coach rolled away.

Liz had recovered her breath. 'Quick!' she commanded, heading for a coach that had just reached the stop and now stood with its door open.

Without pausing to think, he obeyed. They hurried along the boarding site and stepped into the coach after the last passenger in the queue.

'Tickets?' demanded the driver.

'We'd like to pay now, please.' Liz was more acquainted with this mode of travel than His Highness, who at this prompt was ready with cash. The currency was accepted without demur, their passports were given a glance, and two tickets were issued – but all that time the coach that Crayshaw had boarded was making its way into the traffic stream for the docks.

'Thank you for travelling with Charisma,' said their driver, and closed his entrance door.

They took their seats. Greg now asked, rather uncertainly, 'Are you sure it was Crayshaw?'

'Absolutely.'

'But . . . but . . . she was wearing a little cap. Crayshaw's hair thing is big and curly.'

'Good heavens, Greg, he's brushed it down, of course! Or maybe even cut bits off. Or bought a new one in a department store.'

'Oh.'

'It was *him*. I know it was.'

Greg got out his mobile to ring Chief Inspector Valmouth. But he got the low-battery message.

'Oh, *merde*! Liz, use yours.'

She fumbled in her huge handbag. She met his anxious gaze. 'I think I left it on the bedside table . . .'

For a moment Greg debated with himself whether to ask for the loan of someone else's mobile; but that would almost certainly mean explanations and he wanted to concentrate on watching the coach ahead. It was quite possible that Crayshaw would ask to be set down at some point en route. He knew his way about the docks, perhaps knew staff entrances that would be inaccessible to others.

But no. The coaches lumbered on, climbing the long circular approach to the port. They at last joined the queue for the Customs check at the big blue boundary that was the end of British soil. Greg stood up and craned to watch through the front window. The Foremost company's vehicle was trundling up to the barrier. Its door opened, but no one got down.

Documents were handed to the official standing at the coach exit, and then handed back with a slight salute. It seemed the coach company's verification of passports was accepted as adequate. Foremost's coach rolled on.

The same procedure followed. It edged forward according to signals from the traffic master. By and by it trundled up the slope into the ferry. And still no one had alighted from Foremost's vehicle.

Charisma's coach later meandered into its allotted space in the echoing hold. Greg and Liz were on the qui vive behind a dilatory row of travellers lining up to alight. They saw Crayshaw swing down from the Foremost coach and expected him to vanish quickly. But he stayed to assist other passengers to get down, like a good and conscientious stewardess.

He helped an elderly lady unfold a wheeled walker; then he

straightened. He was confronting them as they at last stepped down from the Charisma coach, but about two vehicle lengths away.

A look of utter horror washed across his face at sight of them. He turned and ran.

Greg went after him at once. He tracked the figure in the uniform and cap as it dodged among the passengers emerging from their vehicles. But then he lost sight of him. For a moment he stood, a tall figure immobile in the surge of travellers making for the way to the upper decks. He craned his head to gaze around helplessly – but there was Crayshaw, running up a stair-case leading to the main deck. He was moving fast. The satchel hanging from his shoulder was bobbing about, banging on the handrail of the steps.

Greg heard Liz calling, 'Where is he?'

He pointed and dashed after him. Others who wanted to get upstairs blocked his path. He ruthlessly shoved them aside, and was on the first steps just as Crayshaw disappeared through the upper exit.

Long legs took him up three at a time. He emerged into a glassed-in passageway with padded leisure chairs and circular tables. Which way? The bar was to his left, a continuation of the passage to his right. He chose to go right, was rewarded with a glimpse of the trim figure slipping through a doorway.

The exit was wide, with sliding glass doors. Outside was the main deck. A few passengers were at the rail, watching the quays slip behind them, saying farewell to the White Cliffs.

Crayshaw was running away from the main structure, above which towered the black funnels of the ship. He was struggling with the strap of the satchel, trying to get it off.

Greg immediately knew that in the satchel was the evidence that could convict its owner. It was a truth that darted into his mind like an arrow. He ran along the deck, with the sightseers turning in amazement at his progress. Crayshaw was at the rail, trying to get the strap over his head.

Greg lunged at him, grappled, tried to hold on to the leather band. Crayshaw made a tremendous effort, raised his hand with the strap in it, and pulled it over his head.

The leather band caught the jaunty peaked cap and pulled it. It should have come off, but was securely pinned to the blonde hair. The hair was jerked askew, revealing a smooth short lock of brown hair. Crayshaw swung the bag on the end of its strap so that it went round in a wild arc and thumped Greg on the back of his head.

For a moment Greg was disorientated. His grasp on his quarry loosened. Crayshaw jerked the strap so that the satchel came sailing back towards him and as his arm followed the swing, the satchel went over into the sea.

They were struggling like untrained wrestlers. Crayshaw was calling out words that were scarcely recognizable but seemed to be appeals for help.

Liz came racing up. She'd followed their passage by dint of seeing where travellers were standing in alarm, staring in the direction of the chase.

'Get security!' Greg cried, wrestling with the squirming figure that seemed all arms and legs in his grasp.

She darted away. She'd hardly regained the interior passage when she encountered an anxious man in uniform.

'Trouble?' he asked, already alerted.

'This way.' She grapped his sleeve and dragged him out on deck. There she could see Greg trying to hold fast to Crayshaw, who was flailing his arms about and sobbing in a pretended female hysteria.

The officer shouted, 'Stop that!' Greg was distracted for a moment, half-turning his head to see who was calling.

Crayshaw ceased struggling. The ship's officer hurried up. 'What's going on here?' he demanded.

'This man assaulted me!' panted Crayshaw. He turned to the passengers who had gathered round now that an official was in charge. He gained control of his breathing. In a feminine whimper he appealed to the onlookers: 'He did, didn't he?'

There was a dubious nodding of heads.

'Call Chief Inspector Valmouth of Dover CID,' said Greg in a breathless version of his princely voice. 'This man is Harry Crayshaw, a wanted criminal.'

'What?' wailed Crayshaw. 'How dare you!' But, ever in tune with his audience as his drag act had taught him, he caught the influence of their uncertainty. This bunch were staring at him without warmth – they showed something like disbelief.

'You're going bald, blondie,' commented a cynical voice.

He put up a hand to his head. There it encountered first the wig, and then the cap, askew at his left temple.

The ship's officer heard an echo in his head of a name on the 'Be on the lookout for' list. 'Are you Harry Crayshaw?' he enquired, trying not to grin at the figure before him.

Crayshaw chose not to answer; but he huddled into himself, trying now to put his headgear straight.

'I must detain you for further enquiries,' said the officer, and took him by the arm. Silent and humiliated, he was led away.

Liz pushed one of the bysanders aside to get to Greg. 'Are you all right?'

'Apart from a few knocks and bumps. But Liz, he got rid of the shoulder bag.'

They gazed at each other in dismay, though they couldn't have said why.

Later, when they were put in touch with Valmouth by ship-to-shore telephone, it was agreed it would be no good to try to recover the bag. The tide was going out; the many cross-currents could have swept it miles out into the Channel.

'I'll talk to my French oppo to arrange about getting Crayshaw back,' said Valmouth. 'They're not likely to want him: all his crimes were carried out in the UK. But they'll keep him safe for me.'

Although Greg and Liz were allowed to have lunch, they had to make the crossing to Calais under supervision. There the local police treated them with a neutral politeness. They were allowed to travel on to Paris by train, where they booked into the Hôtel Raimond Dufay.

Greg telephoned Mme Wiaroz with the news. She was so elated that she had to be calmed and soothed by Céleste. 'I will telephone you later,' Céleste said, 'when she has recovered.'

When she did, it was to invite them to dinner. Though they were both weary enough to want a quiet evening to themselves, they accepted.

The meal was produced by the resentful Doranne, but was excellent. However, hardly anyone could pay attention to the food because there had to be explanations and re-explanations until the old lady at last understood what had been done.

'I do not know how to thank you, Grégoire,' she said at length, when they were sitting with liqueurs and little glacé fruits. 'And of course you must prepare an account of your expenses and any other moneys you require in lieu of the time you have given up to this task. To think that the monster will soon be before a judge for what he did to my darling Marzelina . . .' Tears threatened again.

Greg said gently, 'It may not be soon, madame. First, evidence has to be collected, and we gather that very little has been found at the home of Mr Crayshaw.'

'And the manuscript is gone to the depths of the sea?'

'If it really existed,' he sighed, 'I'm afraid so.'

'It must have existed. Why else was this brute so determined to get rid of it?'

'The shoulder bag may only have contained the equipment to make counterfeits.'

'Alas,' she sighed, clasping her arthritic hands together. 'Is it better not to know the truth?'

For a week Harry Crayshaw kept a stubborn silence under questioning. His fingerprints had already been found on the letter of credit and the receipt for the money transfer: the fake countess had had to remove her gloves to sign them. The police showed a head-and-shoulders photograph of him in his stewardess outfit – but with his wig on straight – to the staff of the bank. One of the clerks greeted it with immediate recognition.

This caused a change in Crayshaw's thinking. He hired a good lawyer. On his expert advice, he set about avoiding a murder charge by claiming that the death of Countess Zalfeda was an accident.

'She got very haughty with me the minute she saw the score of the mazurka,' he explained. 'I couldn't understand it – it had been in my family for generations!' Here he put on an indignant and offended expression. 'My great-grandfather picked it up off the floor of the cabin occupied by Frederic Chopin on the Folkestone-to-Boulogne ferry.'

'You're saying it was genuine?'

'Of course it was. But she said she could see it was a forgery and went for her mobile to report me. So I tried to get the mobile from her, but it got tangled in her long scarf. Of course I yanked at the scarf. Before I knew what was happening she was on the floor! I just scarpered – I never knew she was dead till I saw it on the TV news!'

Likewise, he claimed to be innocent of shooting at Liz and Greg on the road to Livingston. 'That was a silly Edinburgh shopkeeper and he's made himself scarce, so I don't know where he is now.'

And so on – if shopkeepers avoided paying tax on their supplies of Chopin memorabilia, that wasn't his fault. True, he himself had kept quiet about his little sideline of selling them, but that was a small matter for which he was willing to go to judgement. As for the fire at Keepsake Curios, he knew absolutely nothing about it.

Despite all that, he appeared before the magistrate on a charge of murder and was remanded in custody. 'He'll be there a long time,' Chief Inspector Glaston said. 'We've got a complicated case to build. And let me tell you one thing: that posh after-shave of his will be a positive handicap rather than an asset in prison!'

'I hope they lock him up for ever,' Liz sighed.

'I think we've got a good chance of doing that.'

The technologists had found their way into the safeguarded areas of Crayshaw's computer. The text of the paperback about the 'romance' between Jane Stirling and Chopin was there, but no evidence of forging the mazurka.

'Could it possibly have been the true lost score of a Chopin composition that he threw into the water?' wailed Liz in distress.

Greg didn't know what to say.

Mme Wiaroz was divided in her view of the outcome when they paid her what they thought of as a final visit; but, strange to say, she was comforted to hear that Crayshaw insisted the manuscript of the mazurka was genuine. She decided to believe that version.

She said in solemn tones to Greg, 'I couldn't bear to think that my Marzelina gave her life over a forgery. And now I have to go to Warsaw for her funeral. The senior branch of her family is there still, and they wish to have her interred with her ancestors.'

'Madame, I'm so sorry.'

'Ah well . . . Céleste is going with me, and we shall visit the birthplace of my beloved Chopin in Zelazowa Wola while we are there.' She blinked away a tear. 'Dear Monsieur Grégoire, you have been so kind to me. I shall be gone from Paris for about two weeks. Would you and your beautiful little *amie* care to use my apartment for a holiday and a time of recuperation after all you have done?'

'Madame ... that is so very kind of you ...'

She managed a smile. 'If you are thinking you would not care to share the place with Doranne, don't be afraid! I have at last summoned up the courage to give her her *congé*. Céleste has helped me to find a replacement, but she will not take over until we return from Poland. So you would have the place entirely to yourselves.' She looked roguishly at them.

'That sounds so nice, but you see, madame – I've got work to do that should have been done weeks ago ...'

'Oh, Liz,' groaned Greg. It had sounded too good to miss.

'We-ell ...'

'All that design stuff for your spectre is on your laptop, now isn't it?'

'Spectre? Spectre means ghost! It's a spencer.' But she saw he was grinning. 'Yes, the design for the spectre is on my laptop; and I could certainly work even better in Paris than in London. Well then ... of course ... Thank you, madame.'

Céleste was showing them to the door when Liz took her by the hand. 'Mademoiselle, would you arrange for some flowers in our names to be sent to the funeral ceremony?'

'Ah, that is so thoughtful! Of course I will see to it. And I thank you on behalf of Madame. You were wise not to mention it to her – it would have caused her to weep yet again, my poor old friend.'

'She's lucky to have you,' Greg said. 'Look after her.'

'I promise.'

They'd had to return to London to attend to a few interim formalities with the police and pack clean clothes. Liz was surveying the contents of her wardrobe when she heard the living-room phone ring. Greg was there, and picked up. She heard him exclaim, 'Ah, Papa!' and then the conversation became inaudible.

After a bit he called, 'Liz? Can you spare a moment? Papa would like to speak to you.'

'To *me*?' She hurried in, accepting the receiver from him.

'Mademoiselle Liz, I gather you have been having adventures with my foolish son.'

'Oh? You heard about that?'

'A friend showed me something about it in the English newspapers. So it is now all over, and Grego tells me you are to spend some time in Paris.'

'Yes, I'm just considering what to pack.'

'You will look beautiful whatever you wear.'

'Aha! Now I know where your son gets his talent for flattery.'

He chuckled. 'I telephoned to say that I very much enjoyed meeting you in Dover and now that I hear you are to be in Paris, I look forward to seeing you there also.'

'You'll be in Paris?'

'*En passant* – I will be on my way to a little place in the Netherlands where there are some horses to inspect. But I hope we can meet for a drink and a chat.'

'Oh, I'd like that, monsieur.'

'So I will ring you in Paris the day before, to let you know which plane I am on. Until then, *au revoir, ma chère.*'

She disconnected then turned with some irony in her gaze to the prince. 'Does Grossmutti know about this?' she enquired.

'Er . . . I gather he's letting drop a few hints.'

'And what's the result?'

'Who cares?' He seized her by the waist and danced her round her studio, humming a tune. 'That's a mazurka,' he informed her.

'Never mention the word to me again!' she protested. But she was laughing.